MW00584377

Knit Together
Amish Knitting Novel

Karen Anna Vogel

He restores my soul

Knit Together: Amish Knitting Novel

© 2011 by Karen Anna Vogel
Second Edition 2013 Lamb Books
ISBN-13: 978-0615941189
ISBN-10: 0615941184

Contact the author on Facebook at:
www.facebook.com/VogelReaders
Learn more the author at: www.karenannavogel.com
Visit her blog, Amish Crossings, at
www.karenannavogel.blogspot.com

Knit Together

BOOKS BY KAREN ANNA VOGEL

Smicksburg Tales
Amish Knitting Circle:
Amish Friends Knitting Circle
Amish Knit Lit Circle

Amish Knitting Novels ~ Standalones
Knit Together
The Amish Doll

Novellas
Amish Pen Pals: Rachael's Confession
~*~
Christmas Union: Quaker Abolitionists of Chester County,
Pennsylvania
~*~
Amish Knitting Circle Christmas: Granny & Jeb's Love Story

Coming soon:
Amish Knit & Stitch Circle: Smicksburg Tales 4

DEDICATION

To Tim, my husband of thirty-three, who shares my love for the Amish and encouraged me to tell their stories. I love you and this empty nest time!

To my four "kids", Evie Lee, Jeremy, Christin and Karamarie...who would have thought you'd all grow up to be my best friends?

To Jack, my faithful black lab, who sat at my feet while I wrote this book. R.I.P. dear friend...

WHAT OTHERS ARE SAYING ABOUT KNIT TOGETHER

"Karen Anna Vogel brings to the table a fresh new Amish series that readers will certainly love based from her own experiences as a friend to the Amish. We 'English' look at the Amish through rose-colored glasses. They seem so peaceful and content with a simple way of life. But we forget they are people like everyone else. Karen's series shows this through the hardships and heartbreaks they face and the faith they cling to or struggle with."
Rita Gerlach , author of *Surrender the Wind, Daughters of the Potomac Series*

"Author Karen Vogel has approached the often misunderstood beliefs or the Amish with tact and tenderness, and I highly recommend this heart-stirring story."
Kathi Macias award-winning author of forty novels, including *Deliver Me from Evil* and *Unexpected Christmas Hero.*

"Karen writes with heart-touching insight and her characters are gripping. Highly recommended."
Jennifer Hudson Taylor, author of *Highland Blessings & Highland Sanctuary*

Knit Together

CONTENTS

Discussion Guide

INTRODUCTION

How honored I am that you bought this book. Thank you. I wrote *Knit Together* while grieving the loss of my mother and two cousins. My Amish friend in Smicksburg, PA, who wishes to remain anonymous, lost a loved one at the same time. This book is semi-autobiographical when it comes to our grief and loss.

I learned that the fabric arts are very therapeutic. I crocheted at my mother's bedside, but found after she passed away, I couldn't pick up a crocheting needle. Just like Ginny in the book, I knew I needed to wrap my fingers around yarn. I met Susan Grim, owner of SuzyB Knits in Smicksburg, PA, and she taught me to knit. Now I understand what this knitting craze is all about. It's really good for your nerves!

In this book, a knitting circle makes mittens for Christian Aid Ministries, a charity run by Amish and Mennonites. This ministry is real and has agreed to partner with Lamb Books to distribute mittens that readers have made using the pattern Susan "spun up". (Please feel free to use your own pattern though). These mittens will be sent to orphanages in Romania, Ukraine and Russia. Winters are brutal and mittens are needed.

Please join Susan and me as we "Knit Together" for charity. Please send mittens marked "Operation Knit Together" to the following address:

Christian aid ministries
2412 division highway
Ephrata, PA 17522

For more information on this wonderful ministry, you can reach them at:

717-354-2434

or

www.christianaidministries.org (website run by Mennonites who use the internet)

SUZYB KNITS COZY MITTS

Written exclusively for Knit Together: An Amish Knitting
Novel by Karen Anna Vogel

Materials: 100 yards of a chunky weight yarn (1 skein SuzyB
Knits Handspun ;)
9 - 9" needles
#9 double points
Stitch markers and a stitch holder
Cast on 28 sts
Place marker join and work in round being careful not to twist
stitches
Knit 3 rounds
Begin Knit 2, Purl 2 and work until piece measures 2"
Knit 4 rounds
Begin Increases
Increase Round: K1, M1 Knit to last stitch M1, K1 (30 sts)
Knit one round
Increase Round: K2, M1 Knit to last stitch M1, K2 (32 sts)
Knit one round
Inc Rnd: K3, M1 Knit to last stitch M1, K3 (34 sts)
Knit one round
Increase Round: K4, M1 Knit to last stitch M1 K4 (36 sts)
Knit one round
Increase Round: K5, M1 Knit to last stitch M1 K5 (38 sts)
Knit one round
Place thumb stitches on holder
Knit first 6 sts place those stitches with the last six stitches of
round on a stitch holder
Knit to end of round then cast on 2 stitches using a backward
loop cast on. Place a marker between the 2 cast on stitches.
Join stitches together and knit
Continue to work on these 28 stitches for 3 more inches.
Shape top of mitten
Decrease round: Knit 5, K2 together repeat to end of round
(24 stitches)

Knit one round

Decrease round: Knit 4, K2 together repeat to end of round (20 stitches)

Knit one round

Decrease round: K2 together (10 stitches)

Knit one round

Decrease round: K2 together (5 stitches)

Cut yarn Leaving long enough tail to thread back through 5 stitches on needles, pull up tight to close stitches together.

Thumb

Divide 12 stitches on holder on to 3 double points

With double pointed needle pick up and knit 1 stitch from body of mitten then knit across remaining stitches on other double points

Continue working in the round on these 13 stitches for 1.5 inches

Decrease round: K2 together to last stitch, K1

Knit one round

Decrease round: K2 together to the last stitch, K1

Cut yarn and thread thru stitches on needles and pull up to close stitches together.

Repeat pattern for second mitten

M1 – make one stitch by lifting the bar in between the stitch on the needle and the next stitch and placing it on the left needle and then knit it thru thru the back.

SuzyB Knits ~PO Box 46 Smicksburg, Pennsylvania 16256 www.suzybknits.com

AMISH – ENGLISH DICTIONARY

Pennsylvania Dutch dialect is used throughout this book, common to the Amish of Western Pennsylvania. You may want to refer to this little dictionary from time to time.

ach – oh

Ausbund – Amish hymn book

boppli – baby

brieder - brothers

bruder - brother

daed - dad

danki – thank you

dawdyhaus – grandfather house

Die Botschaft – An Amish weekly newspaper

dochder – daughter

Gmay - community

Guder mariye. Good morning.

goot - good

jah - yes

kapp- cap; Amish women's head covering

kinner - children

maedel - maid

mamm – mom

oma – grandma

Ordnung – order; set of unwritten rules

rumspringa – running around years, starting at sixteen, when Amish youth experience the Outsiders' way of life before joining the church.

wunderbar – wonderful

yinz – plural for you, common among Western Pennsylvania Amish and English. A *Pittsburghese* word.

PROLOGUE

$\mathcal{S}$tanding at the top of the hill behind her house, watching spring unfold over the distant rolling hills, calmed Katie's nerves. The scent of apple blossoms spoke of new life, a life in heaven where her dear sister-in-law, Sadie, was taken two days ago. The brevity of life hit Katie like cold water from the pump on a winter day. Everyone was saying Sadie had a full life, having six children. She felt a deep emptiness when she heard this because Sadie was thirty years old, just like her, but Katie had little hope of finding a husband she could truly love and have his children.

Her mind wandered to Levi Miller, who made it clear he wanted to court. She knew he was a wonderful man and she loved his little three year old son. He was a tall muscular man with brown puppy-dog eyes; Levi was strong, yet gentle. She had no romantic feelings for him, but she wondered if her heart was so broken years ago that it was numb.

She'd been engaged to Judah, Sadie's brother, and was to marry him when she was twenty-one. He had a thriving construction business but complained that he didn't have a phone and truck. One day he simply said he wanted to leave the Amish and asked her to make a life with him in the fancy world. She felt so betrayed, since Judah knew she had no choice; she was Amish to the core of her being. Since then, it was hard to have romantic feelings toward a man.

She arched her back and massaged the strain in her neck. She remembered what Granny Weaver told her at the knitting circle…that she spun her sheep's fluffy wool into strong yarn, and God spun people together….hearts together…to be stronger. Katie's heart ached to be spun together with a man she could love. She bowed her head and prayed a bold prayer:

Dear Lord God and Heavenly Father,

Bind me together with a man I can love. If it's Levi I'm to marry, knit our hearts together in a romantic way. If I don't know this man yet, bring him to me. But Lord, if I'm supposed to remain single, I beg you to take away this desire to be loved by a man and have his children…Until then, I'll do my part. I'll try to be content in whatever state I'm in, just like your Good Book says to do. Amen.

CHAPTER 1

Katie lifted the pie to her nose and could tell it was raisin and walnut, her favorite. Her dear friend, Lottie, had left it in a basket on the front porch, and such kindness warmed her heart. Today was Sadie's funeral, but she wouldn't face it alone.

Looking over at her *mamm* sitting at the kitchen table, Katie could tell by her shaking shoulders that she was still crying. She poured some coffee into a mug and sat it in front of her.

"*Danki,* my daughter." Millie stared into the cup. "Sadie and I had coffee together the other morning." Fresh tears ran down her cheeks.

Katie sat beside her on the oak bench. "We'll all be missing Sadie."

"I loved her like my own. A heart attack? With no warning?" Millie gripped Katie's hand. "You'll help Reuben with the *kinner, jah*?"

"*Ach,* they're not a problem, and *Mamm,* you know how wonderful the People are at times like this."

"*Jah,* I'm sure you're right. Our church is like the healing oil we put on the bruises of our sheep." She dabbed her pudgy cheeks with her white cotton handkerchief edged with pink embroidered roses, a gift from Sadie for her sixtieth birthday. "I've been missing your pa something awful lately. His funeral was in the barn five years ago."

Katie put her arm around her. "I'm so sorry he's not here to help. He would have been your best comfort."

Millie tried to smile. "Katie dear, you're a great comfort." She looked at her fondly. "You've always been here to help raise the boys and now Reuben's *kinner,* but please don't ignore Levi." She pinched her cheek. "He's so taken with those big brown eyes of yours."

Katie got up to cut two pieces of raisin and walnut pie and set them on the table. "Levi's a *goot* man, but only a friend."

Millie stared at her pie. "*Daed* and I were friends since childhood, just like you and Levi. A trusting friendship is the best foundation for romance. Judah broke your trust, so maybe it's harder to love again."

Katie leaned her elbows on the table. "I know, but what am I supposed to do? I can't deceive Levi."

"The Allegheny River begins as a spring up there in Colesburg. That's how love is. It starts small, as a tiny trickle. Don't you feel a tiny bit of romance…a trickle?"

Katie sighed. "*Jah*, sometimes I do…a trickle…I'll be thinking hard about what you say, *Mamm*. You and *Daed* had such a *wunderbar goot* marriage."

"Can I come in or is it a bad time?" their trusted *English* friend, Ginny, called through the back screen door.

"*Ach*, come in Ginny. You're like family," Millie said.

"I just wanted to bring over these doughnuts for breakfast. It's all so sad about Sadie; I thought you'd need some comfort food."

Millie got up to embrace Ginny, almost knocking the small framed woman over. Katie thanked God for such a good neighbor, who helped her get through the loss of her *daed* and now Sadie, but she couldn't help but worry; Ginny was in mourning herself….

~*~

Ginny waited for a buggy to pass, and then crossed the street to her house with a heavy heart, thinking of Millie's grief. She wished she could take a day off from the online bookstore. She wanted to stay with the Bylers and help prepare for the funeral, but she and James had a full morning ahead. They didn't work on Sundays, so Mondays were always busy. She walked into her house and headed to the kitchen to take the rhubarb strawberry pies she'd prepared last night out of the refrigerator. She popped them into the oven, and then went into the office and nestled into her overstuffed blue chair with her laptop, checking her emails first. She smiled when she saw one from her brother.

Hi Sis,

I just picked up my art degree, and am holding it in my hands. I finally graduated at thirty-five...

It's been on my mind to tell you something for a while. I tried after Mom's funeral, but I choked, so I'll put it in writing. I'm so sorry for all I put you through since I was sixteen. Leaving for New York City without telling anyone where I was going; it was immature and I'm really sorry. I know you worried as much as Mom about me. Will you forgive me?

After Mom's stroke, God gave me a wakeup call. When I came home to visit her at the rehabilitation center, she held her arms out and hugged me like she'd never let go. She shared from her worn out Bible about God's love. I cried like a baby.

No, now that I think of it, God started waking me up before that, on September 11, 2001. When I saw the North Tower fall. When Flight 93 crashed in some field in Southwestern PA, I thought of you and fear gripped me.

I love you, Sis, and want you to know how much I appreciate you and James and your kids. Even though I made a ton of money dealing drugs, I'd rather be poor and know God and be reconciled with my family.

I've been working with the placement agency here at my college. They suggested I take my photography to a rural setting to get peaceful scenes. There's a real market for Amish farms and one-

room schoolhouses, and you live in the heart of Amish Country up there in Smicksburg.

I don't live on campus anymore and need a place to land until I get my footing, so I was wondering if I could stay with you for a while. I have some jobs lined up doing web design, but you know how hard it is to make a living when a business is just starting up. It will only be for six months, tops.

Talk to James about it and let me know. I know you were thinking about taking in foster kids. Maybe I'll be practice?

Love,
Joseph

Ginny's stomach tightened into a knot. She loved Joseph too, but relished time alone with James. She needed solitude to heal; to get over the death of her mother. Yes, she was going through the empty nest syndrome and eventually wanted foster children, but not for a long while. She ran her fingers through her short, wispy brown hair and closed her eyes, shooting up a prayer for guidance.

~*~

Ginny marveled at Bishop Mast's composure as he stood in the back of the barn as people came through the many open barn doors. He seemed to not notice the people filling the rows of benches in the overflow section outside. Two-hundred people would be depending on him for comfort, yet his tall, lanky frame seemed calm.

When everyone was seated, he stroked his long gray beard. "A funeral to us is a much more important thing than the day of birth because we believe in the hereafter," he said as he placed his hand on Sadie's closed pine casket next to him. Ginny wrote the words in her green leather prayer journal. It wasn't a prayer but a profound thought. Having had several years of German in high school and college, and lots of practice over the years, she could understand a lot of Pennsylvania Dutch.

She reflected on her mom's funeral. No simple pine box, they got the best one in cherry, her mom's favorite wood. There was a paid violin and flute duet to play as people entered the church. Here the music was the chirping of barn swallows up in the rafters. She hadn't really paid close attention at funerals before her mom's death. She'd been to Amish funerals before, but this one seemed like her first.

Ginny listened as the bishop spoke about God and everlasting life, but nothing was said about Sadie. She thought of her mom's eulogy given by her aunt; it was a real honor to her sacrificial life. She knew the Amish always wanted to move forward and focus on God, but why couldn't someone say Sadie's light blue eyes were like deep pools of pure joy?

Bishop Mast spoke at length from Genesis, about the creation of the world, emphasizing the fact that Man was made from dust and will return to the earth. Then Reuben got up to speak, and Ginny thought maybe there would be a eulogy after all. He cleared his throat and opened up a piece of paper, and through tear filled eyes read:

> *"God grant me the serenity to accept the things I cannot change;*
> *Courage to change the things I can; and wisdom to know the difference,*
> *Living one day at a time; enjoying one moment at a time;*
> *Accepting hardships as the pathway to peace;*
> *Taking, as He did, this sinful world as it is, not as I would have it;*
> *Trusting that He will make all things right if I surrender to His Will;*

That I may be reasonably happy in this life and supremely happy with Him
Forever in the next.
Amen."

Reuben folded the paper and placed it against his heart. "The Serenity Prayer was special to Sadie. She kept this paper tucked under her pillow to try to memorize it. I find it a fitting prayer to say today." He slowly turned to touch the casket with both hands and then bent over it and wept. Bishop Mast bowed his head in silent prayer, and then lent strength to Reuben's sagging shoulders, pulling him into an embrace. Ginny looked around to see heads bowed in prayer as the bishop took time to console Reuben. He whispered something in his ear, and then Reuben returned to his seat where his brothers shook his hand and kissed his cheek.

Ginny grabbed a tissue out of her purse. Reuben had suffered a terrible loss and she prayed for God to comfort him. She stared at the notes just written in her journal: *Trusting that He will make all things right if I surrender to His will.* She sighed. Was God trying to get her attention? Surrender meant lack of control, and she didn't like that feeling. So many things had been out of control over the past several years; her kids all moving out and her mother's slow decline and death. She flipped to the page in her journal where she'd written her favorite C.S. Lewis quote: *To love at all is to be vulnerable. Love anything, and your heart will certainly be wrung and possibly broken.* She marked stars around it, and in the margin wrote, *C.S. You know exactly how I feel.*

She closed her eyes and focused on the words the bishop read from the *Ausbund.* The long hymn told of how their ancestors faced death daily but remained faithful. The Amish had more peace in tragic times, she thought. Was it the constant reminder of death in their hymnal that kept them in touch with its reality?

The Bishop spoke about everlasting life at length and then everyone stood for "The Lord's Prayer". The hour-long funeral service was over. After her mom's funeral, there was a dinner at a restaurant. Ginny watched as women brought meals from the house and set them on the long tables being quickly assembled all around her. She made her way to the corner of the barn to retrieve her basket which held warm strawberry rhubarb pies, covered with a new tea towel. She spied Katie and handed the present to her.

"*Danki.*" She felt Katie's warm embrace. "To have you here helps bear the pain," she whispered in her ear. "Will you come over tonight and sit on the porch with me?"

"I'd like that," Ginny said.

~*~

Later that evening, Ginny shared the cedar porch swing with Katie. Peeper frogs sang their nightly lullaby. There was a chill in the air, and Ginny was glad she brought a sweater. "There's no more chance of a frost so we'll plant our garden tomorrow, but it's nippy out here tonight."

"It's always colder on clear nights," Katie said. "You can see the Milky Way so clearly. It always reminds me of little ice crystals falling from the heavens. I love watching stars." Katie tapped the porch floor with her foot, helping the swing keep motion. "*Mamm* is so tired; she's in bed already."

"Grief makes you tired," Ginny said. "After my mom's funeral, I couldn't move for days."

"You couldn't move for *weeks*. You look so much better now, but today you seem run down again."

"I'm bewildered. My brother wants to come live with us. He has plans to start a business and needs a place to stay for a while." Ginny took a sip of the root beer the Bylers were known for.

"*Wunderbar goot* for you. *Ach,* we all need family." She squeezed Ginny's hand. "You have one *bruder* ? And he's a grown man, about my age?"

Ginny knew the sacrifice Katie made to help her mother raise eight brothers, and she was complaining about one. She sighed. "Joseph's a grown man, but I've always treated him like one of my kids. I'm so much older than him." She changed the subject. "Was the funeral hard for you today? I'm here for you to talk. This was a rough day."

Katie's eyes welled up with tears. "I miss my Sadie. It's so hard to accept. She made me laugh and always saw the bright side of life." She cleared her throat. "Granny Weaver told me that if I stand up next to one of her quilts hanging in her shop, so close that my nose touches it, everything will look dark. But if I step away, I'll see its beauty and design. She said life's like that. We won't see the beauty of our life until we step away into heaven."

"That's a profound thought…"

Katie shook her head in agreement. "Granny also says we don't fully appreciate someone until they're gone." Her chin quivered. "After losing *Daed* and Sadie, I look at helping Reuben with his *kinner* as a blessing, since we never really know how much time we have together."

She thought of Joseph and all the years they'd missed. Her husband's comment about her forming an unhealthy aversion to change was true. She was creating her own little utopia full of kind Amish people and her closest friends at church. She knew right then she'd be emailing her brother tonight to tell him he could come live with them. James was right; it would be good for her in many ways...

~*~

Kirsten Rowland put her freshly baked apple dumplings into the display case. How she loved being the pastry chef at the Country Sampler for the summer! She was glad to be home. She could watch Jane Austen movies with her mom and play cards with her dad...and see Noah every day. While away at pastry school this past year, their letters to each other had only deepened their love. Now Noah was talking about marriage. But he was Amish...

"I hear your uncle's coming to Smicksburg," Antonio said, counting the number of doughnuts in the display case aloud in Italian.

"Yes, he's coming up tomorrow. *Sono content!*" Kirsten looked at Antonio and grinned.

"Okay, smarty. So you remember the little Italian I taught you." He laughed. "Well, I can tell by that smile you're happy your uncle's coming. *Buena.*"

"Uncle Joseph's a photographer. Maybe he can put some pictures up in the restaurant. You sell wreathes from the Drying Shed and plates from Smicksburg Pottery..."

Antonio finished wiping down the display case. "The apple doesn't fall far from the tree," he chuckled. "Your mom asked to hang Amish quilts in here to sell for her friends. Tell your uncle I'll make room somewhere for his pictures." Antonio leaned up against the kitchen door. "We better get moving. The lunch crowd will be here soon." He pushed the door and was out of sight.

Just then, Kirsten spied Noah Mast coming into the Sampler. She wanted to run and hug him, but knew such a public display would reveal their secret. "Hello, Noah."

Noah winked at her. "What pie is on special today? Want to surprise my *mamm* by bringing home dessert."

"Peach pies are buy one get one free," she said. "You treat your mom like gold, coming in here to buy her pies."

Noah leaned closer and whispered. "You know I kill two birds with one stone. I make my *mamm* happy and I see my girl." He grinned. "So your uncle's coming tomorrow, *jah*?"

"Yes, and you'll love him. He's worked construction before. You two will have something in common."

"Has he ever built a barn? Seen a barn raising?" Noah asked. "We're raising one next week. I can take him."

"Noah, you are forever talking about barns. You played with Lincoln Logs too much with Aidan and Ian growing up," Kirsten said, angling an elbow on the counter, very near him.

"I came over to your house to protect you when your *brieder* picked on you, and I'm Amish; we're non-resistant. Maybe you'll be non-resistant someday? Become Amish?" He took off his straw hat, showing the curly auburn hair Kirsten found so attractive.

She straightened the tall glass jars full of old-fashion candy displayed on the counter, then looked at Noah evenly. "I can't turn Amish. We have to think of a more practical way for us to be together." She studied his amber-brown eyes. "I love the Amish, you know that right? But to live with no conveniences?"

Noah opened one of the jars and took out a root beer stick. He put a nickel on the counter. "I've been giving this a lot of thought. I passed up baptism classes again and at twenty-one, it looks real suspicious, especially to my *daed*." He chewed on the end of the stick. "I have an idea, but I don't know if you'll like it."

Kirsten looked at him fondly. "I want to be with you, Noah. I'm truly open to all your ideas."

"Well, since I'm not baptized I'm free to choose another path without being shunned," he said, looking around at the growing crowd. "Someone might hear. Can you meet me after work at our tree in the Old Smicksburg Park? Then we can talk."

She smiled broadly and turned toward the kitchen. "I'll see you at one."

"Aren't we forgetting something?" Noah asked. "I need two pies. I'll take two peach pies from my girl, who's a peach."

Knit Together

CHAPTER 2

Katie took a deep breath to savor the smell of the lilac bushes that lined the back of the house. She loved the last weekend in May, Memorial Day weekend as the English called it. She was glad to have so many customers, people putting in their gardens or buying flowers to decorate gravesites. She turned the gas stove down in the greenhouse as the clouds floated by to unveil the sun.

She walked to the front of the house to wipe clean the white sign with black lettering that read, "Plants for Sale. No Sunday Sales". Having a business, she was glad their big white house was near the road and not in the middle of the land, like many Amish farms. The farm was purchased from an *English* family when she was twelve. She remembered their barn being raised to the right of the house. The structure was up in one day, and painted red the next. She was sad when the beautiful gingerbread trim on the house had to be torn off. All the red velvet curtains in the living room had to be changed to plain white cotton curtains, but her *daed* told her it was a small price to pay to live plain. Had it really been eighteen years ago she moved to this house? *The years can fly past like a flock of birds.*

She heard a car and turned to see Ginny and James' car pull in their driveway. A tall handsome man with shaggy brown hair emerged from the car. This must be Ginny's brother. She expected someone shorter, since Ginny was so petite.

Before Ginny could call her over to introduce him, she walked quickly to the back of the house. She had dirt all over her from working with the potting soil, and looked like a mess. She rinsed her hand and splashed her face with water from the rain barrel on the side of the house, just in case they came over. She pinched her cheeks so her face would have more color. She heard a buggy and turned to see Levi Miller pulling up the driveway. He was carrying something in his lap, wrapped in a black cloth.

"Hello Levi. Are you here to get more eggs or do you want some plants?"

"*Daed's* coming over later for plants. *Mamm's* putting in a huge garden this year." He hopped out of his buggy. "But I'll take some eggs. You know how my wee Mica loves them and it's my favorite thing to cook too. Ready in two minutes."

"Will you need any green pepper plants this year? Peppers and eggs are one of my favorite meals. If you throw in cheese, you have an omelet."

"*Mamm's* sure to put in at least a few dozen" Levi said, as he handed the item in the black cloth to her. "I made this present for you."

Katie felt her cheeks grow warm. She nodded and uncovered the beautifully carved cuckoo clock. "*Ach,* Levi, you shouldn't have."

Levi stepped closer and put his hand on her shoulder. "I know you've been sad about Sadie's death, and you love birds so I thought a little cuckoo clock would cheer you up."

Levi pierced her heart with his sympathetic dark brown eyes.

"When you see the little bird come out of the clock, remember the proverb, 'Live each short hour with God and the long years will take care of themselves'."

She held his gaze. "What a beautiful thought. I'll do that." She held up the walnut stained clock to admire

Levi's intricate carving. There were two doves looking at each other at the bottom with a nest between them. Did the picture have some kind of hidden meaning?

Levi gripped her shoulders. "You're so precious to me."

More heat rose into her cheeks.

"Could we take a buggy ride soon? A nice long ride to see all the blossoms, then get ice cream at the Country Sampler?"

His hope filled eyes pulled her in. "I think I would."

Levi broke into a broad smile, accenting his chiseled jawline. He cupped her cheeks in his hands. "How about Thursday? I'll come pick you up at six?"

"Okay," Katie said, feeling comfortable so near him. She felt a tinge of romance and wondered if this was the answer to her bold prayer she prayed a few days ago. She saw him draw closer, and then she felt her knees buckle and Levi's arms were soon around her, breaking her fall. Her black Labrador retriever wanted attention too.

Levi chuckled. "He thinks he's your boyfriend."

Katie hugged her dog around the neck. "You rascal. Always need to be the center of attention." She looked again at Levi, this time feeling shy. "Reuben's in the barn helping *mamm* bottle feed some baby lambs. I think a talk with him would be *goot*. You understand what it's like to be a widower and know what to say. He's grieving awfully hard."

"*Jah*, I know how he feels, but we need to keep moving forward, not letting the past drag us backwards." He put his hand on her cheek again. "I'll see you Thursday at six."

~*~

Kirsten showed her Uncle Joseph his new bedroom, lavender walls and a purple flowered bedspread, just like her room. "Mom let me decorate Aidan and Ian's room when they left and I love all shades of purple. Sorry, Uncle Joseph."

"I can handle purple. I can handle a paint brush too. Where's the closest Lowes?"

"We have a hardware store in Dayton, only four miles up the road. They have everything we need. Dad goes there all the time."

"How far away is a bigger town? I think it's gorgeous up here in Farmland, USA but I need conveniences. Any Wal-Mart around?"

"Fifteen miles to the Wal-Mart in Indiana and fifteen to the one in Punxsutawney. You can get to either one in less than half an hour"

"And that's close to you?"

"Plenty close for me. You wait and see, Uncle Joseph. There's nothing like living in the country." Kirsten looked at his three pieces of luggage. "You pack like a girl. You have enough clothes for a year or more."

"This whole suitcase is full of camera stuff." He unzipped the suitcase to reveal a few cameras, several zooms, a tripod, and a large black case.

Kirsten picked up a camera. "This one looks new. Must cost a fortune!"

Joseph crossed his arms. "It took me a while to save up for it. No easy money any more. I work for all I earn, fair and square."

"It's so hard to believe you were a drug dealer. When Mom told me I was shocked."

"When you're empty inside, you need something to fill you up. I obviously picked the wrong thing," Joseph said. "So tell me Kirsten, any lucky guy in your life?"

"I'm not telling you. You'd tell my parents." Kirsten put a shirt on a hanger and hung it in the closet.

"Come on, you're not five. I bet you have men beating down the door to get a blonde haired beauty like you."

Kirsten took a pillow and threw it at him, hitting him in the head. He collapsed on the bed. "Hey, you might hurt an old man."

"You're not old. Any woman in your life?"

"Well, there used to be, but it's over. Actually, I haven't dated anyone in a while."

Kirsten saw how open her uncle was and sat on the bed next to him. "I have a problem nobody would understand."

"I'll try."

Kirsten looked down. "I do have a boyfriend, but he's Amish. Mom and Dad don't know."

She looked at her Uncle Joseph's eyes, now as round as buttons. "You thinking of turning Amish?"

"That's the problem. I can't give up modern conveniences. I'd die if I couldn't wear make-up and clothes that are in style. Do you think it's wrong to like these things so much?"

His eyes softened. "You're so much like your mom. Always struggling with the deep issues of life." He put his hand on her shoulder. "Kirsten, you're way too young to be thinking about whether to turn Amish or not. Maybe you should date other people and get some perspective."

She looked at her uncle evenly. "I've known Noah my whole life. I'm twenty and have met plenty of guys, but my heart belongs to him."

He sat up and scratched his chin. "It's nice you have a lifelong friend. It's rare today. People move so much."

She moaned. "I know what I want, even though I'm young: a big family with Noah." Kirsten looked down. "Noah thought he had a plan, but it won't work. He said some Amish drive black cars and have modern conveniences, but they still dress plain. It's too confining. But, we'll find a way to be together. Love always finds a way."

At that, Joseph made the sound of a dove by cupping two hands over his mouth.

"What are you doing?" Kirsten asked with a crooked grin.

"I'm making a mourning dove sound. It's how you sound when you talk about your Noah. All lovey dovey."

Kirsten gave Joseph a good slap on his arm and laughed. He grabbed Kirsten and tickled her until she said uncle.

~*~

Ginny heard Joseph and Kirsten laughing upstairs and it startled her to realize that she never heard Joseph laugh growing up. She remembered her dad coming home from work and flying into a rage after Joseph spilt grape juice all over the linoleum kitchen floor. The image of her dad yelling about Joseph's green eyes, accusing her mother of being unfaithful, enraged her and she slammed the lid on the pan. Her grandmother had green eyes and her mother was a complete saint.

She held on to the side of the granite counter, feeling weak.

James came into the kitchen talking about something he just read in the *Pittsburgh Post-Gazette* but stopped when he saw Ginny. "Thinking about Sadie, Tink?"

"Oh, James, I'm not as little as Tinker Bell anymore," she snapped.

James readjusted his round wire-rimmed glasses and drew her near. "What's wrong?"

She rested her head on his chest. "Sorry, Honey. I'm a bundle of nerves with Joseph here. I'm having flashbacks of how sad his childhood was, and I didn't help him."

James lifted her chin. "Look at me. You were fifteen when Joseph was born; you can't blame yourself."

Ginny pulled James' salt and pepper beard. "You said the same thing when Aidan got in trouble in high school…to not blame myself." She sighed. "Oh James, I know, I try to rule the universe and it is exhausting."

"Yes it is. God's not up there in heaven wringing his hands over Joseph's past."

Ginny grinned. "You always make me feel better." She reached up and put both her arms around his neck. "You're my rock."

He bent down and squeezed her. "I wanted to show you something I just read in the paper. Knitting is good for your nerves and I think it's time you took classes at Suzy's."

"But how? It takes two to run the business. I don't have time."

"Let's hire Joseph so you have more free time. He can handle foreign orders and returns. He has the personality for customer service, and he can revamp the website."

Ginny put up a hand in protest. "He's here to start a photography business. He needs to focus."

"Okay, I'll spill the beans. Joseph thinks you look too tired and knows you've been crying at night…he wants to help you. He said grief has a way of waking us up to what's really important…and for him, it's you."

"H-He really said that?"

"I tell you what, take some time off. You said you need time to settle your mom's estate. Take a vacation for a month or so and take those knitting classes." He hugged her tight. "Knit me an alpaca wool scarf. The almanac says we're going to have a very hard winter this year."

CHAPTER 3

*J*oseph sat on the front porch, looking through his camera lens at the children playing across the street, when the image turned black. He peered over his camera, shocked to see a pretty Amish woman with her hand over his lens. Her white head covering accented the dark brown hair that peeped through the front. Her almond shaped brown eyes seemed shy, even though she made a bold move in blocking his scene.

"We don't allow our pictures to be taken," she said.

"My sister warned me. I'm sorry," Joseph said. "I came up here to get some scenes of the Amish and everywhere I try to shoot, the people turn away."

"It's because we believe the same thing."

Joseph got up. "Let's start on the right foot. I'm Joseph Hummel, Ginny's brother," he said, extending his hand.

She shook his hand. "I'm Katie, your neighbor across the street. This is the busiest time of year at my greenhouses or I would have come over to welcome you sooner. I believe my *bruder* Reuben has though."

"Yes, I've met Reuben and your mom, Millie. I'm so sorry about Reuben's wife. He's definitely in my prayers."

She took a deep breath. "*Jah*, Sadie is sorely missed, but we move forward. I'm teaching her little ones all about plants so they can help me. We're so busy and need all the little hands we can get."

"I see so many children over at your place. Do they give you a hard time? Kids seem allergic to work sometimes."

Katie's eyebrows shot up. "Ach, the children love to work with me. We relish the family times together."

"The children love to work? I've never heard that before."

Across the street three little girls played with their dolls. Several boys were taking turns pulling each other around the house in their red wagon. "Seeing pictures of how Amish children play would be great to show parents whose kids are too hooked on electronics. And people like to see pictures of the Amish because it makes them feel peaceful somehow."

"We can't have our pictures taken because of the scripture that says to not make any graven images after a person's likeness."

"Oh, I see." He fidgeted with the camera strap. "Don't you ever wish you could have a picture of something in the past? A picture of you as a little girl?"

"My *daed* passed away a few years ago, but I can still see him with his long gray beard, just as if someone showed me a picture," Katie said fondly. She looked up at him and grinned. "Why not take a picture of me watering some flowers from behind. We don't have a problem with pictures from the back, only our faces."

"So I can take a picture of the kids playing around here, or at the little schoolhouse down the road, if their backs are turned?" Joseph asked.

"*Jah*, but they're afraid of the camera, thinking their face will be put in a picture."

"I have a zoom lens on this camera and I can see things far away. The children won't even know I'm there. Want to take a look?"

"*Jah*, I suppose."

He took the camera strap off his neck and put it around Katie's, holding the camera up to her eyes. "Now just keep looking while I move the zoom." He tried to ignore the closeness between them. Katie was such a doll.

"*Ach*, I can clearly see the big oak tree on the hill behind my house! There's a blue heron standing in the pond!" she exclaimed. "It's like a telescope, isn't it?"

"Yes, the lenses magnify everything," Joseph said. "Have you ever looked through a telescope? I have a good one if you'd like to look at the stars some night."

Her cheeks turned pink. "I can name most constellations," she said, looking back into the camera. "Maybe some night I can have my nieces and nephews go outside with us and we can watch the stars. It would be such a treat for them."

"I'd really like that," Joseph quipped. "The summer sky is amazing."

Katie's eyes locked with Joseph's and held for a moment. "I need to water plants. Want to take some pictures of me from behind?

Joseph nodded and tore his eyes away from hers. He thought Amish women would be unattractive, not being able to wear make-up, but Katie was s natural beauty from a Dove soap commercial.

They walked across the street, up the long driveway between the house and barn to where the two large greenhouses stood. He noticed how the clear plastic walls were meticulously clean. Everything was so orderly, no clutter anywhere.

"Vegetables are in this house," Katie said, pointing to the one on the left. "And this one's for flowers," she said, pointing to the other. "It's so much easier when selling the plants. I find customers are either vegetable or flower people."

"And let me guess. You're a flower person."

"Well, being Amish we put up most of our food, so we have large vegetable gardens, but you're right. If I had time, I'd have an acre full of flowers," she said, leading Joseph over to the flowers for sale.

An earthy aroma welcomed Joseph and he inhaled deeply. He walked around the three long aisles, looking at all the six packs of red and white geraniums, pink and purple petunias, and countless amounts of marigolds, lined up neatly on the wooden shelves. The hanging baskets above had flower arrangements with lots of ivy hanging from the sides. "Do you make these baskets too?"

"Yes," Katie said. "I enjoy trying different patterns and colors to see how they'd look together. It's like trying to arrange a pattern for a quilt."

His eyes fell on a white sign with black lettering. It read, "All baskets *$15.00* and all six packs *$1.00*." He read it again, in disbelief. "How come so cheap?" "It's mostly Amish that buy from me, and I don't want to charge more than I need to."

Joseph was amazed at the fulfillment her work appeared to give her. "I'd like to buy two hanging baskets for Ginny."

"I have some on hold for her already. But she didn't get any red geraniums this year. She usually plants them in her window boxes. It looks so nice up against her blue house."

"I'll get what she usually orders and plant them for her as a surprise," Joseph said as they walked up and down the rows of plants. "Which flower is your favorite, Katie?"

"I like tea roses, especially the yellow ones. They're right over here." She walked toward the back of the greenhouse. She started pinching dead leaves and flowers off the roses.

"I hear roses are hard to grow. Is that some kind of trick?"

"*Jah*," Katie said. "It's called deadheading. By pinching back the dead leaves and flowers you encourage the plant to grow."

"Hold that pose and let me get in back of you for a picture." He snapped several pictures. "Here's the pictures. You can approve them." Joseph handed her his digital camera.

Katie's eyes lit up. "You can see the image just like that, right after you take the picture?"

"Yes, it still amazes me."

"I'll take you to the schoolhouses in the afternoon when the *kinner* are playing. You can show me the picture and I'll let you know if it's okay."

Joseph didn't know what to say. She'd just said how busy she was. "I really appreciate your help, Katie; if you have time....I didn't think Amish people would be so nice to a stranger."

"I'll make the time...and as far as *Outsiders*, your sister and her family have been trusted *English* friends for years. We're cautious of some *Outsiders* though. They might try to entice us with worldly ways and cause trouble in our community." She gave him a contemplative look. "Your family has gained our trust; so you have it too. Ginny put in a *goot* word for you."

Joseph grinned. "Ginny always says if she was raised Amish, she'd make a good one. She loves your ways."

"She's a *goot* woman of God as a Baptist. It's having a heart relationship with God that really matters." Katie said, placing her hand on her heart.

He'd known many Christian women, but never seen such sincerity. "You have a strong faith don't you?"

"It's the most precious thing to me," she said, holding Joseph's gaze.

"I feel the same too, especially knowing I have a loving, heavenly Father. My dad and I fought a lot. So knowing God really loves me means everything...I call him Abba; it means dad or papa." Joseph cleared his throat. "God helped get me the straight and narrow when I was a prodigal son. Don't know if Ginny ever told you anything about me."

"She did. But we all need forgiveness from time to time. In our *Gmay* if someone sins, they confess to the People and no one ever mentions it again. All is forgiven."

"Never mention it again? That's amazing. But what's a *G-Gmay?*"

"It's our word for community. It's what you'd call church. We try to focus on relationships and not maintaining a building, so we take turns meeting at each other's houses.

Joseph crossed his arms. "Interesting. I guess I thought Amish spirituality was different. Do you read the Bible?"

Katie put her index finger over her mouth to hide her laughter. "We believe everything written in the Bible."

Joseph leaned up against one of the shelves with his arm. "What's so funny?"

Katie deadheaded more flowers. "The misconceptions people have of the Amish. We're Christians. How could we not read the Bible?"

"Do you believe you can have a real relationship with God?"

"Of course, but we also believe we need to take care of that relationship, nurture it, like I do my plants."

Joseph stroked his chin. "Katie, I am so glad I met you today."

~*~

Ginny walked into SuzyB Knits. The little gold bell on the door jingled, announcing her arrival along with the yapping of two little dogs: Jack, a noble Jack Russell and Mollie, a toy fox terrier, as round as she was long.

"Hi there!" Suzy said, "Come in Ginny. Jack and Mollie were just asking for you." Suzy let the dogs out of the back room, picking yarn debris out of her strawberry blonde hair.

"Hi Suzy. I see you're back there spinning wool; you're wearing it." Ginny picked up tiny Mollie as she bent over to pet Jack "And how's my Jack and Mollie today?" Ginny sighed. "You're what the doctor ordered."

"Now are you talking to me or my dogs?" Suzy asked.

"You silly. I had a meltdown the other day and James said it's time I take those knitting classes I've been talking about…"

"For two years. I've been counting. How wonderful." Suzy moved a spool of green yarn off a chair. "Here, have a seat."

Ginny sat with Mollie on her lap. "You know Suzy, coming in here calms me down." Ginny looked around the small room, shelves from floor to ceiling filled with neat spools of yarn, hand spun and dyed by Suzy herself. "You're more at peace since you moved above your shop."

"I am. No high heating bills to worry about and less to clean. I still miss my staircase in our old Victorian place though." She picked up her knitting needles and yarn and sat next to Ginny. "It's been three months that we've lived here but I feel like it'll add years to our lives. Plus, I have the shortest commute to work, next to you!"

"Working from home has its advantages, but sometimes it's lonely. I look across the street and see how the Amish women work in groups during their frolics."

"But it seems like we have work frolics at church. Our women's ministry cleans, landscapes, has bake sales, runs the food bank...I could go on," Suzy said.

Ginny's eyes widened. "You're right. We do have our own work frolics."

"Yes, we do." She put her needles on her lap. "I compare my life with the Amish too. After all these years, I'm still gleaning some truth from them; they have a totally different culture."

"I know. Sadie's funeral gave me a lot to think about."

"Granny Weaver told me it was a nice service. She's been coming over to dye her yarn. When she saw the mittens I made, she said she'd like to have some ladies from her knitting circle come over to learn. Would you like to join our knitting circle?"

"Yes! I'd love to. But...they'll be so far ahead of me."

"No, they're beginners. They're used to using Amish knitting looms, not needles."

Ginny's eyes misted. "I am nervous. It looks hard, but I can't crochet anymore. It reminds me of the hospital and mom's chemotherapy treatments...all those long hours crocheting while sitting at her side..."

"He'll give you wings again. He did that for me after cancer took my mom."

The little gold bell on the door jingled again. "Hi there, girls," Janice said, flashing her brilliant white smile, set off by her black skin. She looked at Ginny. "Honey, you okay?"

Ginny got up to hug her pastor's wife. "I miss my mom."

Janice held her tight. "I know life has been tough for you. Sometimes you just need a shoulder to lean on, and you know I'm always here for you. You have our whole church family to lean on."

Ginny let Janice hold her in a warm embrace.

Janice jiggled a white bakery bag. "I know something that will cheer you some. White walnut fudge from the Sampler! It's buy one pound get a half pound free day. I can't resist a sale."

They sat down, and Janice opened the bag, holding up a piece of fudge, but Ginny and Suzy put their hands up. "We just joined Weight Watchers online last week and we're keeping each other accountable," Suzy said.

Janice gawked. "You girls are trim. Where you going to lose it?"

"We're getting thick around the middle, but are determined to take it off and be as skinny as you." Suzy said, staring at the fudge.

Janice laughed. "Okay. I won't be the tempter." She took a bite of fudge. "I'd love to sit and talk, but I'm on a mission today. We need to have some flowers put in around the church. I bought four flats of petunias from Katie. Are you girls up for it?"

Suzy looked at Ginny and smiled. "Of course we are."

~*~

Katie opened the oven door to spread apple chutney on the baking chicken. She quickly wiped down the kitchen counter and icebox. She'd lost track of time, showing Joseph the greenhouses and posing for all those pictures. *Time flies when you're having fun*, Ginny always said. She loved her spunky *English* neighbor and looked forward to getting to know her brother.

"Are you ready to go?" she heard someone ask from the back screen door. Katie turned to see Levi.

"*Ach*, Levi. Is it six o'clock already? Come in…Reuben and the *kinner* are coming over for dinner and I'm running late."

Millie welcomed Levi and asked him to sit down. "You can have dinner with us."

"*Danki,* but I ate already," he said, a little bewildered.

Millie looked at Katie with raised eyebrows.

"Levi and I are getting ice cream at the Sampler, but like I said, I lost track of time…actually, I've had a long day. Could we go out for ice cream tomorrow?"

She saw her *mamm* put her head in her hands. She looked at Levi and saw a look of rejection on his face, and immediately regretted what she said. She remembered her *mamm's* advice about not neglecting her friendship with him, since it might turn into romance. "*Ach,* what am I thinking? It's probably just the heat making me tired and ice cream is just what I need. It would be rude to not have dinner with my nieces and nephews though. They've talked about it all week.

Millie walked out of the room sighing.

Levi got up and put his hand on her shoulders. "You eat dinner with your family, I'll water and deadhead your plants, and then we'll get some ice cream."

"*Danki* for understanding." She looked up at his hopeful eyes. He was always so patient with her. He understood her attachment to Reuben and his *kinner*. She could easily eat a meal at the restaurant, and here he was, willing to wait for her. "I'll eat real quick, Levi."

"Take your time. I can wait…""

~*~

Kirsten plucked some apple blossoms off the tree and tapped them against Noah's nose playfully. "I met some Mennonites in the restaurant," she said. "They go to a church in Punxsutawney. But they don't dress plain like the Mennonites in my homeschooling books."

"You found out my plan B," Noah grinned. "Since you can't be Black Car Amish, I talked to a Mennonite friend, a new coworker. Do you think you could be Mennonite?"

"That's a question for you, Noah."

"It's the only solution. But the Amish and Mennonites are both Anabaptist denominations and they won't take it so hard."

Kirsten touched the lettering that Noah engraved on their secret tree in Old Smicksburg Park. *N & K Forever.* She thought of their secret tree on the Trillium Trail. He had engraved *N loves K.* She couldn't tell any of her girlfriends about these trees. It would seem juvenile to them, something you'd do in elementary school. Kirsten loved how Noah seemed like he was from a different era, one that hadn't fallen into the macho man syndrome and could express his feelings openly to her.

If he left the Amish, he wouldn't be shunned, but he'd always be looked at as someone who had strayed. It pained her to think he'd always have that over his head, like a dark cloud. She reached up to put her arms around his neck. "Do you really think I'm worth it, Noah? Your family and the whole Amish community will be so hurt. Now that we have a real plan...I'm afraid of all the repercussions our decision will make..."

Noah picked up a massive rock and flung it into the water, throwing up muddy debris from the bottom. "That's my life without you in it Kirsten...a total mess.

I'm sure about this." He leaned over and washed his hands in the stream, then turned to look at her. "Are you having doubts?"

Kirsten drew close to him. "I don't have any doubts about you at all; I just don't want you to be hurt."

Noah stared at her with a crooked grin. "'*You Amish are as slow as molasses in January.*' How many times have I heard you say that? Now it's time to make a decision and look who's dragging her feet." He bent down and kissed her. "We've kept our relationship a secret for how many years? Now that I'm older, I want a life together."

Kirsten leaned up not to steal a short kiss, but to get one that lingered. "I agree, Noah. This could be the answer to our prayers, but let's not tell anyone until we know for sure the Mennonite church is something we both like."

Noah ran his fingers through her long, wavy, golden hair. "I say we visit the church in Punxsutawney to start. We can go on a non-preaching Sunday. The Mennonites meet every week, so I won't be missed."

"Okay. I'll make sure I'm not scheduled to play guitar at my church too." She leaned her head on his chest. "The trickiest part is my parents not finding out. I'll be beaming, finally with some hope for our future, and they'll sniff out that something's up, like one of your coon dogs."

~*~

Katie stared at Levi, trying not to turn and gawk at the children sitting at the table next to them.

"I'll have a chocolate cone daddy, please, please, please," a chubby little boy begged his father, pulling on his sleeve. "A chocolate cone with sprinkles on top!"

"Be patient son. The waitress will be here in a second to take our order," the father chided.

"Adopt the pace of nature; her secret is patience." Levi whispered the Amish proverb in Katie's ear.

"Remember how impatient we were when the teacher passed out snacks in school?" Katie asked. "Seemed like an eternity back then to wait for five seconds."

The family sitting next to them soon had three whining, impatient children. The older brother had set the tone. Katie was glad patience and respect for elders was taught at such a young age among the People.

"So Katie, you've been busy with Reuben's *kinner*, *jah*?" Levi asked, leaning toward her.

"The *kinner* are helping me. You know how they learn to do a chore as soon as they're able. Little Anna pulls off dead flowers, but lots of times she pulls off *goot* ones, but she's learning," Katie smiled. "I think work helps them grieve and heal."

Levi nodded in agreement. "I started carving more detail on clocks after I lost Hannah. It took my mind off of her. It helped me recover. I'm healed for sure and my heart is free to love another."

Katie put her head down, her cheeks hot.

"What I'm saying is that I think my heart is with another already. I think you know who has it, *jah*?"

Katie didn't know if a public restaurant was an appropriate place to say such things, but it was noisy and no one could hear except her. She sat in silence.

"Katie, did you hear what I just said?" Levi probed. "I think you understand my meaning. Would you be my girl?"

She looked his way, but found it hard to make eye contact. "I'll be thinking and praying about that, Levi," she said. "I have so many responsibilities at home, as you know…"

Levi fidgeted with the salt shakers. "You're afraid to love, Katie. Judah's deception changed you." He grabbed her hand. "I'm scared too."

"Of what?"

"Of loving someone again. Love has its painful side, too."

She knew what he meant. They were both hurt by someone they loved; of course Judah could have prevented the pain. Maybe she couldn't trust a man, like her *mamm* said. "Remember when we talked about this before Sadie's death?" Katie asked. "I said I was happy being single."

"You mean you're safe being single." Levi readjusted his straw hat and sighed.

"Hi," Antonio said. "Can I take your order?"

"I think I'll take a banana split." Katie said.

"I'll take a hot fudge sundae with chocolate ice cream, instead of vanilla. Can you do that?" Levi asked.

"Oh, no problem. Two orders coming up."

Katie was silent. She didn't know what to say to Levi about courtship. Maybe he was right; she was safe being single. Safe from pain. "Let me pray about this."

Levi crossed his arms and slouched in his chair. "Well, I'm glad I'm here. Chocolate is good for your nerves."

Katie let out nervous laughter. "So that's why you ordered so much chocolate. I know you like strawberry ice cream better." She looked into Levi's brown eyes. She did admire this man so. "I am scared, Levi. But the more we talk, my fear seems to ease. *Mamm* said friendship is where romance starts... Could we spend more time together before I give you my answer?" she asked.

Levi winked at her. "Sure."

.CHAPTER 4

Ginny put the platter of roast beef on the table. "Joseph, thank you so much for planting my flower boxes and putting them up. Did you get the flowers from Katie?"

"Yes. I also picked up your hanging baskets. They're on the back porch. Katie's a nice girl. I like her a lot."

Ginny smiled. "She's a sweetie. I'll pay you back."

Joseph put his hand up. "It's on me. Hey, how's the knitting lessons coming along?" he asked as he passed the mashed potatoes.

"Crocheting comes more naturally to me. I needed something new to get my mind off Mom and settling the estate…" Ginny brushed away a tear.

"You know, Sis, maybe you need to talk to someone. Does your church offer counseling?"

Ginny forked a piece of roast beef on her plate. "Yes, and Pastor Jerry's good. He really helped me with perspective – to see beyond this time of pain. He also suggested I read Psalms because it helps me express my emotions to God. Maybe you should do it too, Joseph. I'm sure you miss Mom too. Guys just don't cry like us women." Looking to turn the conversation, Ginny smiled brightly. "But, good news, I had quite an answer to prayer today."

James leaned forward, admiring his wife's spunk. "What, Tink?"

"Well, Millie, Katie and I are all grieving. There's great therapy in the fabric arts, so we're making a quilt for the auction in August. They'll teach me. I've been taking Lottie's quilts to festivals for years, and admire their craftsmanship. So God answered my secret prayer: to learn how to quilt like the Amish."

Joseph beamed. "Great. I know you like to sew. I remember when you used to stitch little uniforms for my GI Joes when I was little. Dad screamed at me to stop playing with dolls. It wasn't like I was playing with a Barbie," he laughed.

"So Joseph, you remember all that screaming?" Ginny asked. "You were so young."

"Dad yelled at me since birth. He was depressed and didn't know God. He didn't have the power the Lord gives to overcome addictive behavior." Joseph poured gravy over his potatoes and meat.

"Addictive behavior? Addiction to anger?" James asked. "That sounds like an excuse to sin."

Joseph's eyebrows went up. "When I was in Celebrate Recovery there was no denying we sinned, but we learned how to break free from its hold." Joseph took a bite of his roast beef and washed it down with coffee. "I guess what I learned was that it was going to take something supernatural - God. I couldn't kick drugs by myself. I needed His help. I still do." He poked at his asparagus with his fork. "I had a friend in the group. Man, the regrets he had about how he treated his family. It helped me understand Dad... and forgive him. I'm over it, Sis."

Ginny leaned forward, thanking God Joseph had come. He wasn't the emotional wreck she'd feared. Maybe she could get over her guilt of not helping him enough. The Lord had intervened.

"You suffered so much, but it really seems like you're over it all. Any other problems your church helped you with? How about 9/11?" Ginny probed.

"They helped, but I still have flashbacks...even after ten years." He bowed his head. "But I can say this, I have more hope now. Hope's a powerful thing; it can get you through a lot."

There was silence at the table. James cleared his throat. "Anything we can do to help with these flashbacks?"

Joseph looked at James and then Ginny. "I didn't have much of a family life." His cheeks slowly grew red as he searched for words. "Well to totally spill the beans, I moved here for more than pictures and starting a business. My family is here, and I want to live near you."

Ginny gasped. "I've missed you little brother." She got up and hugged him from the back, leaning her head on his shoulder.

"I've missed you too, Sis." He pinched her cheek.

"You have us as family, and I know you'll find a girl to start a family of your own," Ginny said, returning to her seat.

Joseph sighed. "Oh, I've dated plenty. Not much hope of finding a wife, though. Not too many women I've met who I'd want to be the mother of my children."

"I knew it! You want children!" Ginny grinned. "Let me see. There are a few single girls at our church..."

James chuckled. "Honey, you watch *Emma* too much. The girl in that movie messed up a lot of people's lives. You and your Jane Austen movies. You have *Emma* in how many versions?"

"Three, and if they make another version, I'll buy it too. And Emma did not mess up people's lives; she only wanted to help them with her matchmaking abilities."

Joseph cleared his throat. "I don't need a matchmaker. Like I said, I've dated plenty, and I've resigned myself to being a bachelor. I'm happy single, honest."

~*~

Joseph and Katie got into his Jeep, and started onto Wilson Road and made a right at Mahoning Road. They pulled into the parking lot of the Smicksburg Baptist Church, which sat catty-cornered to the schoolhouse. Tall field grass and wildflowers bordered the edge of the school property, and he was glad the children couldn't see them up close.

They got out of the car and sat on the wooden steps leading up to the white clapboard church. Joseph looked through a new zoom on his camera, clearly seeing children's faces, and was tempted to click his camera, but didn't. *Girls* painted on one outhouse and *Boys* on the other. The schoolhouse didn't look big enough for the twenty-five children Katie said attended. A blonde-haired little boy with a straw hat played baseball. When he bent down to pick up the ball, Joseph clicked his camera. Girls on the swings with their braids flying in the air caught his attention and as soon as they turned their heads, he took the picture, and then showed Katie each image and she nodded in approval.

After a hundred or more clicks, Katie said she trusted him to keep his word, and Joseph took more shots. A car slowly pulled up to the school and Joseph watched as it came to a stop, and put his camera down. Sweat formed around his upper lip and his face felt hot.

Katie wrinkled her brow. "Joseph, what is it?"

He rubbed his hands on his thighs. "Nothing. Praying through my fears."

"Fears of what? Taking bad pictures?"

"No, no, not that." He ran his trembling fingers through his hair and cleared his throat. "It's just that I was living in New York City. Was close by when the Twin Towers fell. I lost some friends."

"I'm sorry, Joseph," Katie said quietly. "I'm sorry for your loss." She sighed. "What made you think back to such a horrible day?"

"You know about the school shootings in Nickel Mine, right? Where a local man shot those girls in their little Amish school? Well, once you go through something traumatic, you start to fear other things might happen." He rubbed the back of his neck and turned to look up at the cross on the church steeple. "I give my fear to God, but sometimes take it back," Joseph said, with a forced grin.

"So seeing that car made you think a man might shoot at the children?" Katie asked.

"Exactly. It rarely happens anymore."

"So you still struggle with things that happened…ten years ago?" she asked.

Joseph turned toward her, holding her gaze. "Yes. Why? Do you too?"

"*Jah.*" She caught a wisp of stray hair and tucked it under her white *kapp*. ""I should have a family of my own by now. I was engaged when I was twenty, but he left the Amish."

"Why hasn't another Amish man snatched you up by now?"

"I passed up a few proposals. I think when I turned thirty it made me realize I may never have a family." She bowed her head. "The Amish believe love can grow after you're married and there's a *goot* man who wants to court me…"

"And you don't love him?" Joseph asked, holding back the urge to put his arm around her.

"I love him like one of my *brieder*." She sighed.

"Maybe give it some time and if the Lord wants you to be with him, he'll put a special love in your heart for him, like a woman should have toward a husband. I certainly couldn't marry someone I didn't love."

Joseph looked at her round, bewildered eyes. How could the Amish encourage her to marry someone she didn't love? And she wasn't too old to have a family. He picked up his camera and started to click more pictures. He watched as Katie got up and walked over to the flowers planted around the church. When she bent over to admire the pansies he clicked a picture. She turned and smiled, and he took a shot from the front.

"*Ach*, you can't do that! Give me the camera."

"If you can reach it, it's yours," Joseph said, holding the camera in the air.

She laughed and jumped up, trying to reach it. He looked down at her and thought what a lovely picture she would make right now. He held the camera down and pretended to take another picture, but she stiffened. "I'll delete the pictures, don't worry."

"*I'll* delete them." Katie grabbed the camera out of his hands and ran.

"Hey, that cost a fortune!" He ran after her and caught her by the waist. She turned toward him; he felt so oddly at peace with this beautiful Amish woman.

~*~

Katie took Levi's hand as he helped her out of the buggy. "*Danki*, Levi, for the *wunderbar* buggy ride. I enjoyed the peach pie, too. Makes me want to go buy a bushel of peaches and put them up for pie filling."

Levi looked at Katie, brown eyes timid. "Did you have as much fun with me as with Joseph?"

"How can you ask me that? I feel one way around Joseph, another around my *goot* friend Lottie and another around you."

Levi took off his straw hat and flicked a small trig off the brim. "Let's walk up the hill to the pond."

"Okay. It's my favorite place on earth. Want an apple orchard up there someday."

He grabbed her hand to help her over some slick, muddy spots.

She pulled her hand away to pick some dandelions. "Do you know dandelions make the best tea? Good when you're sick. The little flowers cleanse the body." She ran about picking flowers, getting further from Levi.

"Katie, you're doing it again. When I'm with you, you're making work."

Katie's cheeks turned pink as he took her hands. "It's only me, Katie. Not some mean farm dog. I don't bite."

She ignored his comment. "Let's continue to the pond," she said, turning to run up the hill.

When they reached the top, Katie leaned on the old oak tree, needing support. Levi sat by the tree, near her. "Come sit down, Katie."

"Don't want my skirt getting wet."

Levi took off his jacket and laid it on the ground. "There you go. No problem now."

Katie sat down next to him. "*Danki*, Levi."

"Has the little cuckoo been reminding you hourly of the promises of God, to heal a heart?" he asked.

"*Jah*, I think it has, slowly, but surely. I do worry about Reuben, though. He's putting on a good face for the *kinner*, but his eyes are so sad. He loved Sadie dearly."

"I know how he feels. It does take time. He's in my prayers, too. You're in my prayer, too, Katie. I hope you know that."

"*Jah,* I do. I appreciate that. I feel the strength of prayer and the love of the People." Levi gabbed Katie's hand. "You're so precious to me; you know that too, *jah?*"

Katie looked at Levi. "*Jah,* I know that." Levi cupped her face in his hands and drew near to kiss her cheek.

The kiss was short, but heartfelt and Katie was surprised....she was touched by how gentle Levi tried to win her heart. He wasn't forward, trying to kiss her on the lips. They sat quietly and watched the sheep below, holding hands. She was feeling more at ease with Levi. Maybe romance would follow in time.

~*~

Ginny hid a giggle as Granny Weaver marveled at all the bold colored yarn in Suzy's shop. She knew the bishop would never approve anything but an earth-tone color, and she couldn't help but wonder that if Granny had been born *English,* she'd have been a famous painter. Her eye for coordinating colors in her quilts was unmatched, but as Granny said, she was tired of quilting.

The knitting circle decided to meet at Suzy's since everything they needed was right there, the store full of yarn in the front shop, the little kitchen in the back for desserts, and the enclosed side porch to soak in sunshine while they knit.

Katie and Millie rode the three miles to the store with Ginny. Suzy picked up Granny and Sarah Mast. They all came in and took a seat at one of Suzy's antique wicker chairs, all set in a circle, and got out their balls of yarn and needles.

Suzy cleared her throat. "We'll continue to practice the seed stitch pattern. Remember, it's just knit one, purl one. Very simple." She grinned. "You're all learning how to really knit."

Granny looked up, eyes wide. "We knit already with our looms, just need to learn how to make mittens so we can send them off to Christian Aid."

Sarah laughed. "You told me you like the clicking of the needles. Why not admit you're bored with the Amish knitting loom, like you are with quilting?"

Granny shifted in her chair. "My *mamm* taught me to quilt and knit on a loom, and I feel like I'm not respecting her memory."

Ginny moaned. What dedication and honor these dear people had to their heritage. She remembered how her mom taught her to crochet...how patient she was. She felt her eyes mist, but willed back tears.

Millie leaned toward her. "You okay?"

"Yes, I was just thinking of my mom and my Italian roots. My mom crocheted and taught me. It's been handed down through the generations." She looked across the room at Granny. "I know what you mean, Granny, but I think our moms would understand that making something from yarn is just, well, *wunderbar goot*, *jah*?"

The women laughed at Ginny's Amish accent. She looked around the room and thanked God, once again, to live in such an unusual place, where Amish and *English* were such good friends.

"Katie," Granny said. "How's Levi? Do you think we'll be busy next November?"

Katie's cheeks and neck grew red. "Granny, such things are a secret, *jah*?"

"*Jah*, but you can tell us...we're all like family," Granny said, her eyes dancing with wonder.

"Levi and I are just friends for now." Katie looked intently at her knitting.

"I hear you've been taking Joseph around town to take pictures. Is he interfering?" Sarah asked.

Ginny gasped and looked at Sarah. "What do you mean?"

"Well, my husband's concerned. He is the Bishop and needs to look after his flock."

Ginny looked over at Katie who was now as red as beets. "Katie? Is Joseph causing... problems?"

Katie looked at Suzy. "Could I have a glass of water?"

Suzy hit her forehead with her hand. "I forgot, ladies. Coffee and punch are laid out in the next room. Granny brought some cookies, too."

Ginny watched as Katie darted from her chair and went into the next room. She turned to Sarah. "Katie has helped my brother over the past month make an income off his pictures. He's starting a business. Is there gossip about them?"

Sarah nodded. "They're seen together, a lot. Seem mighty happy, too."

Katie reappeared into the room. She sat in her chair, shoulders drooping.

"Katie, I think Sarah's teasing you. Aren't you Sarah?" Millie asked.

Suzy stood up before anything came out of Sarah's open mouth. "Does anyone need help? That's what I'm here for. This is only your fourth lesson and I'm sure someone's having trouble." She moved around the room checking everyone's work. "I think next week we can move on to another pattern."

"Can't wait to make little things, like mittens...and baby booties." Granny turned to Katie. "Should we be making baby booties for your hope chest? You'll probably need them in a year or two."

Katie sat up straight as a board. "I'll be able to make my own booties, if I get married."

Ginny saw the pain in Katie's eyes. Could it really be true she didn't care for Levi and preferred Joseph's company? Surely this was all country gossip that would soon blow away.

CHAPTER 5

Ginny heard the Jeep pull in and soon saw her brother come in the front door.

"Hey, Sis, I left for Pittsburgh this morning and now there's the shell of a house built across the street?"

She loved that her brother was so verbal about all he noticed about the Amish. She was so familiar with their ways and his comments made her once again look at them with new appreciation. "Joseph, you'll see barns up in a day all over Smicksburg." She looked up from her knitting. "They're building a *dawdyhaus*. It's German for grandparents' house. The Amish build them for their aging parents. Millie and Katie are moving into it and giving their house to Reuben."

Joseph folded his arms and stared through the screen door. "That's amazing. So kind of Millie, but isn't she attached to her house?"

"The Amish look at their life as a pilgrimage. They hold all things loosely."

Joseph scratched his chin. "I'm more than impressed. They're not materialistic at all." He ran up the stairs and thunder bolted back down the steps and started snapping pictures on the porch. "There's a man walking on a roof beam with no safety belt."

She got up and joined him on the porch. "No faces."

"I know. Ask Katie. She trusts me."

"Seems like you two spend a lot of time together. I'm surprised one of her brothers hasn't said anything...yet," Ginny said, continuing to knit from the cedar chair.

"What do you mean? Is it wrong that we talk?"

"Not at all, but body language is eighty percent of communication and I see you saying things to each other that cannot be," Ginny said. "Can we have a little chat, Joseph?"

"I can chat and snap pictures at the same time. Go ahead. What's on your mind?"

Ginny put down the little black mitten she was knitting. "You and Katie seem like you're more than friends. You can't see the way you two look at each other, but others can."

"Are others saying anything...about what we're supposed to be saying?"

"Yes, half the town," Ginny informed. "And it's serious for Katie. If she's suspected of forming some attachment to an *English* man, she'll be confronted. People see Katie with you more than Levi Miller."

"Maybe she wants to be with me." Joseph sighed.

Ginny poked him with her knitting needle. "Don't get flippant about it. I'm talking about something serious."

Joseph sat in the chair next to her. "Okay." He ran his finger through his brown hair. "I've never met a girl like Katie. She gives me hope there are still decent women out there."

"Just be careful. I smell trouble.

He grinned. "Sis, maybe James is right. Maybe you do watch too many Jane Ashton movies."

Ginny threw her ball of yarn at him. "Jane Austen, dear, like Austin, Texas. If you're going to cut her down, at least say her name right." She retrieved the yarn off the floor. "Well, she was the expert on love and heartbreak." She reached over and took Joseph's hand. "I just don't want to see you hurt. She'll never leave the Amish for you. She was engaged you know, and never left when Judah did."

"She told me about that guy. What a fool to give up a girl like that!"

"She told you something that personal?" Ginny felt her mouth grow dry. She knew Katie was so guarded around men, even the Amish fellows that tried to get her attention, even if they were five years younger.

"Yes. She's so easy to talk to. Feels like I've known her for years."

"But you haven't..."

Joseph grinned. "Sis, I'm going to save my money and get you a pet; a baby pug dog. You've always wanted one and since you obviously need someone to baby, you can baby the dog."

Ginny got up and slapped his arm playfully. "Joseph, I am not babying you."

"Yes you are."

She poked him in the chest with a knitting needle again. "Well if I am, I have good intentions. I don't want you to hope for something that can't happen."

~*~

Joseph went up to his room. He looked at the walls and was thankful he found brown paint on sale. The room felt like a cave, his man cave. He thought of Katie. He didn't want to do anything to hurt that dear girl. He knew he couldn't be Amish. Yes, his feelings were growing for her, and he'd only met her several weeks ago. She enjoyed being his tour guide around Smicksburg, and he already sold quite a few pictures, thanks to her. There was a company interested in making a calendar if he got all the seasons captured just right. Katie had an eye for photography even though she didn't know it. He sighed. *Who am I kidding? I love being around that girl!*

Joseph looked out the window and prayed God would give him the grace to be around Katie and feel just a brotherly-type love and nothing more.

~*~

Katie, Millie, and Reuben sat around the oak table. Reuben shook his head. "Maybe I shouldn't have read the letters."

"They were your wife's. You had every right. Such secrets should not have been kept between you two." Millie took his hand.

"She wrote to Judah all these years. She even sent him money. Lord help me." Reuben gripped his *mamm's* hand.

"Times like this, I wish your *daed* was here. Ach, I do feel for you, Reuben."

Katie felt a lump in her throat and stood behind her brother. "I was the one cleaning some of Sadie's things from your bedroom and found the letters," she said softly, putting her hand on Reuben's shoulder. "Maybe I did the wrong thing and should have just burnt them."

Reuben seemed to not hear her. "She corresponded with her *bruder* all these years, without telling a soul."

Katie went to the sink to pump water into the tea kettle. She felt dizzy and lost her footing, but caught herself on the counter.

"Are you alright, *dochder*?" Millie gasped.

"*Jah*, I'm fine. Just clumsy today, I suppose." She put the tea kettle on the gas powered stove, and then sat next to Reuben again. "Sadie said she had no idea where he was once he was under the ban."

Millie slummed her shoulders. "She must have loved her *bruder* too much, Reuben. She made a mistake in not telling you, though."

"She lied. There was money missing in our bank account. In some of the letters, Judah thanked her for sending money. Hundreds of dollars." He hit the table with a fist. "She broke an oath. She didn't follow the *Ordnung*. She feathered his nest outside the *Gmay*!"

Millie stiffened. "Son, the *kinner* can't hear you speak in that tone about their *mamm*. You have to forgive your wife."

Katie didn't know if it was appropriate to ask, but her head was spinning now. "Do the letters mention if Judah ever married?"

"From what I've read, no. He's single and living in Pittsburgh."

Judah had never married? What did it mean? She remembered him saying if she didn't leave with him, he'd be a lonely bachelor the rest of his life. *He was being truthful.* She forced herself to think of her brother. She had her hand on Reuben's shoulders and squeezed them tight. "Sadie was such a loving wife. Maybe there was a *goot* reason to send him money."

Reuben's chin quivered. "I must forgive...I wish I could talk to Sadie and ask her why..."

"Katie, are you ready?" She turned to see her best friend, Lottie, at the back screen door. "Eli's finished working on the *dawdyhaus* for today and is anxious to get going."

"Oh, ah, Lottie, I'm not feeling up to going into Punxsutawney tonight. We have all we need from Wal-Mart."

Lottie walked into the kitchen. "Seems like you folk got some bad news. Are *yinz* all right?"

Katie took Lottie's hand. "Just a bump in the road."

Lottie looked around the room, her blue eyes wide. "Katie, can I have a word with you?"

They walked out to the front porch and sat on the cedar swing. "Does all this have to do with you and that *English* man, Joseph?"

Now her head started to spin faster. "What? What makes you ask such a thing?"

Lottie nervously tucked stray blonde hair under her *kapp*. "There's just a little talk among the grapevine that you and this Joseph are more than friends. The Bishop helped on the *dawdyhaus* today and I saw him come in. I thought he might have had some words with you." Lottie looked at her evenly.

"The Bishop said nothing. Only visited with *Mamm*." Katie looked into Lottie's eyes for some explanation, but there was none. "I take Joseph to Amish farms and schools for pictures, that's all."

"*Ach*, Katie. The *English* can pull us away from the Gmay, *jah*. You shouldn't be alone with him."

"Our neighbors across the street are our trusted *English* friends, you know that."

"But this Joseph is a mighty attractive man. Be careful. Guard your heart."

Katie knew her friend meant well. "I will. *Danki*, my dear friend," Katie said, reaching over to hug Lottie.

"Levi Miller is another attractive man, *jah*?" Lottie prodded.

"He is. We're enjoying our friendship and seeing if it leads to love, like *Mamm* and *Daed* did."

"Eli and I did the same thing. When hard times come, you have a solid foundation to lean on. It'll be two years next month that he lost his *mamm;* he drew strength from me, and it felt *goot* to see he didn't carry the burden alone. That's love." She looked at Katie evenly. "Don't let a silly schoolgirl romance on an *Outsider* ruin your chance for real love with a *goot* Amish man like Levi."

Katie nodded her head, letting Lottie know she understood her warning. "I need to get back inside... please pray for Reuben. He's having a very hard time." Katie leaned forward and gave Lottie another hug. "I think I felt the baby move!"

Lottie took Katie's hand and put it on her right side. "Feel right here. It's his foot. I think he's kicking to get out."

"*Ach*, Lottie, I'm so happy for you. God blessed your womb after all these years. I hope you have twins like Rachael in the Bible." Katie embraced her dear friend, but couldn't ignore the emptiness she felt. It threatened to choke her at times. How she longed to have children.

She headed back into the kitchen and sat with Reuben. After praying with him, she went up to her room. Her spacious bedroom was a comfort. She knelt down by her bed and looked at the wedding-ring pattern quilt. *Would she ever be married*

Katie laid her head on the quilt and felt a tug on her heart toward Judah, like it was yesterday. Would he ever come back to the People? If he knelt and confessed his sin of rebellion, he would be forgiven and it would never be spoken of again. Getting up, the room began to swirl so she laid on her bed and looked at the ceiling.

Should she try to get the address from Reuben and write him about Sadie? Maybe he didn't even know his sister died. What would *Daed* do if he were alive? "Abba, Father, help me," Katie whispered. She thought of Joseph and how he called God, Abba. He'd shared his painful childhood that led to his teenage rebellion. His spiral down into drugs and sinful living would have alarmed her if he wasn't such a changed man. When she was with him she felt attracted to him in a romantic way, unlike Levi.

Images of Joseph, then Judah, and then Levi swirled in her head. Her heart raced and she jumped off the bed to retrieve her knitting needles and yarn from their basket by her dresser. She soon heard the tapping of the needles and she took a deep breath. If knitting was good for nerves, like Suzy claimed, Katie needed to knit for a week straight.

~*~

Noah looked at Kirsten and appreciated that she wore a brown skirt and white blouse, something plain so he wouldn't look so out of place. It had taken him a month to get up the nerve to go to the Mennonite church, and Kirsten waited patiently. He gripped her hand as they walked up the stairs to the old, red brick church. When they entered, Noah looked around the church in shock. He wanted to turn and run, but someone warmly greeted him.

"Welcome to the Punxsutawney Mennonite Church," the young man in blue Dockers and white Polo shirt said. "I'm Pastor Sheldon. You're early. Church doesn't start until ten-thirty

"Hello," Noah said, feeling numb. "I'm Noah and this is my friend Kirsten."

"Where are you two from?"

"Smicksburg," Noah said.

"It appears you're Amish and Kirsten, you're not, am I right?

"Yes," Kirsten said.

Sheldon motioned for them to take a seat and they sat in a pew near the back. Noah wiped his sweaty palms on his black pants. Soon Sheldon sat in the pew in front of them.

"I don't mean to be, well, nosy, but you two seem like you're more than friends?"

"Is it so obvious?" Kirsten asked.

"Yes," Pastor Sheldon grinned. "I've had this situation in my church before. I'm not saying it's impossible, but very difficult. We're more *English* here than an Old Order Mennonite congregation, as you can see by the style of my dress and all the instruments up on the altar."

"That's for sure and certain," Noah said, still feeling numb.

"If you'd like some information about what we believe, I can give you a visitor's packet."

Noah nodded in agreement. The pastor ran to the front of the church to get a packet. He gave it to him along with a visitor's pen, with the church's name and phone number on it. Noah took the packet, but felt like he was betraying the People. He kept reminding himself that he hadn't made a baptismal promise to them. He was doing nothing wrong.

As the church slowly filled to capacity, Pastor Sheldon greeted everyone and asked them to rise and sing a song. Noah was shocked when a man playing the guitar started singing while the people in the congregation read words projected onto the wall. Everyone sang in English. Some closed their eyes, some lifted their hands. The words were beautiful, describing how Christ's blood cleansed from all sin. His love was new every morning, and steadfast, and faithful. Noah never saw *English* people worship like this.

Pastor Sheldon stood up after several songs were sung. "We'd like to welcome any visitors," he said. "Please raise your hand if you're a first time guest"

Kirsten and Noah raised their hands. A girl with short hair turned and waved at Kirsten and she waved back. Noah was shocked again. Why the attention on people and not strictly on God? Then Pastor Sheldon talked about the offering. He had plans to expand the church building, since the congregation had grown. Giving money in church was so foreign to Noah, as was having church in a building that wasn't a home. He didn't see the need for more room; people just needed to sit closer. If Amish benches were put in the church, they could pack in four-hundred people easily.

Pastor Sheldon gave a sermon on the Beatitudes, something Noah was familiar with. He agreed with what the pastor said. He talked for forty-five minutes, and then another worship song followed. The pastor thanked everyone for coming and church was dismissed.

A girl raced over to Kirsten and gave her a hug, while others grabbed Noah's hand, introducing themselves and welcomed him to their church. Kirsten introduced Noah to Susan, explaining that this was the Mennonite girl she'd met at the Sampler. Noah shook her hand. Parishioners mingled for half an hour or more after church. There were coffee and doughnuts at the back of the church. Kirsten was all smiles after the service, telling everyone they'd be back.

They got into Kirsten's car. "I loved it, Noah. What do you think?"

"Feel as strange as if I just flew to the moon."

"Different from your Amish services, huh?" Kirsten probed.

"*Jah*, it was nice, though, to see *English* worshipping God, but why do you need a guitar?"

"You've only known the Amish way," she said. "Most churches use instruments."

"I like the Amish way better. It's more reverent. So much attention on money, too. They don't need a bigger building. It's wasteful." Noah turned from her and stared out the window.

Kirsten sighed. "Maybe the music was too much of a shock, but Noah, the church was crowded. They do need more room."

"Kirsten, we need to pray for God's will to be done."

"I pray that all the time but we need to take action, though. Can't expect a church to just fall out of heaven. We need to visit other churches if you're uncomfortable."

"Could we try a more conservative Mennonite church?"

"You mean Old Order Mennonite?" Kirsten's eyes went round. "We may as well be Amish, then. I don't see the difference

He saw the look of hopelessness on her face. "Maybe a Brethren Church then? They're Anabaptist, too. There's one in Plumville." He took her hand. "We do need to keep praying and trying, as hard as this is for me. It would be harder to not have a future with you, Kirsten."

CHAPTER 6

*W*eeks passed, and Katie rarely thought of Judah; she was having so much fun with Joseph. She was also busy with summer chores, putting up preserves and canning peas, beans, and other bounty from their garden. She adored her new kitchen of the *dawdyhaus*, it being so small, anything was in arm's reach.

Today she was making *whoopie* pies for her nieces and nephews. Joseph would be teaching them the constellations of the late July sky. He said he wanted to get them ready for the Perseids meteorite shower in August. Katie chuckled. He didn't believe the children could sit quietly for an hour and he was making them practice. She told him they sat for three hours through a church service, but he didn't seem convinced.

She was glad the rumors about her and Joseph had died down, now that a few nieces and nephews went with them to photo shoots. Sometimes her *mamm* came too, knowing some historic spots in Smicksburg Katie never knew about. She heard a car drive up the long driveway to the little house. She went to answer the knock at the front door, assuming it was Joseph, but he was early.

"Hello, Katie," Judah said. "Can I talk to you?"

"I-I…" Katie shut the door, not knowing what to do. She leaned up against the door. Should I open it? She began shaking and felt her knees grow weak. She ran to the sink to get some water. Another knock at the door. Katie took a deep breath and stood tall. Judah had a right to know about his sister after all these months. She'd talk to him, even if he was under the ban." Katie opened the door and saw Judah; he had aged well, but his blue eyes seemed empty, almost lifeless. She saw his blue car parked out front of the house. She stepped outside to talk.

"What are you here for, Judah?" she asked, clenching her shaking hands.

Judah stepped forward and put his arm on her shoulder. "How are you Katie? It's been years…"

"*Jah*, a long time." She backed away. "Why are you here?"

"I-I was wondering how Sadie was. I stopped over at your old place, but no answer."

"Reuben lives there now. He isn't home."

"Is Sadie home? It's her I've come to see."

Shaking, Katie motioned for him to sit on the swing. "Would you like some root beer?"

"No," he said. "I know I'm shunned, but Sadie wrote. I haven't heard from her and got worried."

"Judah, we know you and Sadie wrote to each other all these years, even though you were under the ban."

"How'd you know that?"

"Reuben found the letters she kept from you."

"He had no right to read those. They were Sadie's. What does she say about all this?"

Katie walked over and took Judah's hand. "She died of a heart attack, in late May."

Judah looked straight ahead not saying anything. "That's not true. You're lying so I can't see her."

"Judah, would I tell such a cruel lie?" She looked at Judah as he looked straight ahead, dazed. Katie ran inside to get him a glass full of orange juice. "Here, drink this. You're in shock."

"He took it and held it in his lap. Then he looked at Katie sharply. "Did anyone see the signs of a heart problem? Did she have any symptoms?"

"No signs at all."

Judah buried his head in his hands for a few moments. The chirping of the birds at the birdfeeder seemed to mock Judah's grief. "You Amish don't know the signs!" he yelled. "You have your heads in the sand." He got up and paced the porch. "Oh, I asked Sadie to leave but she couldn't with all her kids. No birth control. How stupid! Having so many babies killed her!" He shouted. "I bet she had heart burn or her arm hurt, but the country bumpkin Amish herbal man didn't see anything, did he?"

Katie was overcome by sorrow again, as if Sadie had just died. "She was healthy.

"Did she go for check-ups at the evil *English* doctors?"

Katie's chin quivered. "*Jah,* she did. We all go into Indiana once a year for that; you know that, Judah."

"I cannot believe this. Are you sure? You saw the body? She didn't just up and run off from the Amish?" Judah bent over and screamed in Katie's face. "You Amish killed her. You and your backward hick ways! You killed her!"

"Katie, if I'm intruding, tell me to leave," Joseph yelled as he walked up the driveway. "But I don't like his tone with you. I can hear him yelling from my place."

"Who are you? And yes, you are intruding!" Judah yelled at Joseph.

"What's wrong with you, man? This is no way to talk to a lady."

Katie shot up. "Joseph, I'll be fine. This is Judah, Sadie's *bruder*. He just learned of her death. He's just upset."

Joseph walked over to Judah and offered him his hand. Judah didn't take it. "I'm real sorry for your loss. Sisters are special. Is there anything I can do?"

"Well, I'm under the Amish ban," Judah snapped. "Amish people don't talk to me; so if you can let me make a call to my fiancé, I'd appreciate that. There's no cell phone connection in this God forsaken place."

"You're getting married, Judah?" Katie asked.

"Yes," he snapped. "Finally. I had myself tricked all these years there was something so special about you and I could never marry anyone else. Boy, was I wrong. Elizabeth really loves me and would have left the blasted Amish for me, unlike a goody two-shoes like you."

"You need to watch your mouth," Joseph said evenly.

Judah ignored Joseph and turned toward Katie. "Are you married?"

"No," she said.

"Miss Goody has her nose in the air thinking she's better than other people. You slammed the door right in my face when you first saw me."

"I'll slam you ..." Joseph said under his breath.

"Stop!" Katie yelled. "Judah, I have another question and then please leave. Why did you ask for money? Sadie sent you money. Reuben didn't know."

"That's because my sister had a heart and ignored the ban. I had cancer. I mentioned it to Sadie how I needed to take pills and she sent me money. I never asked for it." Judah ran his hands through his hair. "I am so glad I wasn't here when I had cancer. Most likely I'd be dead, just using homeopathic remedies and old housewives' tales." He looked at Katie and his icy gaze penetrated through her. She wanted to run into Joseph's arms.

Reuben pulled into the driveway with his buggy. Judah ran down and started yelling at him, accusing him of killing Sadie. The hurt in Reuben's eyes was pitiful. Judah opened the buggy door and pulled Reuben out, and then punched him in the jaw. Katie screamed for him to stop. Reuben slowly got up and turned to go into the house. Judah lifted his hand to smack Reuben again, but Joseph caught it in midair. Judah turned to punch Joseph, but he was no match. Joseph put him in a headlock. Judah fought against him, but Joseph dragged him over to the horse's watering trough and dunked his head in the water. "It seems like you need to cool down," Joseph said after letting him go. Judah turned around and spit in Joseph's face. Joseph clenched both hands into fists, but simply said, "I'll be praying for you. You're lost and need of a savior."

Judah stared at him, his eyes wild, and then turned and ran to his car and sped down the driveway.

Joseph rushed over to Katie. "Are you okay, Sweetheart?"

Katie stared at him. He called her sweetheart. The look of concern and love in his wonderful green eyes was undeniable. She wanted to run into his arms but only stared at him. "*Jah,* I'm fine." She couldn't tear her eyes from his. "Maybe you should check on Reuben?"

Joseph walked up the three front porch steps and put his hand on her arm. "If you need me, I'm here for you, too, but I'll go and check on Reuben if you want."

Katie felt Joseph draw her to him. He gently cradled her head against his chest, saying everything would be alright. He told her to go inside and lay down while he checked on Reuben.

~*~

Katie still felt his embrace around her as she lay on her bed. So many emotions drained her. The shock of seeing Judah and seeing he was such a changed man. No, he was not the Judah she knew. He was bitter and mean. Yes, the shock of Sadie's death affected his behavior, but he was so arrogant. He ridiculed the People with venom in his mouth. He ridiculed her. Katie shook uncontrollably and slid under the wedding ring quilt on her bed. She tried to make the scene of Judah striking Reuben go away. He spit in Joseph's face and Joseph acted like Jesus did when people spit on him. Joseph said he'd pray for him…that he needed a savior.

She continued to shiver, but raised her eyes and prayed silently.

Father, I've wasted all these years believing Judah was the best man you ever created and no one could match up to him. But I was so wrong. I think I was waiting for him to come back all these years. I believed a lie. Abba, Father, help me and bless Joseph for all he did today.

~*~

Later that day, Joseph carried his huge telescope over one shoulder to Katie's place. "Looks like we have a big patchwork quilt out here," he said.

"A crazy quilt, *jah*?" asked one of the children.

Millie clasped her hands and smiled. "*Danki* for bringing your telescope over with the big zoom. The *kinner* have been ever so excited to sit under the stars and find constellations."

Joseph began to set up the tripod for the telescope. "How are you Millie? I'm sure Katie filled you in on Judah's visit."

"Oh, I'm fine. Judah's troubled inside. I forgive him completely."

"Does Reuben? He has quite a shiner on his jaw."

"We forgive immediately. It's the Amish way."

"You know, Millie, the more I'm here, I see the Amish take the hard scriptures in the Bible and try to live them, not change them. Forgiving is tough."

"Oh, we forgive before the feelings come. Don't be thinking we aren't hurt by Judah's behavior."

Joseph saw Katie come out of the house with stacks of whoopie pies. The children all yelled "Whoopie". Though Katie put on a brave front for the children, smiling at them as she passed out the pies, her shoulders where slumped and she walked slowly.

"And how is Katie?" Joseph whispered to Millie.

"She feels as I do. Hurt, but we're moving on. I think she'll be freer to court a nice man now that she isn't comparing them all to Judah anymore. It's a blessing in disguise."

Joseph put the large telescope in place. He explained to the children not to touch the telescope, just look into it to see the stars up close and one at a time. He handed out the July and August star charts Ginny copied for them, and they all took their places on their blankets.

Joseph walked back and set his blanket beside Katie. "I passed out twenty-three charts. How many nieces and nephews do you have?"

"Sixty-five, last count. Many couldn't come."

"You're kidding. How nice to have such a big family. I only have Ginny's kids."

They looked up into the stars. "Katie, how are you really?" Joseph whispered.

"I'm talking to Abba a lot." She sighed. "I sure wasn't expecting Judah to come here as the villain and have an *English* man show the love of Christ. He spit in your face."

Joseph groaned. "Katie, I wish you'd stop this *English* thing with me. Non-Amish can be Christians, too"

"*Ach*, I'm sorry Joseph. I've just never known a man who isn't Amish to turn the other cheek."

Joseph and Katie lay back on their blankets and looked up at the stars. "Seems like you can touch the bigger stars, doesn't it?" he asked Katie.

"*Jah*, it does."

"But they're millions of miles away, and you can't. It's impossible." Joseph took Katie's hand.

"I know," she said, not letting go.

Joseph wanted to encircle her in his arms and hold her again. To keep her from Levi Miller and any other Amish man who might take her from him.

He turned toward her. "Katie?" he whispered.

"*Jah*, Joseph?" She looked at him, her brown eyes timid.

"I've never known anyone like you. Everything Judah said about you isn't true. You don't walk with your nose in the air and your goodness is what I love about you."

"*You love...?*" Katie asked.

"I'm s-sorry... I didn't mean to say that out loud." He squeezed her hand. "Sometimes I think I do love you, but it's impossible for us to be together. You're Amish."

"Maybe this is something we need to put in Abba's hands?"

"Maybe, but how could it ever work? I couldn't be Amish and you couldn't leave your plain life."

They held hands and looked at the stars. Joseph had that feeling that he'd come home again. The more he was with Katie, the stronger his desire to have a family with her, but how? Millie stepped over to their blankets, without them hearing a sound. Joseph was glad there wasn't a full moon, because she would see they were holding hands.

"Katie, you think it's time to serve the children more whoopie pies?"

Katie quickly withdrew her hand from his. "*Jah*, but I'm so tired."

"I can get them," Joseph said.

Millie laughed. "A man's place is not in the kitchen. Katie, you rest; I'll get them."

Katie looked at Joseph and let out nervous laughter. "You could never be Amish because Amish men never work in the kitchen."

"You mean never wash a plate?"

"Never."

"Maybe I do want to be Amish then…"

~*~

Ginny cut hearts from pink calico material, took the battery operated iron and pressed back one-quarter inch around the edges, and then handed them to Millie and Katie who was painstakingly stitching them on to the quilt they were making for the auction. "I saw Judah from our front porch," Ginny said. "I told Joseph to stay out of it, but he ran right over, afraid someone would get hurt."

"He's a *goot* man and had *goot* intentions." Millie pushed her needle in and out of the white material stretched out on the quilting rack. Ginny was amazed she made such even stitches.

"So once the background is done, we sew on the flowers?"

"*Jah*," Katie said. "It's so nice to have this big room to quilt in. Reuben is ever so generous."

"It's *yinz* who are generous. You could have kept this house for yourselves."

"Ginny, you know by now we Amish hold all things lightly. We're pilgrims here, *jah*?"

"I'm still amazed at it though. I must admit; I'm a little jealous." She walked over to the icebox to get another glass of root beer. "Some of my friends already tease me about being too Amish." Ginny grinned. "Compared to most *English,* James and I live without a lot. We don't watch television, though we do watch movies on the internet. We grow a lot of our food and I can, which is a lost art anymore. We raise our own chickens."

"It's not living without and being self-sufficient that makes a person Amish," Katie said. "It's having the power to say no to what the world says we need. We have enough already. We're satisfied in here." Katie put her hands on her heart.

"Wow, that's a lot to think about," Ginny said.

"Ginny, this isn't the first time we've talked about this. I found an article in the *Budget* and would like for you to read it. It may help," Millie got up to take the paper from the big oak cupboard and gave it to her. "Start here."

"A common question now in America. How can I become Amish? Answer: If you admire our faith, strengthen yours. If you admire our sense of commitment, deepen yours. If you admire our community spirit, build your own. If you admire the simple life, cut back. If you admire deep character and enduring values, live them yourself."

Ginny set the paper in her lap and was silent. She picked it up and read a line out loud again. "If you admire the simple life, cut back … But to get James to go along with it is another question."

"Go along with what?" Katie asked.

"Selling the house and buying one of the houses in the village. The house next to SuzyB Knits was just put up for sale. James and I could live on the second floor and have a small bookstore on the first. It has a large enough yard for a decent garden, too…"

"You seem so attached to your house though," Millie said.

"That's the problem. I hold all things tightly!" Ginny read the article again. "If you admire our community spirit, build your own." She sighed. "You Amish have community that would be hard to match, but I know when I was a little girl, before all the technology gadgets, there was much more community. People knew their neighbors."

"Knew their neighbors?" Katie asked. "How can you not know your neighbors? They live next door."

"Many don't today. They wave to each other, but don't talk. It's more common the closer you get to the city, but it happens in the country, too."

"That is so sad," Millie said.

Katie's brow's shot up, hope filled. "But Ginny, you Baptist seem to have community. When your people bought that old dairy barn down the road and turned it into a church, it was amazing. People came as far as Alabama to help,"

"Oh, the Southern Baptists are known for their community spirit. Yes… you're right. I do have a wonderful church family."

"You have a lovely family, too, Ginny," Millie said. "I know Joseph says it's small, but when he finds the right girl, I hope he has a dozen *boppli*."

"Not many women want a dozen children." Ginny grinned.

"Joseph's a family man, for sure and for certain, and God sees that. He'll grant him his heart's desire. He's such a strong Christian too. Judah spit in his face, and

Joseph said he'd pray for him." Millie remarked. "I just love him and want to see him find a nice girl.

"Let me see. There are a few girls I've wanted him to meet… But he says he's happy being single."

Millie laughed. "I don't believe that for a minute. It's not good for man to be alone, the Good Book says. No, I see him with a large family and will be praying for him along those lines."

"What do you think, Katie?" Ginny asked.

"I'm getting more root beer. It's hot in here," she said, her face beet red, as she opened the icebox and walked outside to sit on the porch.

"Did I say something wrong?" Ginny asked.

"Katie seems to have a lot on her mind lately. The shock of Judah coming back and Sadie passing on, it sure has been hard on her." Millie pulled her needle through tight stitches, and then stopped. "Did you see any signs that Sadie had heart problems?"

Ginny reached over to take her hand. "No. I didn't see any."

"Judah accused us of being uneducated about health problems…"

"My mom was a patient of the top doctors at the Cancer Center in Pittsburgh, and she passed away. Medicine can't cure everything. No one's to be blamed. I remember feeling guilty right after Mom passed on. I kept wondering if we'd done everything possible. I still struggle with it at times, but Mom's gone and I can't change that." She cleared her throat. "The Serenity Prayer that Reuben read at the funeral has really helped me. I see there are some things we can't change…like Kirsten and Noah. They're always together and I think it's more than friendship. I cast that whole situation on God daily.…I don't want my Kirsten getting hurt."

CHAPTER 7

$\sim\!\!\sim\!\!\sim$

Noah looked up at the blue sky that seemed to laugh at his pessimism; the Brethren church service they just attended bothered him too. "Kirsten, I just can't get used to all the noise. All those instruments made me pay more attention to the music than the words."

His heart sank as Kirsten looked aimlessly at her car's dashboard. "You've only known the Amish way."

"A way I'm starting to appreciate more."

Kirsten pulled out of the church parking lot, leaving a trail of dust behind.

"Are there any other churches like the Amish that are Anabaptist?"

"I've searched the internet. No." Kirsten sped up.

Noah put his hand on her shoulder. "Not so fast Kirsten. You're making me nervous."

Kirsten started to drive slower than an Amish buggy. "Is this okay?"

"Kirsten, what's wrong? Do you think I'm being too picky or something?"

She pulled the car over to the side of the road. "Maybe I do. You've only tried two churches."

"I know but you've never been to an Amish service to know how different it is." Noah looked out the window past the barbwire fence that separated them from the dairy cows grazing in the field. "So many obstacles..."

"Maybe it's just not meant to be."

Noah put his arm around her, and drew her close. "I know you don't mean that..."

They sat for a few moments in silence, and then Kirsten's eyes widened. "Noah, the Amish say the Lord's Prayer all the time, right?" She reached for her MP3 player and searched for a CD. "I want you to listen to something. It's The Lord's Prayer by Andrea Bocelli "

Our Father
Which art in heaven
Hallowed be thy name
Thy kingdom come
Thy will be done on earth
As it is in heaven
Give us this day our daily bread
And forgive us our trespasses
As we forgive those who trespass against us
And lead us not into temptation
But deliver us from evil
For thine is the kingdom
And the power
And the glory, forever, Amen

As the prayer was sung, Noah looked up into the blue sky again, now glorious. He felt his eyes moistening. "That's beautiful. He sings it like he really means it. He even sounds a little German, *jah?*"

"Well, he's Italian. But Noah, do you hear how reverent he sounds? Is that it? You feel like the music in the churches we've tried is irreverent?"

"*Jah*," Noah said. "There's too much attention given to the music and not the words."

"I like the guitars and drums, but it's not the most important thing to me. It's worship from the heart that counts. There are plenty of churches that just have a choir and little musical accompaniment. Let me look online again and see what I can find. But we may need to drive further, maybe in toward Pittsburgh where there are more churches. "

Noah kissed her on the cheek. "We can look, but can we listen to that song again?" Noah asked. They held hands and listened again to The Lord's Prayer.

~*~

Katie looked at Levi, sitting on the porch swing next to her. *He has brown eyes like my black Labrador retriever...always wanting to please.* "You're so thoughtful, Levi. With it being harvest time, I know every minute counts."

"*Ach, Mamm's* garden isn't hard to put up and I'll have plenty of time for clock-making when bad weather hits."

Katie got up from the porch swing and went into the kitchen to take the lemonade out of the icebox. She poured two glasses and went back on the porch and sat next to Levi.

"We'll need to make several trips to the auction site. *Mamm* and I've made several quilts, knitted shawls, made baskets and put up so much jelly; we hardly have space to store it." She took a sip of lemonade. "The Rowland's across the street usually take our things in their cars."

"I can manage. I'll take the flat bed wagon and we'll have plenty of room. It should only take two trips. Makes twice the fun for us, *jah*?"

"We'll have the Rowland's take the jelly, though. The jars are fragile and I'd hate to see any break."

Levi took Katie's hand and gently pushed the swing with his feet. He leaned forward to steal a kiss on her cheek. "You look different somehow. You're more at peace. Do you have something to tell me?"

"Well, the image I held all these years of Judah being such a *goot* man, just wasn't true. It took more energy to live in the past than I thought."

"And the bird in the clock, it still reminds you of His promise...to make all things beautiful in His time?"

"*Jah*, I have a scripture promise written down for every waking hour and they're like stepping stones across a roaring river at times."

They continued to swing, hand in hand. "My, do the hummingbirds like my new recipe for nectar. I put in a little more sugar," she said, looking up at the red feeder full of clear liquid. "That little ruby throat's having a feast."

"Hannah loved hummingbirds. She had feeders hung up all around the porch. She must have put more sugar in, too."

Katie looked up into the wispy clouds. "I love anything that has to do with God's creation. Joseph has all my nieces and nephews interested in stars. Tonight is the Perseids meteorite shower. There'll be thousands of stars falling from the heavens, making streaks across the sky. I've never seen it, but Joseph said it's spectacular." She looked into her glass. "Would you and Mica like to come over and watch with us?"

"Well, Mica's only four and he'll be in bed. I'll have to see if *Mamm* can stay with him. If she can, I'd love to. What time?"

"The *kinner* bring their blankets out and scatter them across the yard at nightfall. Bring a blanket if you can come."

~*~

Katie looked at the magenta sunset that stretched across the sky. *The heavens declare the glory of God...* She swung on the porch swing and closed her eyes. The repetitive sound of a squeaky chain mixed with the song of hooting barn owls calmed her heart, something she felt she had little control over lately.

"I see another patchwork quilt," Joseph said, as he walked up the driveway, making the children laugh.

"A crazy quilt!" yelled the swelling group of kids.

"That's right!" Joseph said enthusiastically, looking around to find Katie. Their eyes met and held.

"Who wants a whoopie pie?" Katie asked.

All the children's hands went up. "Okay, you *kinner* listen to Joseph as he tells you which constellations to look for while I get the pies." Katie went into the house and with shaking hands, started to assemble the pies. She took the large chocolate cookies off the cooling racks and stuck two together by smearing the sweet white filling in between. When she washed her hands, she sat at the oak table and bowed her head and prayed the Lord would give her strength to be around Joseph and feel nothing for him but friendship. Surely God didn't want her attracted to an *Englisher.*

Then she picked up the metal tray of pies and stood behind the screen door, watching Joseph point up at the stars as the *kinner* listened to him intently. Katie felt defeated already because as she watched him, she longed for him again. She bowed her head and prayed for more strength. She heard giggling and looked up to see Joseph had taken a hat off little Moses and put it on, running slowly around the yard until Moses caught him. He was so good with children...

She walked out onto the porch and the children yelled, "Whoopie!"

"Let me help you," Joseph said. He ran up to her and put his hands over hers to take the tray.

"*Danki*, Joseph," she said, not making eye contact.

The children sat down on their blankets and waited as Joseph passed out all the pies. Katie walked up on the porch to sit on the swing again, and Joseph followed her. "Katie, have I done something to upset you?"

"No, Joseph, nothing," Katie said, a little bewildered.

"I can read you well enough to know I have." He sat next to her.

She looked up into his questioning green eyes. "No, I'm fine, honestly."

"My sister said you seemed a bit on edge at her quilting lessons."

"*Ach*, Joseph, such a dilemma."

"A dilemma?"

"*Jah.*"

"Did you and Levi have a fight?"

Katie moaned deeply. "No, we get along perfectly fine."

He sighed deeply. "It's hard seeing him over here. Does he ever leave you alone?" Joseph froze. "Oops. I'm sorry, Katie. I guess I'm jealous. I can't come over here because there'd be talk."

"*Jah*, there would. The Amish grapevine."

"Don't you ever feel like you're suffocating, having everyone watching you?"

"It's not easy, but the way I see your world, it's sad. Everyone seems disconnected."

Katie could now hear the beating of her heart. She loved being near Joseph and was flattered to know he was jealous. To know he wished to see her more…

"What's this dilemma you talked about?" he asked.

"You know what it is. Do I marry a good Amish man like Levi and hope love will follow?"

"No," Joseph blurted out. "You know how I feel about that. You love first, and then get married." Joseph turned to her and put his hand on her shoulder. "Are you really thinking about marrying Levi?"

"*Jah*, I am, Joseph. You're not Amish and refuse to be." Katie bit her quivering lower lip.

Joseph grabbed her hand. "I need time. I'm confused. Some days I feel like I want to be a farmer...the way the Amish do it."

Katie wasn't sure what he meant, but he seemed to be softening to the Amish ways. They sat quietly on the swing, as shooting stars fell all around them and the children cheered and pointed to the sky.

"Will you take me to Lottie and Eli's soon? I need to get in some shots of the farm with the trees loaded with apples."

"*Jah*, we need apples for jam."

"Can it be just the two of us?"

"I suppose," Katie said, "if you want to ask me more questions about the Amish way of living. Can't see any harm in that."

~*~

The red blinking light woke Katie up. She ran to her window and saw an ambulance in the Rowland's driveway. She called for her *mamm* and they quickly dressed. Katie grabbed a loaf of friendship bread and some jams and put them in a basket. The two went over to meet Reuben, who was standing on his porch. Katie saw the ambulance take James out on a stretcher while Ginny got into the ambulance. Fear gripped her and she ran across the street and held Kirsten in her arms. She turned to Joseph. "What's wrong?"

"They think James had a heart attack. He woke up with pain in his chest."

"Katie, can you stay with me?" Kirsten asked, visibly shaken.

Katie held Kirsten in her arms and rubbed her back. "Of course."

Reuben shook Joseph's hand. "Give me a holler if you need anything."

Katie led Kirsten into the house and sat on the couch. Millie and Joseph followed. "I left a basket of bread and jams on the porch. *Mamm*, can you get it?"

She saw the shock on Joseph's face. "How nice…so unexpected."

Millie put the basket on the counter. She sliced the bread and laid the jams on the kitchen table. "Everyone needs some comfort foods in stressful times."

~*~

The doctor at Indiana Memorial Hospital pulled back the white curtain and sat down. "I'm Doctor Palmer. We think you had a panic attack, Mr. Rowland."

"What?" Ginny and James said in unison.

"The symptoms are similar to a heart attack. Have you been under a lot of stress lately?"

"No, not really."

Ginny groaned. "You've been running the business by yourself. I should have known better."

"Joseph's helping."

Dr. Palmer cleared her throat. "Take a look at your lifestyle. Eliminate the stressors. As a precaution, we're keeping you overnight for observation. I'll see you tomorrow and talk about exercise and diet that can help relieve stress." She got up and shook both their hands. "Goodnight."

"Thank you doctor," Ginny said. She took James' hand. "I'm going back to work tomorrow."

"No, you're not. I said Joseph's working out fine."

She kissed James' forehead and pulled his beard. "I love you, my gentle giant. You need to take care of yourself for my sake." She reached for her cell phone. "I need to make some calls."

~*~

Joseph let out a sigh of relief. "They think he had a panic attack. Ginny's staying with James at the hospital overnight." He yawned. "Please, go home and get some rest."

"We're right across the street if you need anything," Katie said, turning to leave. "I'll bring over breakfast in the morning."

Kirsten hugged Katie. "We're fine. We eat cold cereal for breakfast. We can manage," Kirsten said. She hugged them as they both left the house.

Joseph collapsed in the recliner. "In the city, sirens go off all the time and neighbors don't even look outside. Up here, they bring you goodies."

Kirsten yawned. "The Amish take the command to love your neighbor literally. I'm going up to bed, but sleeping with the cordless phone in my hand in case Mom calls." She hugged Joseph goodnight.

Joseph felt wrung out, but needed to wind down. He picked up Ginny's prayer journal she wanted him to read. When he opened it, he read:

May 24rd: Pray if Joseph's supposed to come live here.

May 25th. Katie helped me immensely today. She told me about Granny Weaver's quilt story. I know Joseph's supposed to come and live with us. I neglected him when he was little. I need time with him. To make up the times we've missed. We can't take life for granted. Also learned a lot at the funeral. The Serenity Prayer is so helpful.

Joseph put the journal in his lap. His sister had never neglected him. He never thought that once. She was always so caring toward him, like a mom. He closed his eyes and thanked God he had a sister. He remembered Judah Yoder being so sad about losing his sister and he prayed for him, too. He seemed like such a troubled person.

Joseph looked at Ginny's journal again. She had the Serenity Prayer written out in calligraphy. She must have thought it important to write it out so fancy. He read it and then went over it slowly a few times. He whispered the prayer, "God grant me the serenity to accept the things I cannot change; courage to change the things I can; and wisdom to know the difference... Lord, I surrender my feelings for Katie to you. Help me to know what can be changed and what I should just accept."

CHAPTER 8

Katie watched as Levi carried boxes of preserves to his flatbed wagon. He carefully layered them in between blankets so the fragile jars wouldn't break. Reuben carried boxes of quilts, one that Sadie had made last winter. She prayed the auction would raise enough money for the hospital fund again this year.

"Katie, is that the last of the boxes?" Levi asked.

"*Jah.* Are you sure the jelly is safe? Maybe Joseph should take it over in his Jeep."

"Everything's packed tight." Levi gripped Katie around the waist and lifted her onto the wagon seat, as if she were a feather. They pulled out onto Wilson Road. Levi held the reins in one hand and his other hand held his hat on, since the wind was kicking up.

Katie yawned. "I'm so tired, but look forward to this every year."

Levi looked over at her. "Nice to see folk from other church districts today."

"I can't wait to see the Weaver kids. Last we heard Mary's given birth to her eighth baby. She's a strong woman to have all those little ones under ten."

"My Mica wishes he had a *bruder*. He plays with his toys and pretends he has one. It's sad at times."

Katie's heart went out to little Mica, but feared Levi was about to propose, so she looked to change the subject. "We got word from Ginny last night that James doesn't have any heart problems. He's just been under too much stress. He had a panic attack."

"Well that's *goot* news. What will he do about his stress?"

"I don't know." As they made their way past the Smicksburg Baptist Church, Katie spied the same blue car Judah drove. "It couldn't be," she gasped.

Levi slowed the horse and put his arm around her. "Katie, you alright?"

"*Ach*, I'm so foolish." She pointed to the car. "I thought that car was Judah's."

"If he's come to start more trouble, I'll be looking after you. You're my girl now."

Katie bit her lower lip. "We're friends, Levi. I told you we need to build a friendship and see if it leads to romance."

"Well, I still call it courting. At least for me, I'm feeling the romance." He took Katie's hand. "How about you?"

She couldn't speak. She didn't want to be deceitful, but if she told the truth, it would crush Levi. She knew there was no future with Joseph, but she had romantic feelings for him. "The more I'm around you, I respect you more. You're a *goot daed* and a good listener."

Levi was silent for a spell as he looked aimlessly ahead. "Love is patient. I'll be waiting when you're ready."

Katie was taken aback. She knew Levi suspected her feelings for Joseph; yet he was so kind. She put her arm through Levi's. "You're such a *wunderbar* man."

~*~

When they got to the auction site, five miles away, Katie started counting all the different states she saw on car license plates that lined the road. They were mostly from Pennsylvania, Ohio, New York, and West Virginia. They pulled into the field and the aroma of smoked meats, apple cider, and baked goods swelled Katie's heart with pride. So many Amish had come together for a common purpose; how could she even entertain thoughts of leaving for Joseph? No, she was Amish to her core.

They passed the church bench wagon and Katie thought it seemed out of place, being out on a Saturday. Levi pulled the wagon up to the Byler stands. Most of Katie's brothers and sister-in-laws were there setting up all kinds of goods: baskets, aprons, braided rugs, homemade root beer, cookies, pies, and jams. Katie's oldest brother, Matthew, had his meat smoker fired up to sell pulled pork sandwiches.

At eight o'clock, the auction officially started. An Amish man spoke through a bullhorn to the swelling crowd. "Do I hear a starting bid of one hundred for this wedding ring quilt?" Several people with bright red numbers in their hands raised them up. The bidding increased, as did the tension among the *English*. After the price being raised in increments of fifty dollars, the man yelled, "Going, going, gone for eight-hundred and fifty dollars to number 103."

Katie looked around at the crowd. She wished Joseph knew this feeling of community, that he could be Amish. She spied Mary Weaver with her eight children. A yearning to have children overpowered her. *Was she the answer to little Mica's prayers?* Levi was so patient with her. He also calmed her. The sight of the blue car in the church parking lot set a chill through her, but when Levi took her hand, she'd felt his strength run through her. Is that what romance is supposed to feel like? Was it a peaceful feeling of deep trust and reliance upon someone else?

She bit her nails when it was time to sell her log cabin quilt. The starting bid was a hundred dollars but it quickly jumped up to five hundred. She looked at the bidders, but it was a sea of people and she couldn't make out faces. She figured it was someone from Philadelphia making the bid jump to seven hundred dollars. They'd sell it even higher in the city. The bidding stopped at eight hundred dollars and she headed to the auction booth to thank the buyer for being so generous. She weaved her way through the people and as she approached the booth, she could see it was a tall man with light brown hair. It was Joseph!

"I'm the lucky winner," he said to Katie as soon as he saw her. "Ginny's going to be so surprised!"

Katie blushed profusely. "Joseph, why'd you buy ours?"

"I know the makers of this quilt and know they don't cut corners; Ginny's so proud of helping out on this quilt." Joseph looked closely at it. "*Yinz* did a great job."

Katie was speechless. She looked up at Joseph and felt a burning in her heart. He treated his sister like gold; most likely he'd treat his wife the same. He looked at her; his green eyes puzzled. "Katie, what's wrong?"

She wanted to run as far from Smicksburg as her legs could take her. Run from the growing love she felt for him. But she did what she always did, bury her feelings and put on a smile. "I'm just surprised you'd pay so much for a quilt."

"Thanks to you, I sold some pictures of Amish kids playing at the school, and I could pay cash," he said. "But Katie...you don't seem happy about it. What's bothering you?"

Was it true everyone could read her feelings toward Joseph? Was her smile not enough to hide the depth of her longing for him? She turned to go back to her family booths, but he caught her arm and looked at her, confused. She pulled away and ran.

He ran after her. "Katie, have I done something wrong?" She stopped and looked at him, but no words came out. "You sit under this tree and I'm getting you something to drink. You don't look good." He ran over to the nearest booth and bought an apple cider, and ran back, trying not to spill a drop. "Here, drink this."

Katie took the drink and stared into it. "Joseph, I don't need a drink. I need an answer to our dilemma! That's what I was trying to say when we watched the stars! I care about you…but it can't be."

Joseph held her gaze and without thinking, cupped her cheek in his hand. "I care about you…"

She heard a man clearing his throat loudly over her. "Katie we need help at the booth," Levi said, standing over them with both hands on his hips.

~*~

Ginny walked in with her knitting and took a seat next to Katie. "You look so pale. What's wrong?"

Sarah sighed. "That *bruder* of yours made a pass at her at the auction. My husband knows…"

Katie put down her needles. "Joseph admitted he was too forward. We talked about it."

Ginny's mouth gaped. "What? Are you sure?"

"*Jah,* we're sure," Granny said. "You need to talk to him. Ginny, you know Amish have to marry in the faith."

Ginny felt heat rise in her cheeks. "I've lived here for fifteen years and am aware of that. As for Joseph, he's a grown man. I can't tell him how to run his life."

"See now that's the difference between the *English* and us," Sarah said. "You don't have church discipline."

"We do, too. If someone's sinning, we humbly try to restore them to their faith…and right living. Joseph didn't sin."

Katie took Ginny's hand and stared at Sarah. "James was in the hospital for stress, you know that. Why bring this up?"

"Because it's better we talk than my husband give you a warning, Dear One."

"Warn her about what?" Suzy asked as she entered the room. "That I'm a tough knitting teacher? The whole town knows that."

Silence filled the room and Ginny clenched the ball of yarn in her hand. She'd come here to de-stress, and here she was ready to knock Sarah's head off. "I'm leaving."

Katie tightened her grip on her. "Ginny, please. I don't see you enough." She looked at Sarah firmly. "Anything you need to say to me can be done in private, *jah*?"

"Only sin is done in private…in secret. You know what I mean."

Granny Weaver sprung to her feet. "Enough already. Sarah, you know James was in the hospital and Ginny's been under so much stress. Why go on?"

Sarah's chin started to quiver. "I'm afraid for my husband. He's lost some of his sheep to the *English*. He can't sleep at night…"

"Because of me?" Katie gasped.

"Because we share this town with our *English* friends and sometimes…."

Ginny put her hand up. "Sarah, go no further. I understand. It's all so touchy when an Amish man leaves for an *English* girl. I know some have left on your husband's watch." She got up and went to sit in the vacant chair by Sarah. "But we women here love each other. We say our 'casting off prayers' together. Why don't we all bow our heads and pray. My Amish friends mean so much to me."

Sarah hugged her. "I've been too harsh, and I'm sorry. I need to cast my husband's many burdens on the Lord. I do fear for him."

The women all got up, joined hands and prayed.

~*~

Ginny looked down at her notebook to review the numbers and then looked across the kitchen table at Kirsten and Joseph. "From what I can see, we can pay off our mortgage and then some. To think Mom had all this money! She was so frugal and knew where every penny went."

"Mom could have written a book on how to save money," Joseph said, eyes misty.

"But Grandma never seemed like she had much," Kirsten said.

"Well, with the estate settled, we all have decisions to make and I, for one, have an exciting prospect to announce," Ginny looked across the table at Kirsten. "Honey, my cousin Carmine, has offered for you to stay with him in Rome to study pastries. You've always dreamt of having your own chocolate shop. No better place to learn about chocolate than Europe." Ginny was beaming from ear to ear. "You have enough from your inheritance to go and chase that dream of yours."

Kirsten's eyes grew round, but she said nothing.

"Carmine said you could live with him and Silvia; his daughter is your age and speaks English. I'd trust them completely to look after you."

Kirsten got up and started to jump up and down, clapping her hands. "I can't believe it. How long are the classes, though?"

"I think four months. You can go online and see what the schools have to offer."

"Rome! Mom, are you kidding? Who would have thought of me, Kirsten from Smicksburg, studying in Europe! I could scream!"

"Go ahead!" Joseph said, as he picked up Kirsten and spun her around. "I'm happy for you, kiddo."

"What are you going to do, Joseph?" Ginny wanted to know.

"I'm in too much shock. Can't think about it right now."

"I feel the same way. It's bittersweet. All the money in the world can't replace Mom."

"Well, let the dust settle and I'm sure it'll all fall into place," Joseph said.

Ginny put her hand up. "There's one thing I want to share that Mom did that is quite inspirational. She had a fund to help children in Haiti. Aidan wrote to her often and his letters really affected her. I think we should keep it open, and add money since….." Ginny's voice broke. "She started it and…"

Joseph went over to Ginny and gave her a warm embrace, and they both broke down and cried.

~*~

"We asked you two to come over to get some advice," Ginny said as she offered cookies to Janice and Jerry. "There's safety in a multitude of counselors."

Pastor Jerry reached across the kitchen table and patted James on the back. "We're always here for you two. What's up?"

"Ginny's settled the estate and we have more money than we thought possible. We have several options," James said.

"That's because I have several ideas." Ginny grinned at James, and then cleared her throat. "I've wanted to sell the house for a while and buy the one for sale next to Suzy's shop in town. We could have a bookstore downstairs and live upstairs. All the kids are gone, almost, and we don't need the space."

"What do you think, James?" Jerry asked.

"After my panic attack, the doc said to get the stress out of my life. Ginny and I talked about it. I don't know. It might be the right choice. I love the business but I'd rather be around real books and real customers."

"This may sound really strange," Janice said, "but I've felt a tug toward buying your house. I told Jerry one day as we were driving past. We know of so many people in need and have been praying about opening a house of refuge of some sorts. Maybe it's for battered women or foster children, just don't know. But I do know from our church headquarters, people just don't have the family they need to fall back on when in crisis and there's a rise in homelessness. We had a young man stop by the church last Saturday asking for help."

"Maybe all the remodeling I've done on this old farmhouse was to house people like that," James said.

"Are you sure, James?" Ginny asked. "You love this place."

"I do. All the memories of the kids growing up…but I love peace of mind more. If we could live at our business, just the two of us, it would solve lots of problems, and it might be romantic, living on top of a bookstore," James said as he winked at Ginny.

Jerry laughed. "Okay, lovebirds. I hear you both saying you want the same thing and that's good. But my advice is to give it some time. Pray about it. I usually tell people to not make a major decision the first year after you lose a loved one, because the grieving process can make you very emotional. But somehow, I believe you two are being level-headed." He clasped his hands. "You know 'simplicity' and 'downsizing' are buzz words today. When I'm at Wal-Mart I look at magazine covers and count how many times I see those words on them. It shows you the pulse of the country."

"Honey, that is profound. You are so smart." Janice winked at Jerry. "Let's pray."

The four of them held hands and prayed that God would direct their paths.

CHAPTER 9

Katie sat in the wagon while Reuben hitched up the horses *"Guder mariye,"* Joseph said, camera gear in tow. *"Wunderbar* day for a ride, *jah?"*

Reuben laughed. '*Vielleicht eines tages wirst du in der lage sein, Deutsch zu sprechen oder?*

Katie frowned and looked at Reuben. *"Ich denke, es ist zu schwer für ihn."*

"German is *not* too hard for me to learn...and I will be fluent someday..." Joseph said with a grin. "I understood you perfectly."

They both looked at Joseph and laughed. Katie turned to Reuben. "We'll be back before the mid meal. I'll be cooking for you and the *kinner*, don't you worry."

Reuben hugged his sister. "Have you've forgotten? The *kinner* are all in school. It's just me now. Go out and have a nice time."

Joseph hopped on the passenger side of the flatbed wagon. Reuben gave Katie the horses' reins, but she seemed too petite to be directing a draft horse. "Want me to drive?"

"Do you know how?" she asked with a smirk.

"No," he laughed. "So, what were you saying in German?"

"Nothing," she said, smirking.

Joseph waved goodbye to Reuben. "How far is this apple farm?"

"Three miles. Lottie and Eli live in a different church district so I don't see them much. I can't wait to see them!"

"Church, or the *Gmay*, is too far if it's three miles?" Joseph asked, smelling the scent of lavender coming off of Katie.

"When the *Gmay* is at two-hundred people, it splits off into another one. We feel community needs to be small enough to have accountability and really know each other." She looked out across the vast fields. "My *brieder* all settling on *Daed's* land added quite a few people to our *Gmay*, so we split off and have our own. Eli, Lottie, and I grew up together in the same *Gmay*, though. We go back a long ways."

"Lifelong friends are hard to come by these days."

"Well, it's common in the Amish community." Katie looked at Joseph, a longing in her eyes for him to understand her People, and he was touched.

They turned right onto Mahoning Road and passed Reuben's sawmill. Lumber and beams were stacked in neat piles all over the yard. As they passed the Baptist church, Katie gasped. Her eyes were as round as saucers.

"What's wrong?" Joseph asked.

"That car. I saw it last Saturday on the way to the auction. It looks like the car Judah drove."

"There're lots of blue Camry's around. Don't worry. That man won't be bothering you anymore." He wanted to put his arm around her, but decided not to, as someone might see. "You still think of him a lot?"

"No, but that car just makes me feel like he's around here. Brings back memories of the day he came..."

They turned around a sharp bend and continued to the Hershberger's farm. A car came from behind and tailed them close. Joseph instinctively put his arm around Katie, trying to protect her. Katie laughed. "They won't hurt us, Joseph. They're just waiting for a place to pass, and then they whiz around us. It's not a problem."

"I'm not used to it. Seems dangerous," Joseph said, keeping his arm around Katie.

"It's rare to have a buggy hit. And driving a buggy makes life slow down."

The car swerved around them and they continued down the road and passed several farms. Joseph kept his arm around Katie.

"Joseph, your arm around me is not fitting for a couple not courting."

"Does Levi Miller put his arm around you?" Joseph felt a stream of jealousy pulse through him.

"Sometimes, *jah*. We're courting as friends."

"No romance yet? Can't you tell by now if you like him in a romantic way?"

"*Mamm* says to build a friendship first."

"I see," Joseph said, a bit sarcastically.

He withdrew his arm and grabbed his camera and started clicking pictures of the houses and barns. Everywhere he looked was a postcard. To take his mind off of Katie and Levi he just continued to snap his camera, ignoring Katie. When they got to Eli and Lottie's, he asked her to stop the wagon so he could get out to take pictures.

Joseph saw the white farmhouse nestled deep behind several maple trees. Men carrying crates of apples and workers picking them in the field. He got out his biggest zoom and intently took pictures. After a hundred or more snaps, he returned to the wagon. To break the tension between them, he aimed the camera at her, pretending to take a picture.

"What's this?" Tears were rolling down Katie's cheeks. "Did I say anything wrong?"

"No, and that's the problem..."

"Then why are you crying?" Joseph took her hand.

She didn't say anything. He lifted her chin and looked into her eyes. He brushed away the tears. She didn't stop him. "It's impossible, Joseph. We'll never be together and I have to consider Levi."

He put his arm around her and drew her close. "You see no answer to our dilemma?"

"No. I could never leave the Amish and our way of life."

She leaned her head on his shoulder, and Joseph felt hopeless. The same feeling he felt while going through drug withdrawal. He remembered his doubts that he'd ever be free and nights when he wanted to give up. But his prayer group was always praying for him, and somehow hope filled him and got him through. The hope God gave him then was the same hope he felt toward a future with Katie. He'd continue to pray. God didn't lead him down hopeless dead-end streets.

~*~

They saw Lottie waving from the porch as they turned into the apple farm. As they pulled around to the back of the big, mammoth white farmhouse they saw all types of apples in crates. Amish workers were carrying multicolored bushels to a white cement block building in the back of the house where the apple press was stored. The noise of the apples grinding in the press mingled with male voices singing in German. Joseph felt like he was transported back in time, to Germany long ago.

Eli took off his hat to fan his face, revealing an abundance of auburn hair. "Hello there, Katie. Your friend, I've met before, but can't remember his name."

Joseph jumped off the wagon. "I'm Joseph. We met when Katie's *dawdyhaus* was being built."

Eli's brown eyes twinkled as he talked. "That's right. Ginny's *bruder*, up from Pittsburgh. How do you like living in the country?"

"Well, after I figured James was teasing about cougars and black bears being in their backyard, I'm starting to ease up."

"I'll be over on the front porch with Lottie. Eli knows the best spots on the farm for pictures," Katie said. She headed to the front porch and Joseph admired her determined walk. He knew she'd just been crying, but no one could tell

Eli took him by the elbow and led him over by his neighbor's house. "I want to show you the *dawdyhaus* next door. Some *Englishers* bought the big farmhouse near the road a while ago, but it burnt down. They've been trying to sell the little thing without much success. Would make a *goot* picture."

The small abandoned white house seemed to call for Joseph's attention. He took a few pictures. "Is it livable?"

"*Jah*," Eli said. "Needs painted and cleaned. Floors might need sanded again and stained. Of course, there's no electricity."

"Good sized, stocked pond too, great for fishing'," an elderly Amish man chimed in as he joined them.

"This is my *daed*, Moses. *Daed*, this is Joseph, Ginny's *bruder*."

Joseph was in awe at the good physical shape Moses was in. Only his long gray beard gave away his years. He took Moses' hand and shook it.

"How much land goes with the little house?" Joseph asked.

"Only ten acres, but the barn goes along with it. Are you interested?" Eli asked.

Joseph looked over at the house and just couldn't explain the draw it had on him. "Maybe."

Moses grinned. "You'd have a neighbor who wouldn't charge you a penny for apples. What's that worth?" Moses nudged Joseph with his elbow. "And you won't be lacking a fishing partner." Moses slapped him on the shoulder.

"Let's go look at the house," Joseph said.

~*~

Katie thought of Joseph as she walked over to talk with Lottie. She'd been praying her feelings for him would go away, but they only got stronger. She felt like a schoolgirl back in the wagon, crying with no self-control. She hoped Lottie could give her wise counsel she was known for. She saw Lottie hanging clothes on her clothesline that extended twenty feet to an old maple tree. She looked bushed. "How's my dear friend Lottie today?"

"Tired. I'll be seeing my sweet *boppli* any day and I don't want to leave Eli without any clean clothes to wear." She yanked at her pulley clothesline. "Katie, sit down. I want to speak to you."

Katie took a seat on the cedar glider while Lottie sat on the rocker facing her. "What is it Lottie? Is the baby okay?"

"*Ach*, the baby's fine, but awful restless." She patted her stomach. "I'm concerned for you. I see how you look at Ginny's *bruder*. If the eyes are the window to the soul, you need to draw a shade. You care for him too much."

"I can't help it. I do try. I give it to the Lord daily, but my feelings don't change."

"We talked before about how he could pull you from the *Gmay*. We also talked about Levi. Aren't *yinz* courting?"

"As friends."

"No romance yet?"

"Well, at the auction I did feel a trickle. Something startled me and Levi was a solid rock right there to comfort me."

"That's *goot*. A little apple seed can grow into a large Macintosh, *jah*? What startled you so badly?"

"Ach, I thought I saw Judah's car on the way to the auction. Silly of me."

"Not silly at all." Lottie pushed back blond wisps of hair back into her prayer *kapp*. "Eli went out the other day to the Chocolate Shop and saw Judah there. That's another thing I wanted to speak to you about."

Katie grabbed her waist, as pain stabbed through her stomach. "Is Eli sure it was him?"

"*Jah*, Judah spoke to him."

Katie felt her mouth grow dry. "He's a shunned man." Katie instantly thought of Eli's kind nature. He would talk to anyone. "Why is he up here in Smicksburg?"

Lottie sighed. "Judah told Eli he's moved up here. He's staying with Jerry and Janice and the Baptist Church is helping him. Seems like the day he spat in Joseph's face and Joseph said he was praying for him really made an impact. Told Eli he realized his worldly ways were wrong and wants to become right with the people he offended."

"Will he confess his sin to the People and be Amish again?" Katie felt her heartbeat pounding in her ears.

"I'm not sure. I wonder why he's not talking to Bishop Mast?"

Katie stood up, but her body swayed like the clothes on the line and she sat down. Lottie brought her a glass of lemonade and she drank it and took a deep breath. "I want to go home," Katie said. "Tell Joseph I want to go home."

~*~

Kirsten looked up at all the colored leaves dripping from the trees. With the sun streaking through the woods, it seemed like a cruel contrast to Noah's feelings. He could never see Europe unless he went on a boat, and that was unlikely. She cupped Noah's face in her hands. "We can write like we did when I lived at college."

"Four months is a long time…" Noah sighed. He took her hand as they started to walk down the deserted country road. "Will you be happy there?"

"That's what surprises me the most. I'm so excited about seeing Italy and learning how to bake from some of the world's best chefs."

She felt him squeeze her hand like he didn't ever want to release her. Kirsten looked up at him and prayed the Lord would ease his pain. They continued down the road, but soon spied a wagon coming in their direction, so they quickly ran into the woods to hide. She watched as Joseph and Katie went by. She saw Joseph's arm around her and Katie seemed upset. When the wagon was out of view, they went back on the road.

"I don't like keeping our relationship a secret," Noah said. "It's deceitful." He took Kirsten's hands and kissed them. "Maybe time in Italy will be *goot* for us to think through our plan."

Kirsten put her arms around Noah's neck. "I do love you, Noah. You'll wait for me?"

"What kind of question is that?"

"I know your dad wants to know if you'll be getting baptized into the church. If you join while I'm away…"

"I said I'd wait for you, Kirsten. I won't join the Amish unless you're joining with me."

Kirsten leaned her head on Noah's chest. "Hold me Noah. I'm scared."

~*~

Katie got out of the wagon and raced up the Rowland's front porch steps, and Joseph followed. She turned to him. "I need to talk to Ginny privately. Do you mind?"

"Joseph, James is picking tomatoes in the garden. Could you help him?" Ginny asked with her eyebrows up.

Joseph nodded and headed to the back yard.

Ginny looked at Katie. "What's wrong? You look so pale."

Katie collapsed into a cedar chair. "Judah is back in Smicksburg. There's talk he's living with Jerry and Janice. Have you heard about this? Is that true?"

"Actually, I got a call from Judah today. He wants to come over and apologize for spitting in Joseph's face. Seems like it was a turning point for him; he realized how low he'd become."

"But why is he staying with Jerry and Janice?"

"Jerry got a call from a pastor friend in Pittsburgh. Judah went to a Baptist church for help and the pastor advised him to go back and apologize to all the people he'd offended. Jerry is counseling him." Ginny reached over for Katie's hand. "God is in control, Katie. Say the Serenity Prayer. Having someone come back into your life that hurt you so badly would be hard."

"*Jah,* it's like I'm twenty again; the pain's still fresh."

Levi Miller pulled into Katie's driveway and Ginny looked in his direction. "He seems like good medicine for you."

"I sure will be saying the Serenity Prayer," Katie sighed deeply. "We must accept the things we cannot change..."

"And you can't change the fact that Judah's here. I'll be praying for you."

Katie groaned. "When you met James, how long was it before you had any romantic feelings?"

Ginny put her head back on the chair and clasped her hands. "It's been over thirty years, but I do know it wasn't love at first sight. James was the big lug jock football player and kind of quiet. I took it that he was, well, an arrogant jock."

"What's a jock?" Katie asked.

"Oh, a guy who's too much into sports. It was like James had no life besides football and hanging out with friends. But there was a Bible club in our high school and we both went. The more I got to know him, I saw he was one hurting guy. His mom was really sick, but James never really told anyone at school.

"That's sad. But after you knew James, how long before romantic feelings?"

"Oh, we were friends for a while. A year maybe."

Katie looked at Ginny and wanted to scream. Everyone was telling her the same thing; romance came from friendship. She thought of the Bible verse, *There's safety in a multitude of counsels.* She just couldn't figure out why she loved Joseph so much…. She looked across the street and saw Levi come out of the barn with Reuben. She mumbled the Serenity Prayer under her breath.

~*~

The women knitted so intently that they barely noticed Janice come into their knitting circle. She sat by Ginny and beamed. "So it is decided. We'll be buying your house and you'll be the new owners of Serenity Book Nook. I like the name," Janice said, as she poured more coffee into a mug. "You and Suzy are lucky. You'll be neighbors."

Suzy set down her knitting needles and looked over at Ginny. "I'm so excited. You can come over and knit anytime. You just have to walk across the yard."

"I'm still a little nervous, but it's all for the best. We'll have less upkeep and a retirement plan." She thought of James' comment about feeling isolated and wanting to be around more people. She looked up at her friends. "He'll get to be around real books and customers too."

Granny Weaver put her yarn in her lap. "Janice, I think the idea of a home for hurting people is touching, but do you feel okay opening that big house up to total strangers?"

"They'll come by referral only through the Baptist church. Anyhow, we already have a person in need and we don't own the house yet: Judah."

Sarah grunted. "He should be coming to my husband."

Ginny saw Janice ready to pounce and spoke up. "Jerry's a good counselor and Judah has so many regrets to sort through. Jerry helped me all those years when my mom was sick." Ginny took a sip of tea. "I'm afraid Katie is one of his regrets. I hope he didn't break off his engagement to be with her. She and Levi are so cute together."

"*Jah*, they are," Granny Weaver chimed in. "I'm hoping for a fall wedding next year."

Ginny looked at Sarah. "We all know he didn't have a normal Amish upbringing. Amish kids are so happy and content, working along with their parents."

Sarah's knitting needles slowed as she talked. "I knew his parents, and something wasn't right. No joy in the wife's eyes, that's for sure. Judah used to come to our place so shaken at times. Why doesn't he come to us like he did before?"

Suzy looked at Sarah evenly. "Should we be joining hands to pray again? I want unity in my shop."

"*Ach*, I'm sorry Suzy. I'm just hurt. Judah became like a son after his parents passed away."

"How'd they die?" Janice asked.

"Well, the father died of liver disease from alcohol. I believe the mother died of a heart attack soon after." Sarah stared at her unmoving needles.

"Sadie had a heart attack. She must have inherited her mom's genes," Janice said.

Ginny laid down her knitting needles. "Judah helped remodel our house. I remember he was upset his dad never listened to your husband, Sarah. If he had, he wouldn't have been an alcoholic."

"Why don't we pray for Judah now? He's really at a crossroads and hurting something fierce," Janice suggested.

All heads nodded in agreement and they sat down their knitting and joined hands to pray.

CHAPTER 10

*J*udah wiped his sweaty palms on his blue jeans as he and Jerry sat at the familiar oak table. How many times had he enjoyed a meal with the Bylers? Amos was missing, though, the father he never had. He looked across the table at Millie, Reuben, and then Katie. His eyes stayed on hers. "I'm asking your forgiveness for my behavior toward you. I've been angry with the Amish for too long."

"We forgive," Reuben said, "but you'll need to confess to the People to be in fellowship with us. You know if you kneel and confess before the People, all will be forgiven, and as best we can, all will be forgotten."

Judah looked at Katie, searching for answers. Was Reuben saying this because he knew Katie wanted him to return? To be reunited?

"Will you be confessing?" Millie asked.

"I'm taking my time so I can make the right decision…before I kneel and confess." Again Judah looked at Katie and their eyes locked. "I might be doing that sooner than I think."

"Well, we can't fellowship with you until you do; so I'm asking you to leave," Reuben said kindly. "But we accept your apology."

"Thank you," Judah said, still looking at Katie.

"Have you a-asked Joseph for forgiveness?" Katie asked.

"Yes, I have. He's amazing. He shook my hand and offered to help me in any way he could. I was shocked."

Katie lowered her head. "He's a wonderful *goot* man. Best they come."

~*~

Jerry pulled out of the driveway and looked at Judah. "Did you come back here for that girl?"

"What makes you say that?" Judah asked.

"I have eyes, don't I?" You wrecked that girl's life and you think a few flirty looks at her, and snap, you can get her back?"

"What are you talking about? I was sitting across from three people and I had to look at her."

"You were staring, man, and I mean star-ring. But it's the glint in your eye I didn't like. You were giving her the green light that you were available."

Judah looked at Jerry, confused. "I am available. I'm not engaged anymore."

"She is not available to you because you aren't Amish."

"Okay, I never met a girl like her and realize I made a mistake in letting her go. Maybe I'd like to have her back."

"Is that why you came here? I mean you were engaged to another woman, and as soon as you saw Katie, you called it off and are right back up here in Smicksburg."

Judah put his head down. "I don't think I came back for her. I don't know. Joseph's response to me spitting at him. I've never....Oh forget it."

"You've never what?" Jerry asked, driving slower.

"This may sound stupid, but it was like I saw a picture of what God would be like. Jesus was spit on and he prayed for the people who did it. Joseph did the same. I just don't know why it caused me to doubt everything I was doing with my life."

"So you saw the Lord's love to you through Joseph, is that it? You want to give God a try? Let him have control of your life for once?"

"I gave God a try before. Just don't buy it."

"How did you give God a try? By being Amish?"

"I went through baptismal classes. At my baptism the bishop poured water over my head and said, 'You who repent and are baptized will be saved.' So I was saved, but it didn't do anything for me."

"You're being vague. What do you mean it didn't do anything for you?"

"I still felt like God's untouchable. I'd listen to Katie talk about her love for God and how she prayed to him every day, but when I pray, I feel like He's not paying attention or something."

"Like your father?" Jerry asked. "What was your relationship with your dad like?

"My dad didn't talk to me. I only remember that he barked orders." Judah looked out the car window.

"You don't have one memory of a decent conversation?"

Judah took a deep breath. "Listen, it's been a hard day having to apologize to so many people. Can we talk about this later?"

"Okay, but I have to say what I saw back there with Katie I did not like. I'm a trusted *English* friend to many of these good people and want to keep it that way. I'm not going to let you stay with us so you can try to get Katie to leave the Amish again. This may sound harsh, but after what I saw, I'm thinking Katie should be off limits if you want my counsel and share my home."

Judah shot a glance of disbelief. "You can't be serious."

"Oh, yes I can."

~*~

Kirsten gawked at her mom. "Carmine said to come in November before Thanksgiving? Before Christmas? Mom, I love the holidays."

"You'll leave a few days after Thanksgiving. He needs time to get things arranged. Classes will start in January. He wants you to see Rome, the Vatican, take the train to Florence and then down to Riccia to see the relatives. Family is so important there and you'd offend the relatives if you didn't visit. They already know what they're cooking!"

"Mom, I need time to wrap things up at the Sampler."

"Just give Antonio your two weeks' notice now. He should be happy. Isn't he talking about you being a partner? He'd have a pastry chef who studied in Europe." Ginny grinned. "Just don't go fall for some dashing Italian man and stay."

"I'd never do that!" Kirsten yelled.

"What on earth? Kirsten, what's going on?"

"Oh, Mom, I can't talk about it."

"We've never kept secrets before," Ginny prodded, concerned.

Kirsten bent over and put her head in her lap. Joseph walked into the living room. "Am I interrupting something?

"No, Kirsten's just getting homesick already, I think."

"Mom, I'm not a baby. It's more than homesickness. It's….love. There, I said it. The cat is out of the bag. Uncle Joseph knows."

"What is she talking about?" Ginny looked up at Joseph.

"Kirsten, you never told your mom?"

Kirsten looked sympathetically at her mom. "We're best friends, right? Think about it. You had no clue I had feelings for Noah?"

"I, ah… I, ah… well, I brought up my fears to Millie but she assured me I was wrong."

"So you're afraid of my relationship with Noah?"

"Of course. He's Amish. It's all he's known. It would be tough, almost impossible to leave his people for you."

"He might be changing all that." Kirsten quickly raised her hand to her mouth

Ginny leaned forward. "What will he be changing?"

"Noah loves the Lord, more than being Amish. We're trying to find a church we both fit into."

"If you find one, let me know," Joseph muttered.

Kirsten looked up at him. "A church for you and Katie, Uncle Joseph? You love her, don't you?"

"I try real hard not to but…."

Ginny got up and walked to the window, staring at all the birds at her birdfeeders in the front yard. "We should be a reality television show. Honestly!"

"What about missionaries, Sis? Women who go to India wear the traditional clothing and follow their customs. They respect the culture and the Amish have their own culture. If you love someone, isn't it worth it to adapt to their culture?"

Ginny was silent again. "Joseph, are you thinking of turning Amish?"

"Sis, maybe some other time. You don't look good."

"I raised three kids! I had three teenagers at once and I'm still standing. I'm tougher than you think."

"Okay. The little farm to Eli Hershberger is for sale and I think I want to buy it."

Ginny eyes were round as buttons. "There's no electricity in that house."

"Well, I can change that if I want to."

"If you want to?" Ginny sat down on her Amish rocker and read the Serenity Prayer she had cross-stitched on the pillow, and then put the pillow up to her mouth and screamed into it.

Joseph walked over to her and sat at her feet. "I'm so fascinated by the Amish and their simple ways. I knew my Post-Traumatic Stress was getting better when Jerry had the missionaries to Haiti visit the church. All the pictures of the buildings on top of people made my heart go out to the earthquake victims. I knew before I moved here, I would have had a flashback to the Twin Towers falling and people being trapped. I see I'm getting better or almost completely healed by living in such a calm place among such wonderful people."

"I'm glad for you Joseph. I truly am, but what does the farm next to Eli's have to do with all this?"

"I think I want to go totally off the grid. Be self-sufficient. No internet, no cell phone, just me and God and nature."

"Is that why you're reading *Walden Pond*? I thought that odd," Ginny groaned, face still in the pillow.

"Thoreau learned a lot about life living off the beaten path in that cabin. It may be for only a year, but I feel I need to do this. The stress of modern life is not for me."

"And where does Katie fit in?"

"She doesn't know anything about this. Yes, I have hopes and I pray, but above all I want her happy. I mean it. God knows of my desire to have children. He's not sitting up there in heaven shocked, not knowing what to do. He has a plan and I can only follow it. All I know is I feel this farm next to Eli is for me."

Ginny grabbed Joseph's arm. "You two heard about us selling the house and feel you need to move, huh?"

"What!" Kirsten and Joseph said in unison.

"We're buying the house next to Suzy's and starting a bookstore downstairs and living on top, like Suzy does."

"Mom, is the business failing?" Kirsten asked. "If it is I'm not taking the money and going to Italy."

"No, the business is fine. Your dad misses being around people. Jerry and Janice will buy the house for the homeless. We figured Joseph could just stay here if he wanted."

"When I come home, where will I go?" Kirsten asked.

Ginny got up to hug her daughter. "We'll have two bedrooms. Always enough room for you to come back to. Sorry this is so sudden. I was going to break it gently."

Kirsten smiled at her mom. "I think it's cool. You'll be a part of the Smicksburg merchants like you always wanted."

Joseph came over and encircled Ginny and Kirsten with his long arms.

~*~

Joseph got out of bed, put on his robe over his flannel pajamas, and tip-toed down the stairs. *Who's knocking at the door this time of night?* He opened the door and saw Katie.

"What's wrong? Are you alright?" he whispered.

"*Jah*, I need to use the phone. We got word Lottie's having her baby and I want to be there. I need to call a driver. The roads are too slippery to take the buggy out."

"You need a driver and you're going to call one from here?" A grin slid across Joseph's face.

"What's so funny? It's too cold to walk to the phone shanty. Ginny and James are used to me coming over to use their phone."

"I'll never be." Joseph continued to grin.

"You don't want to see me, Joseph?"

"Not under these circumstances."

"Oh, you think it wrong I see you in your robe. I'm sorry." Katie blushed and turned to go. "I guess I'll walk to the shanty then," she said, looking hurt.

"Joseph grabbed her by the shoulders and turned her around. "I'll drive you to the shanty, okay?"

"If you want to. Maybe get on some clothes, though."

Joseph started to take off his robe and Katie covered her eyes. "I'm fully clothed. Katie, you're half awake. I am your driver, *jah*?"

Katie looked puzzled and stared at him. Then let out a laugh which turned into a giggle, one she couldn't stop. "Oh, Joseph, I thought you were being mean. You have a car and can drive me." She doubled over laughing and Joseph joined in, trying to be as quiet as they could, not to wake up the whole house; before they knew it they were holding each other up.

"I think we're both exhausted, *jah*?" Joseph asked. "Hence, the giggles?"

Katie put her head on his chest and laughed until tears came down her cheeks. "When you say '*jah*' it makes me laugh. Stop it."

He realized the distance between them for the first time. She was in his arms, and the scent of lavender on her was intoxicating.

"Joseph, I miss you," Katie said in a whisper.

"I see Levi Miller over your place a lot more and don't want to intrude."

Without thinking, Katie grabbed Joseph around the waist. "I don't feel for Levi like I do for you."

Joseph pulled her away. "You're tired Katie. We should speak in the morning."

"I'm not tired. Remember, I'm Amish. I get up at four to milk cows."

"You really want to talk about this?"

"*Jah*, I do." Katie followed him to the couch and they sat down.

Joseph looked down at her. "Remember I told you about the stress I've been carrying since 9/11?"

"*Jah*, I do."

"I feel so much better, even healed being out here in the country and seeing how you Amish live. I'm planning on buying the little farm next to Lottie and Eli."

"You won't be across the street from me?"

"No. I need to get away. I feel the Lord leading me to live in that little house by myself to reflect and get direction. I'm at a crossroads in my life and it's an important one." He reached over to get the Bible that stayed on the coffee table. "This scripture popped out at me the other day and it's the one I believe the Lord wants me to stand on. Jeremiah 6: 16. '*Stand at the crossroads and look; ask for the ancient paths, ask where the good way is, and walk in it, and you will find rest for your souls*'."

Katie asked him to read it again and he did.

"God says to stand, look, and ask. I don't think it's a minute-long process. I think God speaks over time, in a still small voice, but we need to be quiet enough to hear him. I need to be alone, too."

"I'll still show you around to take pictures, *jah*?" Katie asked.

"Of course. I won't be a complete hermit," Joseph said. "I'll have the animals."

"You're getting pets?"

Joseph grinned. "Promise not to laugh."

"I would never laugh at you…"

"Okay" he said, taking a deep breath. "I want to farm."

Katie gasped. "This is one step closer to becoming Amish! You said some days you didn't want modern technology and others you wanted to farm like the Amish. That's *wunderbar goot*! What will you farm?"

"There's a barn on the property and ten acres. What do you think I should do?"

"Well, you need a cow for milk and chickens for eggs. I'd get a beef cow for meat or some sheep. This is for your food. You could raise Nigerian pigmy goats. They let out the richest cream and the best for making cheese. *Ach,* you could make cheese and sell it. I can teach you!"

He looked at Katie's eager eyes. She *did* want to be with him even though she was going through the motions of courting Levi. She even remembered what he said about throwing his computer out the window and being a farmer. Was she praying for this to happen? He cleared his throat, knocking out the feelings he felt toward her. "So I have to get these Nigerian goats from Africa? Doesn't sound realistic."

She grinned. "They're just called that; they're not from Africa. They're expensive, since many people like to keep them for milk but don't have the room for a farm. If you bred them, you'd turn a nice profit. We can go to the auction in Dayton and get some there."

Joseph took Katie's hand. "You make me feel like I can do anything. I don't know what the future will hold. I wish I did. But like I told you a while back, I know God loves me like a real son. He cares about every detail of my life, and your life, too. If we're to be together, He'll move mountains." He raised her hand and kissed it. Katie took Joseph's hand and brushed it against her cheek.

"I never felt like this for Judah..." she whispered.

"I'm glad about that. He has me worried. He looks like the Prince Charming type."

"Handsome? *Jah*, he is, but so are you, Joseph, and your handsome in here, too." She placed her hand on his chest. "You have a heart like no other."

Joseph tilted Katie's chin up to him. He stared into her eyes. "For some reason, I feel so hopeful about us. We'll just keep walking on the path God shows us...*jah*?"

Katie didn't laugh at his Amish words, but just stared at him. He kissed her on the forehead. "We need to get over to Lottie's before she has the baby."

"What?"

"Remember, you're here for a ride to Lottie's. She's having a bambino, *jah*?"

"Oh, Lottie! The *boppli*! Joseph, we have to hurry!"

CHAPTER 11

Moses put his hand on his son's shoulder. "I remember when you were born, Eli. Your dear, sweet *mamm*, God rest her soul, screamed like that, too. Lottie will be fine."

There was a knock at the front door and Joseph ran over to open it.

"Anything I can do to help?" Leah asked. "My *oma* must be exhausted by now."

Moses chimed in, "*Jah*, you can help, dear one." He turned to Joseph. "Leah, this is Joseph. He came to live with his sister six months ago. They're trusted *English* friends. Live across from all the Byler's on Wilson Road."

"*Goot* to meet you Joseph. I haven't met your family yet. I only know the people in this neck of the woods." Leah flashed a pearly white smile at Moses. "Having you live across the street has been fun. I love hearing about the history of Smicksburg."

"Well, I did come here from Millersburg to help start this settlement in 1962; so I've collected a few stories."

"You live here?" Joseph asked.

"Have my own place in the back of the house." He pointed to a door off the kitchen. "Just go through that door and you'll be at my place."

"That's real nice. Family living so close by. You can help with the baby." Joseph grinned.

"I can't wait. I love the wee *boppli,*" Leah said.

Joseph looked over at Leah and smiled warmly.

~*~

Katie came out of the bedroom and gripped the wooden banister as she descended the stairs to get more water. When she turned to go into the kitchen, she saw

Joseph practically gawking at a pretty blonde-haired woman. *Who is she?* Katie coughed to announce her entry into the kitchen.

"How is Lottie?" Eli asked, with a furrowed brow.

"She'll be ready to have that baby any minute. I need more water. Lottie needs to be cooled down." Katie went over to kitchen sink to pump some water into the large pitcher.

Joseph took the pitcher from her. "I can help you, and Leah is here to give you a break."

Katie heard Eli introduce her to Leah, Granny Weaver's granddaughter. Granny mentioned she'd be visiting but why did this girl hit such a nerve in her. Was it that she was so beautiful, blonde hair and with big blue eyes? *Lord help me if I'm jealous.*

"I've come from New York to live with my *oma*. I can sew and she's sick of it. *Oma* wants to give up her quilt shop for knitting, of all things."

Katie stared at Leah's eyes. She has such long eyelashes. She looked like she was wearing makeup like the *English*. Katie asked, forcing a smile. "*Goot* to meet you. I need to get back to Lottie."

Joseph held Katie by the shoulders. "Sit down a bit and have a cup of tea. It's been two hours since you took a break. Leah's here. She came to help."

Did Joseph think Leah could do a better job? "Joseph, I am f-f-fine." She yawned hardly able to keep her eyes open.

"Maybe you should take her home," Moses, looking at Joseph. "She's exhausted."

"I-I am not." Katie went and sat in the Amish rocker next to the wood burning stove. "Fit as a fiddle."

Moses bent over to whisper to Katie. "Leah's here to help. She's had a *goot* night's sleep and she's younger than you. Only twenty-five."

Katie looked at Moses like he was daft. "I'm not an old lady," she snapped.

"Neither am I," Moses laughed. "Seventy going on twenty."

She put her head back on the rocker. Maybe she was exhausted, but she longed to see the *boppli*. "You're right, Moses. I am tired."

"You come see the *boppli* after you get some shut-eye," Moses said with a twinkle in his eye. "Lottie will want to see you for sure and for certain."

Leah had already gone upstairs with the pitcher. Katie let Joseph lead her out to his Jeep.

Even though the Hershberger's lived only three miles away, Katie fell asleep when they pulled up to her little house. Joseph carried her inside and laid her on the sofa in the living room. He bent over and gently kissed her on the forehead. *Sleeping Beauty...I hope I'm your prince someday...*

~*~

Sarah knit another row and then held up a green mitten. "Now I need to learn to cast off."

Suzy came across the circle and sat next to her. "It's easy; just watch my hands."

Sarah looked intently at Suzy's hand's fly. She'd waited all week for knitting circle so she could get advice from her friends. Sarah felt hot tears blur her vision.

"Sarah, what's wrong?" Granny Weaver asked.

Sarah took a handkerchief from her apron pocket and dabbed her thin face. "My husband is just beside himself, and I am, too. I found a pen with Punxsutawney

Mennonite Church written on it when I was washing Noah's trousers."

"Maybe he did construction there," Millie said. "He does work in Punxsy a lot."

"Jacob confronted him and he said he was trying their church."

Granny Weaver, Millie, Katie, and Suzy all stopped knitting and stared at her.

"Why would he do that?" Katie asked. "Do you have any Mennonite relatives that asked him to go to their church?"

"No, and the church isn't Old Order Mennonite. They live like the *English*."

"So he wants to go fancy?" Granny Weaver gasped.

"I'm glad Ginny isn't here, to be honest. I'll tell her when I've calmed down. Noah is in love with Kirsten Seems like Ginny allowed her kids to play with mine when they were little. We gave them permission to go to your place, Millie, but not the Rowlands. Seems like Ginny doesn't respect the line we have to draw."

Millie looked at Sarah, mouth gaping open. "You know that's not true."

"Well, Noah snuck over there plenty of times when he went to play at your house, and no one told us. *Yinz* are too cozy with the Rowlands." She looked helplessly at Millie and then Katie. "You should have stopped him!"

Katie went over and sat in a chair next to Sarah. "We're so sorry. My younger *brieder* and Noah always played with the Rowland boys, but we saw no harm in it. Aidan and Ian were such *goot* boys."

"But Kirsten lured him into her fancy ways," Sarah snapped. "Seeds of doubt were planted long ago. Noah tried to tell us all about Kirsten's dedication, and my dear Jacob almost had a stroke when Noah told him that he'd read her Mennonite readers. Her homeschooling books...he helped her study."

"Noah's not baptized," Millie said. "He's free to choose his path. Kirsten is a *wunderbar*, God-fearing girl."

"Ach, all your sons have married *goot* Amish girls to keep them in line. You've never had a worry. Remember, we almost lost our Gideon to the world..."

"But he's Amish now and that was long ago. Don't look back," Granny warned, "or you'll turn to salt, like Lot's wife. Keeps you from moving forward."

"Well, Jacob has forbidden Noah to write to Kirsten when she goes on her fancy trip to Italy," Sarah said, "and I'm sure glad Noah agreed to it."

"You mean forced him into it..." Millie said evenly.

Sarah looked at Millie in disbelief. She'd often thought the Bylers and Rowlands were too close-knit. "Millie, how would you feel if Katie were to leave the Amish for Joseph?"

"Ach, Katie's baptized into the Amish church."

"But what if the ties between you and the Rowland's are too strong?"

Katie took Sarah's hand. "You're in so much pain now and we need to pray for you. I understand. I lost Judah to the world, but we can't shut out all outsiders. The Rowland's have been trusted friends for years."

"*Humph*...trusted by you, but not us."

~*~

Ginny slipped her red gloved hand into James's as they walked down Wilson Road. "So we'll own the house before Christmas." She breathed in the fresh smell of pine trees and looked up to see Canadian Geese migrating in a V shape over them. "So much change...but we can get a head start on remodeling."

James squeezed her hand. "You know I love taking something old and broken down and fix it up, whether it's furniture, cars, or houses."

"Or people?"

James stopped and turned to her. "People?"

"Oh, Honey, you're too modest. Ever wonder why so many youth in the church come to you to 'pal around' after church?"

"They're hyper?"

"No, it's because you listen and kids need that. Ours were blessed to have you as a dad. They've all turned out fine and I didn't do it alone."

"Did you think you'd be homeschooling a missionary, a doctor, and a pastry chef?" James asked.

Ginny sighed. "I thought Ian would never read. How I worried about him and here he is in medical school. Did you read the email from Aidan?"

"Yes and boy does our money go a long way in the Dominican Republic. Hard to believe we can fix all Yohany's teeth for a hundred bucks. He said she can't sleep at night because of the pain. I say we do it."

Ginny looked up at James. She knew he would send the money. It was what she loved so much about him, his big heart.

James put his arm around her. "It was great seeing all the kids together at Mom's funeral, but it went by too quickly. I miss the boys. No more Thanksgivings together, it seems."

"Kirsten will be home. We do have traditions to maintain, like Black Friday."

"*Yinz* are nuts getting up at four o'clock to shop."

"No we're not. The Amish are up at four all the time."

James laughed. "You just can't pass up a bargain, can you? Tightwad."

Ginny slapped him on the arm then put her arm through his. "I feel like a new chapter in life is opening up to us. I'm so excited about our store and home on top."

"I felt bad selling the house at first. Felt like I was letting you down, but now you look like a weight has been taken off you. You look younger."

"Thanks, but it's Weight Watchers. I've lost ten pounds."

"Whoa!" James yelled as he slid an icy spot. "It's too cold for early November."

Ginny braced James as best she could. "Millie worries me. She said we're going to have a hard winter and is already checking their pond for ice skating. Shouldn't she wait until January at least?"

"The pond's shallow, right? If someone falls through the ice, it won't be over their head."

"Just the same, I'm going to talk to Millie about it." Ginny saw a man walking toward them. It was Judah.

"Howdy, Judah. We're walking to the church for exercise. You must be walking away. Shame on you Judah...walking away from the church." Ginny laughed at her own joke.

"Just walking and thinking," Judah said somberly.

"No one's talking to you still?" James asked.

"I'm a shunned man." Judah kicked at a rock stuck under ice.

"I've only known the Amish to be the kindest people on earth. Maybe repent and make things right with them," Ginny said. "We all need family. Joseph was a loner like you until he moved to be up by us."

"Joseph has a sister who's still alive...."

Ginny cringed. How could she be so insensitive? She went over to him and put her hand on his shoulder. "No Yoder's living around here? Surely there are. I see it on mailboxes all the time."

Judah continued to kick at stones frozen in the ice.

"Joseph would be a good person for you to talk to," James said.

"How come? Looks like he's had an easy life, riding around, taking pictures with Katie. Now, buying a farm from big inheritance money, I hear."

James crossed his arms. "Let's just say God is restoring the years the locust has eaten away in his life, like the Bible promises."

"The Bible's full of broken promises."

"Your life's been that rough, here in Amish country?" James asked.

"Not all Amish are nice. My dad should have been put in jail the way he treated his kids and wife..." Judah kicked the frozen stone free. "Don't know why I'm saying this....Sorry."

Ginny gave Judah's stiff body a bear hug. "When we're hurting we tend to bottle things up, but when a friend listens, you begin to talk. Can we help you in any way?"

Ginny saw intense fear in Judah's eyes and empathy gripped her.

James put his hand on Judah's shoulder. "We used to talk all the time when you helped us remodel our house. Remember, you picked out our 'fancy' front door."

"I'll think about it."

"Think about this, too," James added. "We're moving to a place in town and we'll need a good carpenter. We'll keep you working until March, at least. We plan to open our bookstore in early spring."

Ginny sat in awe as silence hovered around them. She felt like she was in a sacred moment as she saw tears form in Judah's eyes. She was witnessing a miracle. God was melting Judah's heart through their love. "We'll take that as a yes," she said. "Good to have you back with us."

~*~

Katie took the baby from Lottie and cradled her in her arms. "She's perfect. I can't believe she's two weeks old already." She kissed little Miriam on the cheek.

"I can't believe I'm a *mamm*," Lottie said as she knitted in the rocker next to Katie. "I love it. When I saw Miriam's face, I loved her with a love like no other. I didn't know her until she popped into this world, and I'd give my life for her."

"That's beautiful."

"You'll be having a *boppli* someday. How are things going with Levi?"

"I think I need to break our courtship."

"Why? He's such a *goot* Amish man."

"I don't feel any romantic feeling toward him."

"You said before you felt a little."

Katie looked at little Miriam and that same longing for a child welled up.

"*Hmm*...something's choking that seed of love from growing. Maybe a weed?"

"What?" Katie looked up, puzzled.

"What causes seeds not to grow? Lack of water and sunshine, or weeds choking the plant. Are you two tending to your relationship? Giving it the things it needs?"

"*Ach*, Lottie, you're my closest friend. I need to talk to someone..."

"Go on..."

"I love Joseph Hummel. There's no room in my heart for another. I've tried."

Lottie's eyes grew round. "Are you serious?"

"*Jah*, I am. What made me realize it was when Judah came back. I never felt for Judah like I do for Joseph."

"Does he feel the same for you?"

"*Jah*. He said he loves me."

Lottie put her head back on her rocker and closed her eyes. "He's moving right next door to us and I'm glad."

"You see how *goot* he is. You're happy to be his neighbor, *jah*?"

"I'm glad he won't be living across the street from you. Katie, he is not Amish. Are you saying you're willing to leave the Amish for him? You never did for Judah, but you would for Joseph?"

"That's how wonderful *goot* Joseph is. He said he'd never ask me to leave the Amish."

"So what will you do?"

"Never marry unless Joseph becomes Amish," Katie said in a whisper.

"Katie, that's unlikely to happen. And you say you both admit to loving each other? When you're alone it could be a place of temptation."

"You don't think I'd act in an immoral way with Joseph, do you?"

"The spirit is willing, but the flesh is weak…you know that, Katie."

"But Joseph's helped me grow spiritually. He really knows his Bible."

"Has he tempted you though?"

"No. He's never tried to kiss me or anything…although I admit I wish he would."

Lottie gawked at Katie, her eyes out of proportion to her face. "So you have no hope of a future with Levi? None at all, or is this Joseph choking your relationship, like a bad weed?"

"Please don't call him that," Katie snapped, surprising herself.

"Let me ask in a different way. You said you felt a seed of romance starting when you and Levi went to the auction. What happened to the seed?"

"Well, Levi's busy making clocks, that's for sure. He makes most of their money on Christmas sales. He started working hard in September."

"There you have it. Lack of water and sunshine. You need to see each other more."

"Lottie, my hearts so full of Joseph..."

"Then spend more time with Levi and let him poke a hole in your heart. Joseph can flow right out, I'm sure," Lottie said, narrowing her eyes. "It could be infatuation you feel for him, or worse, lust. Your *Mamm* told you to build a relationship on friendship."

"Lottie, lust is such a bad thing. You exaggerate. And I did try friendship, but found romance with Joseph. It didn't happen with Levi."

"I'd give it time. You want children, *jah*?" Lottie asked, bending forward to take her friend's hand.

"More so now than ever."

"God put that desire in your heart. Would he do that to make you miserable?"

Katie looked down at baby Miriam. She literally ached to have a baby sometimes. How many baby blankets had she knit, and with each one hoping someday the blanket would be for her own dear *boppli*? Lottie was right. Surely God wasn't so cruel to give her a desire and not fulfill it. But she didn't love Levi...

CHAPTER 12

Ginny reached across the table and took Kirsten's hand. "You tired honey? Not used to getting up at four to shop, huh? We'll take a long break here, and then we'll shop the other end of Pittsburgh Mills. Oh, and we need to stop at the Windgate Winery and get our raspberry cordial so we can have our *Anne of Green Gables* marathon party before you leave." Ginny took another swig of coffee. "Oh, and then we need to pick up pastries at the Oakmont Bakery. Wouldn't be a tea party without tarts."

Kirsten stirred her soup.

"I'm sorry honey, I'm hyper on all the coffee I've been drinking. Is something wrong?"

"Noah is. He won't write to me while I'm gone. He promised his *daed*."

Ginny put her hand on Kirsten's. "Sarah told me and I think it's a good idea. You two need to get away from each other. You'll need to withstand temptation."

"What do you mean?"

"You'll meet lots of dashing Italian men. The relatives know you're single and will be setting you up with a good boy from Riccia. That's my fear, but you need to live your life."

"Mom, you've overdosed on coffee. You're talking nonsense."

Ginny took another sip of coffee. "No, I'm in my right senses. You could fall for someone else, and so could Noah. This test in your relationship is important. You need to make sure it's made of metal before you think of a future with him."

Kirsten looked lost. "I need Noah. I've never been without him. I prefer him to all others."

"You sound like someone out of a Jane Austen book. Maybe we do watch those movies too much. You need to get out there and live your own love story."

"I've already found my Mr. Darcy," Kirsten said evenly.

~*~

Joseph looked at all the boxes in his room and sighed. He needed a break from all this packing. Looking outside the window at the freshly fallen snow, he thought he could get some great pictures. He got bundled up from head to toe, and went outside and headed down the road to see if any deer were on the Byler land. He saw an eight point, trying to make a meal from dry corn stalks. After taking several pictures, he spotted more deer and snapped away.

"*Goot* morning, Joseph," Reuben said, as he came by on his buggy.

"*Goot* morning, Reuben. Looks like you need to get your sleigh out."

"*Jah,* looks like a hard winter is upon us. Going to get the *kinner* from school and take them to my *bruder's* house for babysitting. There's always a pot of hot chocolate there and they love playing Dutch Blitz with their cousins."

"Ginny and James play that game. Have to be quick."

"*Jah,* you do." Reuben chuckled. "I hear you're moving into the little farm by Eli. What will you be doing with the land?"

"I hope to raise goats and possibly miniature horses. Living without electricity, too."

"Why would you do that?"

"Since I was a boy I've always dreamed of living in a cabin with no modern conveniences. I've also lived without electricity before in New York City and it doesn't bother me. Actually, there were months when I didn't even have a house to live in; so I'm looking forward to having my own place."

Reuben rubbed his hands together. "Well, let me know if you'll be needing any help moving."

"*Jah,* I will. *Danki.* Have a *goot* day," Joseph said, with a grin.

Joseph shivered and headed back to the house to get his heavier coat. He looked behind Katie's house and thought he saw a blue heron land near the pond. He focused his camera until he saw the bird, but was surprised that it was Katie. She was skating, and in such frigid weather. He clicked a few shots, making sure not to get her face. He admired her grace; she twirled in the middle of the pond like a little ballerina. He took more pictures of her, and then to his horror, Katie fell through the ice.

He dropped his camera on the road and raced as fast as he could toward the pond. He didn't have boots on and slid. He felt like he was in a nightmare, trying to run but only getting slowed down. The path Reuben's kids made with their sled was slick, so he moved off the path and grabbed tall weeds and latched on. He pulled himself up the hill, screaming for Katie, hoping to hear her voice. When he finally got to the pond, he only saw a crack in the ice.

"Dear Lord, no! NO!" Joseph yelled. Then something bobbed up to the opening. It was Katie.

"Good Lord, let her be alive!" He went onto the ice and laid down flat to steady the ice. He reached for Katie and with supernatural strength pulled her out of the water. Joseph put his arms under hers and slowly slid her off the pond.

He put his cheek against her mouth and realized she wasn't breathing. "Lord, God, help me remember CPR!" Joseph screamed. He tilted her to one side and hit her back hard. Some water came out of her mouth. He continued to hit her but no more water came out, so he turned her over on her back, lifted her neck with one hand and pinched her nose with his other. He put his mouth on hers and blew in air with all his might. No response. He blew again and she started to cough up water. He tilted her to one side again, and she started to gasp for air.

"Praise God!" he yelled. But she looked so cold, lips blue and shaking all over. He took off his coat and wrapped her in it. Joseph picked her up, went to the kid's sledding path, and sat down, and after saying a prayer, started to slide down the hill with Katie in his lap. Tall field grass laden with snow was high on both sides. He was relieved to reach the bottom, and carried her into her house, shielding her from the wind.

"Millie! I need help!"

No response. "Millie?" He yelled as he ran through the little house. She wasn't home.

"Katie, we need to get these clothes off of you, now." He held her tight. "My sister and Kirsten aren't home. I don't know what to do." But instinctively he took off Katie's apron. She didn't object. Then he unpinned her dress and peeled it off. He was relieved to see she had on undergarments. He ran and took the quilt off her bed and wrapped her in it, then laid her on the sofa, rubbing her feet and then her hands. He took off her bonnet and ran to the kitchen to get a dry towel. Taking out the tight bun pinned to the back of her head, he wrapped her hair in the towel.

"*Danki*," she whispered. Her lips were blue as was her skin. Joseph took her pulse. It was slow.

"Katie!" Joseph said, choking back tears. He picked her up and sat her in his lap. "I need to warm you up some more. Do you mind if I hold you? My body heat's the best thing for you now. Your fire in the woodstove is low."

"*Jah.*"

Joseph took off his shirt and unwrapped some of the blanket so she could feel the warmth of his body. He continued to massage her hands and feet. Katie soon fell asleep and he shook her to wake her up, but she didn't, so he just held her tight. After a few minutes, Joseph took her pulse and it was gaining strength. When he knew her hands and feet were warm he started to relax. Five minutes passed while Joseph held Katie in his arms. He kept saying, "Thank you Lord, I couldn't live without my Katie," as he cried like a baby.

Katie's eyes slowly opened. "W-what are you s-saying...?"

"Just talking out loud. You rest." A sob escaped as he talked.

"*Ach...*" She looked up at Joseph with concern. "*Danki.* You s-saved me."

Joseph looked down at her. How he loved this girl like no other. He lifted her head up and kissed her on her cheek, then the forehead, then on her mouth. Tears rolled down his cheeks. "I thought you were dead." He squeezed her close to him.

Katie's eyes glistened with tears. "Do y-you think my l-lips are warmed up? They s-still feel c-cold."

He laughed and kissed her again and found he couldn't stop.

"I l-love you, Joseph. So m-much...." Katie said, breathless.

He held her tight. He took her pulse and then sobbed again. "You're alright. Do you feel warm?

"*Jah*..."

"Oh, God, I thought you were dead. I can't lose you. I've never loved anyone like this before."

She looked at him and smiled faintly. "Go to the c-crossroads...." Then she fell back to sleep.

Go to the crossroads? Was that where medical help was? She was fine now. Was Millie at the crossroads in Smicksburg? Was she asking for her mom? What did she mean?

Joseph held her for a long while. He didn't want to let her go, ever. No girl he'd ever met came close to Katie.

He felt her jerk in his arms. "I can't breathe."

Joseph rocked her back and forth. "A bad dream. I'm here. You're okay"

She looked up at him and gave a weak smile. "Pray...at the cross..."

She fell back to sleep. He would pray at the foot of the cross, like she said. But for what? She was safe now. *What did she mean?* He was having a hard time keeping his eyes open. He fell asleep, and hours later, a car's headlights woke him up. He saw Ginny's Jeep backing into her driveway.

He pulled Katie away from him and wrapped her up again in the quilt. He picked her up and took her back to her room, putting her on her bed. Fumbling in the darkness, he grabbed one of the dresses hanging from the peg on the wall. "Here, you get dressed. I'll go out and make a better fire in the woodstove. It's almost dead." Joseph quickly went out of the room and shut the door. He headed to the stove and opened the door, he threw in some kindling and it quickly caught on fire. Then he lit the oil lamp on the wall and threw more wood on the fire. When the fire was roaring, he put on his shirt.

When Katie emerged, her long brown hair flowing down her back, he couldn't look away. "I need some matches to light my bedroom lamp." She walked past him to go to the kitchen, but stopped and looked at him. They quickly embraced. Joseph stroked her long brown hair, and no longer could trust the passion he felt toward her.

"Good night, Love. I'll go get Ginny and have her stay with you."

"Joseph, I'm *goot*, really." She clung to him. "You saved my life."

He held her and wanted time to stop; to be in this moment forever. "I'm going to get Ginny now." Joseph said, and walked away, wanting to run right back into her arms.

"Joseph," she yelled. "Pray at the crossroad, for my sake."

Then he understood what she meant. He'd shared Jeremiah 6:16 with her, the scripture he was meditating on, about praying at the crossroads, *their crossroad.* There had to be a way for them, a path to walk down hand in hand, as husband and wife, and he would pray that God would direct them. "I will dear one; I will."

~*~

Eli took a swig of coffee and bit into a gingersnap cookie. "Joseph, it's all over town how you saved Katie's life yesterday. *Goot* thing you saw her fall in the pond,"

"That's what I've come over to talk with you about. I no longer trust myself to be alone with her."

"I can see the sparks between you two, and it does create a problem, you not being Amish."

"Yes, *indeed*," Lottie said, as she entered the room, holding little Miriam.

"I'll be moving in next door. Will you be my accountability partner, Eli?"

Eli grabbed another cookie. "What's that?"

"It's usually a good friend you've known for a while and one you trust to keep you on the straight and narrow. I haven't known you long, but I feel like I have. Like I said, I don't trust myself around Katie anymore. Until I figure out if I want to join the Amish and be able to marry her, I need you to be there whenever she comes over. It will keep me accountable, understand?"

Eli and Lottie stared at him, gawking.

"You are a moral man, and I admire that, but do you want to be Amish for Katie or for yourself?" Eli asked.

"For the Lord," Joseph said. "I want His will in my life. I'm very drawn to the Amish way of living, though. It's like God can speak to me so much better without all the distractions of the *English* world."

"You know you'll have to be taking baptismal classes and pass to get into the church," Lottie said, a bit coolly. "And the People will vote whether they will accept you in."

"I'm waiting on God to show me if He even wants me Amish. I get the feeling the Lord wants to show me something living next door in that little house."

"How to live with no electricity?" Eli asked.

"I've done that before. Was homeless at times in the city."

Eli got up to get a large book off the shelf. "Here's my English-German dictionary. Get started. Never hurts to learn another language."

Joseph looked confused.

"You need to learn German before you turn Amish, and also live among us to know our ways."

"I've lived here six months…"

"If you're serious, you'll need to live without a car, too."

"I don't want anyone to know about this and giving up my car would give it away."

Lottie glared at him. "What if this is some kind of phase you're going through? Where does that leave Katie and Levi?"

"Katie and Levi? What do you mean?"

"I'm encouraging Katie to take a fresh look at Levi. She wants a family badly. Levi's a *goot* man."

"She doesn't love him…" Joseph wanted to scream this to Lottie but restrained himself. Why were people almost forcing her to marry Levi?

"She's going to be spending more time with him to give the relationship time to grow. She had a little romantic feeling toward him and that can grow when properly nourished."

"When did she tell you that?"

"Last week."

"I see. Well…I don't want anything but happiness for Katie, even if it means my unhappiness at seeing her marry another, if she loves him."

Lottie's eyes softened. "You mean that?"

"I'd have a broken heart, for sure, but when you love someone you put their happiness before your own."

Eli's eyes shone. "You know Him in the heart…there's not much dividing us. You'd make a *goot* Amish man, if that's the path God has for you."

Lottie looked at Joseph with new admiration.

Joseph took a little notepad from his pocket. "Ginny writes her prayers and favorite quotes, and I started to also. This is how I feel about Christ." He opened the notebook and read, "'There is a God-shaped vacuum in the heart of every person, and it can never be filled by any created thing. It can only be filled by God, made known through Jesus Christ.'... Blaise Pascal. This quote best tells my story. I was empty and tried to fill it with everything under the sun, some things sinful. Nothing satisfied me, but when I met Christ ...well...I was satisfied. My heart was full."

Eli grabbed his Bible on the table and flipped through until he found the passage he wanted, John 6:35: 'And Jesus said unto them, I am the bread of life: he that cometh to me shall never hunger; and he that believeth on me shall never thirst.' Is that what you mean?"

"Exactly. Is that what the Amish believe?"

"You carry a little notebook about your faith. We have a little booklet about ours." Eli got up and ran into the living room and came back with a little blue book in his hand. "This is our belief. It's called the *Dordrecht Confession of Faith*. You can have this copy."

"Are you sure?" Joseph asked.

"*Jah*, sure. There's scripture references to all we believe below each article. If you have any questions, ask me or my *daed*. He would love to talk with you about it. He may even enlist you in one of his classes."

"Classes?"

"*Daed's* a Senior Bishop. He used to be active as Bishop for years but retired two years back. I think he misses teaching the Bible."

"I'll visit him. Moses likes to talk. I thought the Amish wouldn't talk to me when I first moved here."

Eli stroked his chestnut-brown beard. "Well, as a People, we believe in separation and living in community. Our human nature wants its own way. When you live in community you can't get your own way all the time. It takes great sacrifice and faith to live as we do. *Outsiders* might destroy our faith, and then our community would be destroyed."

"So you need faith to live in community?"

Lottie laughed. "*Jah*, for sure and for certain. You need the *Goot* Lord's help a lot."

Joseph contemplated what they just said. He scratched his newly forming goatee. Living next door, he was sure to learn more about the Amish. Was this part of God's plan? A step toward being Amish?

CHAPTER 13

Ginny's hands flew as she knit. If Sarah continued to treat her like a heathen, she'd leave the knitting circle for good.

"So, did Kirsten have a good trip to Italy? No flight delays?" Suzy asked. "Sometimes those change-overs are brutal."

"She had a direct flight. It was more expensive, but I couldn't imagine Kirsten changing flights in a foreign country."

"I couldn't imagine flying at all," Millie said. "I'm glad we're not allowed."

"Unless it's an emergency," Granny Weaver added.

"Well, I'm glad Kirsten's gone..." Sarah said.

Ginny clenched her ball of yarn. "I'll miss her. She's a dear girl and one of my best friends."

"I suppose she does have a way with pulling at people's heartstrings. Quite a charmer."

Ginny shot up. "She's sweet is what she is." She looked over at Suzy. "I'm leaving."

"Ginny, I'm not ready to go. Please, let's stay," Millie said. "Do you want me to get you some hot chocolate? You don't look good."

"Chocolate won't fix how I'm feeling." She turned to Sarah. "Do you know my *English* brother, Joseph, saved Katie's life yesterday? Imagine that, a heathen saving a saintly Amish life."

Suzy put up her hand. "This is my place, and I won't have bickering here."

"I'm sorry, Ginny," Sarah said. "I think you misunderstood what I said about Kirsten. What I mean to say is that she's easy to love. She pulls at my heartstrings. She's always so kind."

Ginny felt the muscles in her shoulder relax. "Sarah, I'm sorry for overreacting."

"I'm so worried about Noah. Let's all pray for my son. He's so withdrawn since she left. He's scaring us. Acting like Gideon when –"

"Remember Lot's wife, Sarah. Turned to salt and couldn't move," Granny Weaver interrupted.

Sarah nodded. "Will *yinz* pray for our family? Jacob feels he did the right thing in asking the two not to write, but deep down doubts his judgment."

"I think he did the right thing," Ginny said. "There's just no handbook on how to deal with us *English*, huh?"

Sarah looked at her with fondness. "Nee, but we've managed to have *goot* relationships for years."

~*~

"Have I done something wrong, Katie?" Levi asked as they walked around his clock shop. "I thought you might want a nice cedar chest. *Daed* and I sell as many chests as clocks. Popular with the *English*."

"It's what you called it: a hope chest," Katie said, looking down.

"That's what they're called. What's wrong with that?"

"I had one of those as a young girl. I got it when I was a teen and filled it with dishes, linens, and all types of things to be a *goot* homemaker. I gave it all away."

Levi took her hands. "Katie, when I helped you and your *mamm* move into the *dawdyhaus*, I noticed you didn't have a hope chest. I thought you could take this chest and start to fill it with hopes of a future...with me."

"Levi, you are such a *goot* man, but I have a confession to make." She sat on the hope chest for support. "My heart is filled with another man. I'm so sorry."

"Judah?" Levi asked.

"Ach, no. It's not Judah. When I saw him I knew what I felt long ago was nothing compared to what I feel for...Joseph."

"Joseph? You can't be serious."

"We were only friends, and it turned into romance."

Levi sat on the hope chest next to her. "Katie, he's not Amish. What are you thinking?"

"That I'll be single my whole life...I'm not unhappy about it."

Levi put his arm around her. "Then why are you so sad?"

Katie was surprised he didn't act jealous, but was more concerned about her Amish roots and happiness. "I'm so sorry I deceived you."

"Katie, you've deceived yourself. You want *kinner* and you won't be happy single."

"I am confused, for sure and certain."

"You said you felt a little bit of romance toward me, *jah*?"

"*Jah*, I did."

Levi took her chin and tilted her face toward his. "I've been too busy with this shop lately. We haven't had time to water that seed."

"That's what Lottie said."

"You told Lottie you loved Joseph?"

"She's my best friend. I needed advice."

Levi let go of her chin and looked down. "Katie, if the bishop finds out about this, you may be reprimanded. Have you told anyone else?"

"No. *Mamm* doesn't even know."

"Well...what was Lottie's advice? She seems wise."

"When I told her my heart was full of Joseph, she said to spend more time with you so you could poke a hole in me and let Joseph run out."

Levi smiled. "That's a *goot* way of putting it." Levi poked Katie in the side. "I would like to make that hole in your heart and make Joseph go away."

Katie looked at Levi. His big, brown, puppy-dog eyes seemed hurt, yet hopeful. She just told him she loved another, yet he was so patient…so kind; not jealous or envious. He was living what the Bible called 'love.'

Levi bent down and kissed her on the cheek. "Will you take this hope chest and try to fill it with things that can lead to a real future? A future with me?"

"I can't make that promise right now."

"Then take the chest and fill it with things that make you happy."

She leaned her head on his shoulder "Levi, you're too *goot* to me."

He took her hand. "How about we plan a sleigh ride? I'll bring a thermos full of hot chocolate."

"Sounds *goot* to me," Katie said, not letting his hand go.

~*~

Judah sat with his arms crossed. If Jerry and Janice hadn't made church attendance mandatory, even on Wednesday nights, this would be the last place he'd be. He watched Janice flash her big smile, and then sing a song:

This is my Father's world, and to my listening ears
All nature sings, and round me rings the music of the spheres.
This is my Father's world: I rest me in the thought
Of rocks and trees, of skies and seas;
His hand the wonders wrought.

This is my Father's world, the birds their carols raise,
The morning light, the lily white, declare their Maker's praise.
This is my Father's world: He shines in all that's fair;
In the rustling grass I hear Him pass;
He speaks to me everywhere.

She sang the last verse, "He speaks to me everywhere," several times. Judah looked over at James, who had his eyes closed. He seemed to be soaking in every word. Anger ripped at Judah's heart, and he darted from his seat and marched out of the church.

He didn't see the patch of ice in the parking lot, and slipped, landing on his back. A strong hand reached down to help him up. It was James Rowland. "Judah, what's wrong?"

Judah got up tried to look at him, but couldn't make eye contact. "I don't know....just needed some air."

"Are you sick?"

He groaned. "Sick of church!" He made a snowball and threw it against a tree. "That song ticked me off. 'He speaks to me everywhere'. What a joke! He doesn't talk to me much." He formed another snowball and hit the tree harder. "Look at all the places in the Bible where God strikes people dead, or allows people to drown in floods...all except Noah, his favorite. It's like we're some kind of joke, like we're guinea pigs under some type of weird experiment. I don't know if I want a God like that talking to me anyhow."

"I wonder why you see that in the Bible, but don't see the love of God."

"Have some scriptures for me to memorize?" Judah bit back sarcastically. "No thank you."

"Actually I do, but your bitterness would keep you from seeing them for what they are. The Bible is the greatest love story ever written, but you can't see that."

Judah shot back, "I'm tired of trying to be a Christian." All the times his father called him 'Judas' instead of 'Judah' flooded his mind. When he took baptism classes and his father would drill him, he called him that wretched name when he missed an answer. No, he was tired of trying to be a Christian. He couldn't do it. He looked squarely at James. "I give up. I'm not Christian material."

"Maybe you should give up," James said.

"Give up. So you think I'm a hopeless case, too."

"No, but I think you need to give up trying to be a Christian. Jesus said we all have stony-hard hearts, but when we put our hearts in his hands, he softens them like clay. He writes his ways, his laws, on our hearts, so we'll want to obey him. He does all the work, not us."

Judah felt like he wanted to punch James, but didn't know why. "Just stop the religious mumbo jumbo, OK?"

James stepped closer. "Give your heart to Christ and let Him soften it."

Judah lifted his eyes to James, "Judah, it's time you trusted someone. Trust God."

Judah raised his fist, but when he looked into the love in James' eyes, he froze as solid as the ice below him. He soon felt James' arms around him. "Give your heart to Christ. He'll give you a new heart, one like His."

Judah felt the tension release from his back and he put his fist down. He could have given James a shiner, but hugged him instead. He thought of Joseph, and how he could have beaten the living daylights out of him when he spit in his face, but Joseph said he'd pray for him. It wasn't normal. Maybe it was supernatural or something.

Maybe it was the God in him showing his love. He felt the glacier in his heart crack and started to melt. Tears slid down his cheeks; then they came down like a river.

He felt James embrace him tighter. "Say a simple prayer from your heart. Tell the Lord you realize you're a sinner, and thank Him that He loved you enough to take your place on the cross. Ask Him to live inside you so you can know His love."

Judah choked back tears and broke free of James embrace. "He died two-thousand years ago. How can He change my heart today?"

"There is no time with God, and Jesus isn't dead…He's still alive…"

"I don't think I'm thick or anything, but how do I do that?"

"By talking to God and telling him you want this new heart…like a heart transplant…ask him to plant his heart into yours. He's not looking for perfect words, only sincere words."

Judah knelt down on the snow and wept. "I can't believe you love me, God. I can't believe you're not mad all the time."

James put his hand on Judah's shoulder. "Let those tears out, Son. It's OK for a man to cry."

Judah clenched his hands, poured out his heart to God, confessing his anger at his father, the People and the world, and begged to have a new heart. There was a stillness, a peace he'd never experienced as he knelt in silence for several minutes, soaking up this new feeling – a burden lifted. He opened his eyes, and looked up at James. "Thank you."

James was beaming. "Let's get together and study the Bible and find out more about God. Maybe you can see with this new heart of yours how much He loves you."

Judah nodded in agreement, swiping a tear off his cheek. James put his arm around him and they walked back into the church.

~*~

Millie plunked her knitting needles in her lap and looked at Ginny across the knitting circle. "So you're moving before Christmas? I'll miss you, Ginny."

Ginny cast on red yarn and started to knit. "I'll miss being your neighbor, too. I was hoping to have one last Christmas at our house. When Janice said a family needs housing already, before the place opens, James and I thought it only right."

"What kind of need?" Sarah asked, squinting to see her yarn.

"A lady with a daughter. Don't know much about her, but she has no place to go. She's been homeless a while."

"Now that's sad. When will she move in?" Granny Weaver asked.

"The week before Christmas, so we're moving next week."

"The road to a friend's house is never long, *jah*?" Katie asked.

Ginny grinned. "I taught you that proverb a while ago. I'm surprised you remember it. I'll only be three miles away....You'll call me if you need anything, right?"

"Of course I will. Janice already assured me I can use the phone and when I go to town. I'll stop in."

Ginny put her needles down. "I'm a little worried about you, Millie. You seem weighed down. Is something wrong?"

"No nothing," Millie quickly said. "Right as rain."

"Millie, what is it?"

"Well, it's private." She looked at Katie, then the other women. "Would *yinz* mind if we went into the next room for a chat?"

"We can manage," Suzy said.

Millie took Ginny's hand as they left the room. She leaned toward Ginny and said softly, "Katie told me something the other day that almost knocked me off my rocker."

"What?" Ginny asked, hoping this was not about Joseph.

"Well, fifteen Amish families are leaving Smicksburg for Upstate New York. Granny Weaver's upset. Didn't want to bring it up. Anyhow, they want to have dairy farms and there's more land there to be had. It's always sad to have to say good-bye, although we'll all keep in touch through *Die Botschaft*."

"The newspaper you write in to keep in touch? The one I call Amish Facebook?"

"*Jah*, but it's not the same as seeing them." Millie stared at the shelves of yarn. "Katie's talking about going with them. I don't want to hold her back, and she may find the right man up there."

Ginny's heart went out to her dear friend. When her boys moved away, she cried for days, but they had so many ways to communicate. "I'm sorry, Millie. It's a shock. Isn't she courting Levi?"

"She is, but there's no romance yet. I think deep down she may care for Judah and want to get away from him. I hear he has no intention of returning to the Amish."

"He's been going to our church and he and James are having a Bible study together. It's hard to tell what he'll do." Ginny sighed. "You really think Katie is leaving because of Judah?"

"She keeps saying she wants to get away. Maybe she's just talking without thinking."

"Well, I can talk to Katie or maybe Joseph can. She seems to be able to talk to him too. Want me to ask him to talk to her when they go out to shoot pictures this afternoon?"

"*Jah*, little Josiah is excited he was invited this time."

"Can't they have a private conversation?" Ginny asked. "What if it is Judah she's running from? Little ears can talk, too, and we know country gossip spreads like wild fire."

"Sure, I'll keep Josiah with me when Joseph picks her up."

~*~

Joseph pulled up the long driveway to get Katie and Josiah. He couldn't believe Katie would leave Smicksburg. He soon saw Katie all bundled up in black garments from head to toe.

Joseph got out of the car to open the door for Katie. "Where's Josiah?"

Katie slid into the front seat. "*Mamm* told me he couldn't go. Said we had important things to talk about. What's going on?"

Joseph took in a deep breath. He didn't want to be alone with Katie, but what could he do? He'd tell Eli it was out of his control. He got back into the driver's seat. "Where are we going to take pictures?"

"I thought Black Angus cows against the snow would make nice pictures. There's a farm a few miles out toward Dayton," Katie said, her eyes locked on Joseph's.

Joseph peeled his eyes from hers and headed toward Dayton. There was silence in the car.

"Joseph, what do you want to talk to me about? And why do you look so angry?"

"Well, I got some bad news."

"What's wrong?"

"I hear you're moving to Upstate New York. Is that true?"

"Well...it's hard being here. I need to get away."

"From Judah? Ginny asked me to talk to you about him, of all things."

"Joseph, I feel nothing for Judah and I haven't made my mind to go. I was talking to the families going and it seemed exciting. They need an old *maedel* school teacher."

Joseph pulled over on the side of the road and looked at Katie. "It's more than that. What is it?"

"Levi asked me to marry him."

"What?" Joseph felt his heart in his throat.

"Joseph, it's so hard. I told him I loved you. I said no, but he said he'd wait. He blames himself for neglecting our relationship due to the clock shop being so busy with Christmas sales. He thinks he needs more time with me."

"What do you think?"

"I'm confused, so I thought moving to New York would be *goot*. I never should have mentioned it to *Mamm*. Reuben needs help with the *kinner* and I have a greenhouse to start in February. It was selfish of me."

Joseph took Katie's hand. "There's not a selfish bone in your body. You're always looking out for other people's feelings but your own. You're like Anne Elliot."

"She's a friend of yours?"

"No, she's in a Jane Austen movie Ginny watches over and over again. This girl lets everyone run her life but herself. She just can't seem to hurt anyone's feelings."

"What happened to her?" Katie asked.

"She went against her family's wishes and marries the one she really loves."

"Joseph, I'll never leave the Amish for you, so I'm not like her at all."

Joseph put his hand on her cheek. "I'd never ask you to leave your people. Captain Wentworth made changes in his life to deserve Anne and the father agreed to their marriage in the end."

"Captain Wentworth is the one she loves?" Katie asked.

Joseph leaned closer to Katie. "Yes. She waited seven years for him to make his fortune at sea, but I won't be asking you that. Only one year."

Katie leaned toward Joseph. He felt the warmth of her breath. "Wait for what?"

"That's the problem. I don't know. I'm just asking you to wait for me until I can figure this whole thing out. Don't say yes to Levi. I love you." He took her head and kissed her. "I couldn't bear to lose you. I told you that before." He kissed her on her lips, then her cheek, then her nose, then back to her mouth. All sense of time and space seemed to disappear to him, until Reuben knocked on the window.

CHAPTER 14

*J*ames dusted off his hands as he looked around his new home. "Well Judah, that's the last box. Can you believe it?"

"And you left a lot of stuff for Forget-Me-Not Manor."

"Forget-Me-What?"

"Forget-Me-Not Manor. I overheard Janice and Ginny talking this morning. They said it will constantly remind the girls coming to live here they're not forgotten by God, and a manor is an old word for castle; they said all girls need to know they're princesses, loved by their king, or something like that."

"I'm watching a miracle." James said. "You would have said that in a sarcastic tone before. Looks like the Lord has softened that heart of yours, huh?"

"Well, I'm reading lots of scriptures on forgiveness, trying to forgive my dad. I even had a good memory of us fishing. So strange; I was six or seven but it seems like yesterday."

"I went through something similar with my own dad. My childhood was something I had no control over, but when I became an adult I had the power to make my own decisions. I decided to forgive my dad, too, and some good memories came back."

"I hope to have a nice family like you someday," Judah said.

"Marrying Ginny was the best decision of my life. We're not perfect and can bicker at times." He grinned. "We've been married thirty years, though."

Judah looked at James and hoped he'd be as lucky as him someday. "So you'll have the store downstairs and live upstairs, huh?"

"Yes. So glad the house was converted into two apartments years ago. We'll keep part of the kitchen downstairs for a cappuccino bar," James said. "Let me show you around my new pad."

Judah stared at the carved wood on the staircase as they climbed the steps. When he looked inside the apartment, he was in awe of the gorgeous hardwood floors and the original woodwork on the windows and doors. "How old is this place?"

"It was built in 1897, at the height of the Italianate period. When Italians immigrated to America they thought the colonial houses were too box-shaped, so they added curves. The two-story bay window makes the outside of the house seem rounder."

"And the scallops around the front porch...I see. I've always been fascinated with architecture."

"Ever think of going to school to study it?" James asked.

"Well, being raised Amish I only went to eighth grade."

"You have your whole life ahead of you. Do you have your GED?

"Yes, I got that and even took a few classes at the community college."

"Why'd you quit?"

"I got leukemia, but I didn't like college anyway; I'm a hands on guy. I was known for my construction business years ago. I contacted some old clients, and they're more than willing to hire me. Lots of remodeling jobs lined up."

"Glad to hear you beat cancer. Nasty disease. Ginny lost her mom to it." James readjusted his wire rimmed glasses. "I'm concerned she'll be really depressed at Christmas. None of the kids will be home. Where will you be on Christmas Day?"

"At Jerry and Janice's place."

"Aren't you moving in with them into our old house?"

"They said I could stay at their place. Women are going to be their main ministry and a guy living in the house didn't seem like a good idea, so they're letting me stay in their house for really cheap rent."

"Want to come to our house for my famous fish dinner? We'll need to cheer Ginny up."

"Sounds good." A warm sensation flooded Judah's heart. He felt like part of a family somehow. He thought of Amos Byler. He was like a dad to him long ago. His days with Katie and the Bylers were the happiest of his life. He thought of Katie's sweet nature. Seeing her made him break up with Elizabeth. He wanted a girl like Katie to be the mother of his children and wished he could talk to her...

~*~

Reuben, Millie, and Bishop Mast sat across the oak table from Katie, waiting for her answer.

Bishop Mast's eyes narrowed. "We're not judging, but you know our Gmay's survival is dependent on the mutual submission of the People. We all abide by the same rules."

Katie thought of Joseph's story; how a girl waited seven years for her true love to come back and how her father agreed to their marriage. Could she agree to never speak to Joseph again like the Bishop was asking? No, she knew she couldn't vow to that. "No! I can't do that."

She looked at her *mamm's* face, so pale and withdrawn. Reuben spoke up. "Bishop, how about she agrees to never speak to him alone? That would solve the problem."

Bishop Mast's face was as red as beets. "Can you keep a pure heart when seeing him? God looks at your heart. Will it lead you into temptation to want to be with this man and leave the Amish?"

"I'd never leave the Amish," Katie said.

"Then you must act like an Amish woman. You can only marry an Amish man," the Bishop yelled, pounding his fist on the table. " I see too many Amish young folk falling for *Englishers* and it can't work."

"What is your advice, Bishop?" Millie asked. "Joseph will be moved in next week to his little farm next to Eli and Lottie. He won't be across the street anymore. I think Katie should be able to see him in group settings. Are you agreeing to that?"

Bishop Mast stiffened and nervously fidgeted with his black hat. "Absolutely no contact until he moves out. Not even a hello or good-bye. When he's gone, only in groups. This is your first warning. If you don't submit, we'll have to take further action." The Bishop paused to take a drink of water. "Now, do you repent of your sin of lust?"

Lust? Is that what the Bishop thinks my feelings for Joseph are? "I kissed Judah Yoder when we were courting years ago. Was that lust, too?" Katie asked, defiantly.

Reuben looked in disbelief. "Katie, it was leading to marriage. Kissing Joseph is like eating of the forbidden fruit. You know you can only marry an Amish man to remain among the People."

Katie did not speak. She loved the Amish way of life, but at this cost? She loved Joseph and she wasn't guilty of an ugly sin called lust.

Reuben reached across the table for her hand. "If you don't think you need to repent of the sin of lust, how about breaking your word to our People? At baptism you made a covenant vow to follow the *Ordnung*; our ordinances have not changed concerning marrying an outsider. Can you repent that the path you were on was leading you from the People?"

"*Jah*, I suppose," Katie said.

"Then you see it's the wrong path and you regret taking it?" Bishop Mast boomed.

"Yes, according to the *Ordnung*, yes it is the wrong path."

Bishop Mast wiped the sweat from his brow. "All is forgiven. But you are not to see this Joseph at all this week and only in a group setting or another warning will be given."

~*~

Levi took Katie's hand and led her to the sleigh. "I brought the warmest buggy robe we have. It's a chilly night." When she got into the sleigh, a small white box was on the seat, tied with a red ribbon. Levi ran around to his side and hopped in. "Open it up, Katie. It's for you."

Katie untied the ribbons and was surprised; a pound of white, walnut fudge from the Sampler.

"Danki, Levi," Katie half whispered. "How did you know this was my favorite sweet?"

"I asked Reuben the other day." Levi pulled another white box with red ribbon from his coat pocket. "I found out your second favorite fudge was maple. It was buy one pound, get a half pound free day," Levi said as he gave her the box. "Let's get the sleigh robe up around us and we'll be off." Levi took the heavy quilted blanket up over them. He put his arm around Katie and pulled her close. "It's cold and we'll need to snuggle."

It was freezing so Katie didn't pull away, although his nearness made her feel shy.

He led the sleigh out onto Wilson Road. "I love sleigh rides, how about you?"

"*Jah*, it's cold, though."

"We're stopping at Granny Weaver's for a little surprise." They soon turned onto Mahoning Road. "Freshly fallen snow always smells so *goot* and hides all the winter mud," he said. "It reminds me of God's forgiveness; though our sin be red as crimson, he'll make them as white as snow."

"So you heard about my confession." She looked up at him. "You're not angry about me kissing Joseph?"

Levi stiffened. "*Jah*. But we move forward." He shifted. " I've been too busy at the clock shop, but that's going to change." He looked down at her. "You can't see Joseph, though."

"*Jah*, I know…only in groups." She sighed out loud, knowing the whistling wind would hide the sound that came from deep within her. "The bishop made me feel like a wretched sinner."

"Maybe you feel shame inside. Bishop Mast is pretty fair, even though I don't know him well. Our bishop would have come down harder. "

They neared the Baptist church and Katie squinted. "Is that Judah helping put up Christmas lights?"

"Looks like it. I see him a lot with James Rowland. The two stop into the Country Junction for coffee and they open their Bibles right there in the restaurant and study them. Seems like Judah's doing much better; seems happy. Don't think he'll be returning to the Amish, though."

As they passed the church, Judah waved over at them. Katie saw a lightness in Judah she'd never seen. She waved back. "He's shunned but it doesn't hurt to give a friendly wave." Snow flew in her face and she put her face against Levi's chest. "The wind is really picking up."

Levi encircled her with his broad arms. "Any warmer?"

Katie looked up at Levi. "*Jah.*"

Levi slowed the horse to a slow walk. "Am I poking any holes in that heart of yours?"

"You're too *goot* for me, Levi."

Levi squeezed her tight as they continued on to the quilt shop. A deer flew out of nowhere and spooked the horse. The sleigh started to swerve and tilt. Levi pulled back the reins and yelled, "Drop down!" The horse put his head down and steadied his pace. "*Goot* boy, Barnabas," Levi yelled. Steering the horse over to the side of the road, he got out and went to pat the horse's head. When it was calm, he returned and got back under the blankets with Katie.

"*Goot* thing a car wasn't on the road," Katie said, her voice shaking. "That could have been a bad accident, but you handled Barnabas with such skill. He listens to you like a *goot* friend."

"He's like family. We should call him Barnabas Miller."

Katie noticed such tenderness in Levi, or had it been there all along, and she hadn't realized? He was so kind, even to his horse. They slowly rode to the quilt shop, snuggling under the blanket. When they arrived, Levi ran to her side of the sleigh and effortlessly scooped her up in his arms and started carrying her to the little quilt shop.

"Why are you carrying me?"

"You're so short; I might lose you in the snow if I put you down."

"Levi!" Katie laughed. She jiggled to get free and he slipped. They tumbled onto the freshly fallen snow, laughing. She made a snowball and threw it at him. He chased after her and she ran toward the shop. "I'm faster than you and half your size," she yelled back at him.

Granny Weaver held the door open to them "Come on in or you'll catch your death of cold."

Katie hugged her and they all went into her small quilt shop. There was a bed in the center of the shop, layered with many quilts that Granny showed to customers. Baskets, braided rag rugs, aprons, Amish dolls lined the shelves on all four walls. How Katie loved this shop since she was a little girl. She looked at the baskets, remembering the first one she made.

Granny's light blue eyes sparkled under the glow of the oil lanterns. "Katie, Levi has a surprise for you. Can you guess what it is?"

"No, not really," Katie confessed.

"I want you to pick something to put in your hope chest," Levi whispered in her ear.

Katie felt strangely warm inside. "I'll take some pot holders."

Granny Weaver let out a laugh. "I think Levi has something grander than a pot holder in mind!"

Katie looked puzzled. Levi said to put anything in the hope chest that made her happy. She liked the pot holders. What did Granny mean?

"Let's take a look at some quilts," Granny said. The door opened and Leah came in. "Have *yinz* met my granddaughter, Leah?"

"*Jah*, we met the night Lottie had Miriam, although I was half awake," Katie said.

Leah looked at Levi and smiled. "We've never met."

"I...ah...I'm Levi," he said.

"Are you in Katie's Gmay?" she asked.

"No, I'm in the one closer to downtown Smicksburg."

Leah smiled at him. "It's nice to be in a bigger community. In New York, the settlement was much smaller."

"There's a group moving from Smicksburg to New York," Levi said.

"Well, it's too cold for me. The damp chill in the mountains goes right through me and my joints ache in the winter. Staying with *Oma* gives me some relief." Leah turned to Granny. "I brought out some rugs I just finished." She draped them over the quilt holder. "I'll be seeing *yinz* around?"

"*Jah*," Katie and Levi said.

Granny's eyes were on Katie again. "You need a quilt for that hope chest." She pulled back the top quilt to reveal an all-white wedding ring quilt. "Do you like this one?"

Katie gasped. She held on to Levi's arm for support. "I need some air...Levi can we go outside? I need to talk to you privately."

Granny put up her hand. "*Yinz* go shop by yourselves. I'll leave the store to you."

"Danki, Granny," Katie said. She put her head down and looked away from Levi. "I can't accept that white quilt."

"*Goot*, because I can't afford it."

Katie looked up at him, relieved. "Ach, I thought you wanted me to get the wedding ring quilt as a sign of engagement. I'm not ready for that."

"I told you to get something that will make you happy," he said. "Granny scared me when she started to show you her quilts. They start at three-hundred dollars."

Katie looked at Levi and laughed. "Then why not let me get a pot holder?"

"A pot holder isn't exactly a birthday present."

Her eyes moistened. "Aw, Levi, how sweet of you...You remembered my birthday. It gets looked over because of Christmas."

Levi took her hands. "*I've* been looking over you because of Christmas." He took her in his arms. "Now pick anything in the store you like as a birthday present, except a quilt."

CHAPTER 15

Ginny looked at the empty room and tears ran down her cheeks. She remembered when they bought the small farmhouse and the boys had to share a room. She looked at the violet colored walls and red cherry-stained floors. Kirsten had covered over the boy's mural. They'd painted the Rocky Mountains on all four walls, inspired by their trip out west. One wall was dedicated to Arches National Park in Utah, so arched red rocks and prickly pear cacti covered the wall. Now the boys hardly saw each other, Aidan being on the mission field and Ian in medical school.

James came into the room, blowing his nose. Ginny ran into his arms. "You're c-crying, too…"

He held her tight. "The kids grew up too fast." He sighed. "I worked too many hours. The Byler boys worked right along with their dad and I have to say, I always envied that."

"You and the boys did all your guy things. You took them out coon hunting with the Bylers. How many kids have that experience?"

"I just miss them…having Judah around helps, though. I've kind of adopted him as my own."

"How's Judah doing?"

"Well, he's studying the whole book and seeing God's mercy and not all the 'wrath of God' in the Old Testament. But he has some decisions to make about returning to the Amish or not."

"How's he leaning?" Ginny asked.

"Sometimes I think he's still sweet on Katie Byler."

"No, you're kidding. After all these years?"

"He does talk about her...he saw Levi and Katie go by the church the other night and he admitted to being jealous."

"Poor Katie. Her life was so serene last year and now she has three men after her."

"Two. Levi and Judah." James looked confused.

"Joseph has dreams of a life with her somehow."

"He's not Amish. Wow, what a dreamer. She'd never leave the Amish."

Ginny smiled at him. "I'm so glad I married my first boyfriend, never having a broken heart over anyone." She kissed him fondly and put her arms around his middle. "Well, we need to say goodbye to the house and hand the key over to Jerry and Janice. If this house wasn't going to be used for Christian work, I'd never be able to leave it... We can always come back to help the girls living here."

"I guess Judah and I didn't build the addition years ago for nothing," James pondered.

~*~

Katie lifted the preserves and headed toward The Drying Shed. Someone snuck up behind –Judah. She tightened her grip on the box.

"This looks too heavy for you. Let me help," he said, eyes locked with hers.

Katie forced herself to look forward. "Judah, you are shunned. I can't talk to you. We want you to miss the community and come back."

"You want me to come back?" Judah asked, stepping closer.

She looked his way and searched his eyes. He was sincere and really wanted an answer. He wasn't flirting with her again. "I love living plain, but that's something you need to decide for yourself, and it seems like you made that decision to leave long ago." She lowered her head. "You wouldn't have broken our engagement for no *goot* reason."

"I never meant to hurt you, Katie. I just never understood a lot about God, like you always have...until recently. Now I want God's will for my life."

Katie watched as he took the box from her. "Can we talk...private like?"

"You're shunned..."

She needed time to think. "Take the box inside and tell them it's from me. I'll collect the money later." She looked around for a private place to talk. Judah seemed like he had more peace, so maybe rumors about his conversion were true. Long ago she was so blind not to notice he lacked spiritual depth. Katie spied a table in the back of the store with a lattice fence around its porch. When Judah appeared, she led him to the table.

She sat down across from him, hungry to know what happened. "I know the problems you had at home; how your *daed* never taught you the scriptures like my *daed* did his *kinner*."

"*Jah*, but he did his best. Had lots of problems." He put his head down. "I was afraid I couldn't provide, Katie. We were so dirt poor and I thought if we left, we'd have a better chance in the outside world."

Katie felt like reaching across the table to console him, but restrained herself. He was shunned and she risked much by talking to him. "Judah, danki for trying to make things right. I forgave you a long time ago..."

He reached for her hand and she took it. "Friends then?"

"Ach, no. We can't talk, unless you repent and return to the People."

"I'm praying about what to do. Will you pray for me, too?"

She squeezed his hand. "*Jah*, I will." She watched as fear crept across Judah's face. She soon heard Sarah Mast from behind her, reprimanding her for talking to a shunned man.

~*~

Katie tore off her clack cape and bonnet and threw it on the wooden peg next to the door. How could Sarah talk to her like that? She didn't believe her when she tried to explain why she talked to Judah. He was asking for prayer. He was thinking about coming back to the People.

She stomped the snow off her feet and looked at the mail. There was a letter and the return address was Lottie's. Why would Lottie send her a letter? She sat near the woodstove and opened it and was shocked to see it was from Joseph. She held the letter to her heart, and whispered a prayer, then read:

Dear Katie,

I know you can't communicate with me, and for that I'm more sorry than you can imagine. I was too forward with you in the car and said some things about Anne Elliot and Captain Wentworth. How she waited for him until he proved himself worthy of her. Ginny watches a movie called Persuasion over and over. It's her favorite. So I hear it a lot and it just came out of me; the part about making you promise to not marry Levi. It was selfish of me. I do love you and because of this, I want you happy. If staying Amish and marrying Levi will give you the life you've always wanted, I don't want you to miss out on it because of me.

I'll be praying for you to make the right decisions in your life.
Love,
Joseph

An image of Leah and her big blue eyes popped into her head. She took the letter and smashed it into a ball.

He's fallen for Leah! Katie remembered how Joseph looked at her the night Miriam was born. He lived across the street from her now. Did he always fall for the girl across the street?

Katie walked to her bedroom and looked into the small mirror on the wall. "I look old," she sighed out loud.

"Katie, are you home?" she heard Ginny yell.

"Just a minute." Katie pinched her cheeks so she wouldn't look so pale.

"We've come to say good-bye," Ginny said, embracing Katie. "You've been a dear neighbor for so many years."

"We'll sure miss being neighbors with all you Bylers," James added.

Katie hung on to Ginny. She couldn't help it. She broke down and sobbed. "Honey, we'll be three miles away. I didn't think you'd take it this hard...I'll still come over to visit. Maybe we can make another quilt."

Katie wiped her eyes. "I know. It's not that."

Ginny looked at James. "Can you go back over to the house and make sure we did everything on the list?"

"Good idea." James nodded, and then headed back out the door.

Ginny held Katie's shoulders. "What's wrong? Want to talk to your old friend? Maybe I can help?"

"You're not old," Katie laughed nervously, and then cried again.

Ginny led her over to the couch and sat next to her. "Did you get bad news? I see a letter crumbled up in your hands."

"*Jah*, in a way, *jah*. Seems like your *bruder* doesn't want anything to do with me anymore."

"He can talk to you in groups, right?"

"Ginny, I have to confess something to you. I love your brother. He's the one I want to marry, but he's not Amish." Katie flattened the letter on her lap. "He asked me to wait for him like Anne Elliot waited for Captain Wentworth, but now he says not to...." Another sob escaped.

"Joseph told me about the letter. I explained to him the lady who wrote the story, *Persuasion*, never married. She was hurt by a romance that could never be and legend has it, never married. I don't want that happening to you or Joseph."

"I see. You want me to marry Levi, too..."

"I want you to move on with your life. First Judah held you back for a decade and now my brother might do the same. I want to babysit your kids someday and Joseph's, too."

Katie went over to the wood burning stove and threw the letter in. She picked up a log and threw it on the fire. "So are you giving Joseph the same advice? Is he moving on, too?"

Ginny did not meet Katie's eyes. "I don't want to hurt you, but I need to be truthful. I'm encouraging him to notice some of the nice girls in our church. It's nothing against you, Katie, you know that, right?"

Katie went over and picked up the basket full of black yarn. She got out her knitting needles and sat in the Amish rocker. "I understand, Ginny. You don't want Joseph to marry a girl who's Amish, only Baptist."

"What?" Ginny gasped. "We *English* don't care what church denominations people marry into, for the most part. There is no shunning in our world, but there is in yours. You would be shunned. I want Joseph to find a nice girl to settle down with and the same for you. I hope you find a nice Amish man and have a house full of kids, like your mom did. You've always wanted that."

Katie looked at the brown basket in her lap; the one Levi got her for her birthday. She leaned over and hugged it. Levi had been like a rock to her over this past year. With Judah popping back into her life, Levi was like an anchor her heart desperately needed. She looked down and turned to see the latest issue of *Family Life Magazine* in the wooden magazine rack. Would she ever have a family of her own? Was God trying to speak to her through Ginny?

~*~

Joseph looked up at his living room ceiling and saw water spots. The little house would need a new roof, but for now, he just painted over them. He liked the simplicity of the place. All the walls were white and the floors oak. The windows were bare to bring in more sunlight. The black wood burning stove that sat in the little living room warmed the whole house. He sat in the rocker he bought from Roman Weaver across the street. He liked the new neighbors, but he missed the Bylers, *missed Katie*.

Joseph laid his head back and thought of all James and Ginny said about going on a double date with Jessica, the new woman at church. He didn't need the distraction; his little Walden Pond experiment was working out fine, so far. It was only a week old, but he liked the place. He even liked reading Moses' used copies of *The Budget*, *Family Life Magazine* and other Amish newspapers. Joseph was amazed at how the Amish sent money to each other, even to people they didn't know. Someone was hurt or in need, and an address was given to send a card with a few dollars stuck in. Granny Weaver said she got nearly a thousand dollars in a card shower when she had surgery. The Amish community was stronger than he thought.

He got wrapped up to go outside to fill the bird feeders. Joseph was determined to keep all five of them full all winter, although the birds ate up the feed in a few days.

"Hello there, Joseph," Leah yelled, waving from across the street.

Joseph walked over to say hello, but saw a buggy coming down the street. It was Katie and Millie. The buggy slowed to a stop. His heart ached when he saw the pain in Katie's eyes. "Good morning, ladies. Have you met Leah Weaver? This is Katie and Millie."

"Nice to meet you, Leah," Millie nodded.

"Nice to meet you, Millie. Katie and I've met. I also met Reuben and the *kinner*. They are all so adorable. Will you be needing any help watching them?"

"No," Katie snapped. "*Mamm* and I take care of the *kinner* fine. You have your hands full helping Roman with their *kinner*, *jah*?"

"My aunt and uncle do have a house full. You're right," Leah said, bewilderment registering on her face.

"We best be off," Millie said. "We're knitting a rug at Lottie's. Should fetch a *goot* price at the auction. Will you and your *oma* be coming?"

Leah shook her head. "*Oma's* not feeling well today. I'm staying home to keep an eye on her."

Joseph had never heard of a knitted rug, and thought maybe he could break the ice with Katie. "Katie, how do you knit a rug?"

She looked at him, eyes hollow. "We take strips of rags and braid them into an oval. We knit the outside edging…"

Joseph hoped to see some tenderness in her eyes, but didn't. She'd acted so coldly toward him and was rude to Leah. He needed to find out why. Maybe the Bishop told her she couldn't talk to him at all. Saying good-bye to Leah, he started to walk over to Hershberger's. Trudging through the snow, he saw Katie and Millie from a distance enter the house, so he missed them. Not knowing what to do, Joseph decided he'd just have to visit Eli, hoping to get a word with Katie.

~*~

Lottie answered the door, and to Katie's shock, it was Joseph. He came in and stared at the large rug and the women who sat around it, but his eyes lingered on her, his eyebrows arched high.

"Lottie, is Eli or Moses in?" Joseph asked.

"No, they went to the harness shop, but The Chocolate Shop is right next to it. They're always late when coming home from that area." Lottie laughed. "They should be back though, any minute. Wait in the kitchen and read the latest *The Budget. Ach*, I forgot to give you something." She went to her oak pantry to retrieve a little brown book and handed it to Joseph. "Moses also ordered a book for you that came in the mail yesterday." Lottie grinned. "He found an Amish book called *1001 Questions and Answers on the Christian Life*. He bought it for you since you're wearing him out."

Joseph tried to smile. "I'll go in the kitchen and wait for them to get back." He looked at Katie, and motioned with his head for her to follow him. She looked away.

"Any news from the Weavers about their new settlement in New York?" Lottie asked, starting the rounds of conversation that would follow."

"Granny Weaver would know, but she's not feeling well to be with us. We saw her beautiful granddaughter on our way here," Millie said.

"Seems like her joints are doing better since she moved out of the heart of the Snow Belt, up there in New York."

"What's wrong with her joints?" Millie asked.

"She calls it Hypermobility Syndrome. She has too much connective tissue in the joints. Damp, cold weather sets in her joints, like arthritis. They get one-hundred fifty inches of snow where she came from. We get maybe forty inches here in Smicksburg. She said she's not in any pain here."

"How interesting," Millie said.

Lydia Yoder looked at Katie. "You've been awfully quiet since you got here. What's on your mind? Levi Miller?"

Katie blushed. "No, I'm just concentrating on my knitting, is all."

"Are *yinz* getting married or not? The suspense is killing me..." Lydia prodded.

"That's my prayer," Lottie said. "Levi's a *goot* man."

"He's not hard to look at either," Lydia said, and everyone giggled. "I bet you're keeping your engagement a secret."

Katie felt intense heat on her face. "If you'll excuse me, I need some water." She marched into the kitchen, only to find Joseph there.

"Have I done something wrong?" he whispered as he got up from the kitchen table.

"We can't be alone," Katie said, looking into the other room.

"We're not. There's a house full of people here." Joseph's seemed to plead to her. "What have I done?"

"You've given up," she blurted. "I thought you were coming to live here to pray and ask for direction for our future. You practically told me in that letter to forget you and marry Levi." Katie got a glass of water and took a sip. "Ginny talked to me, too. She wants you to find a nice girl and for me to find a nice Amish man. She called our relationship 'impossible'."

"Katie, I want you to be happy, even if it hurts me. But I don't want you to marry Levi!" Joseph folded his arms and slumped back into his chair. "Ginny shouldn't have said anything about our future being impossible. She loves me too much sometimes, always interfering." He sighed. "Remember when we had our first real talk while I took pictures of the children? You said you believed in God's sovereignty, but you didn't trust yourself to make the big decisions in life, and mess up His will. I'm asking you to really listen to the still small voice of God in your heart. I don't know much past today; I wish I did. I just know there's a divine plan at work here."

Katie heard Lottie yell from the other room. She wanted Katie to bring out the doughnuts. "*Jah*, sure," Katie said. She felt the tension in her neck ease. "So you don't want me to marry Levi." She wanted to run in his arms, but kept her distance. "So we're back at the crossroads, waiting and praying for God's will for our future." She looked at him, not wanting to leave. She saw Joseph get up and come closer to her, so she grabbed the doughnuts and ran into the other room. She didn't trust herself not to embrace him and never let go.

CHAPTER 16

Ginny put the needle through the piece of popcorn and slid it down her growing chain. She remembered doing this on Christmas Eve as a child and memories of her mother flooded her heart. She looked up at Joseph and Judah across the table, stringing their popcorn and then over to James, who was cooking his annual fish dinner…another tradition she shared with her children, but they weren't home. She wiped a tear that escaped. "Nothing stays the same, huh? Remember how Mom was at our Christmas Eve dinner last year?"

Joseph reached for her hand. "Mom was in pain last year, but not this Christmas."

"I'm sorry everyone. Excuse me," Ginny said, gasping for air as she ran out of the kitchen. When she entered her room she looked at the picture of her mom that was on her nightstand, and sobbed. The black and white photo showed her mom giving her a piggy back ride. She heard James come into the room. "We did everything we could to keep her alive, you know that, honey?" he asked.

"I miss her. It just hit me out of nowhere. I thought the grief was going away."

"They say the holidays bring back a lot of memories. We wondered if you'd breakdown at Thanksgiving, but you had the house full of people and didn't."

"I had a houseful for a reason. Too busy to think of Mom." She wrung her hands. "I'm ruining your dinner and I'll never be able to sing my song at church tonight."

James sat next to her. "I have a surprise for you."

"I'll wait until after dinner," she said.

"No, I think you should open it now. Let's go out into the living room." James led her out to their new little four foot Christmas tree. Joseph and Judah joined them. "Look in the tree," James said.

Ginny was puzzled, but then she saw a white envelope tucked into some branches. She opened the envelope and saw a card. She read it out loud. "One child in Dominican Republic will get a goat this year, giving milk and cheese to a needy family. Thank you for giving. Compassion International."

Ginny felt her heart lift. "Oh, I love it. Is this goat for our sponsored child?"

"Read the other card," James said, pointing to the other white envelope in the tree.

Ginny ripped it open. It was a picture of a little girl with pink ribbons in her hair. "The goat is going to her. We have enough now to sponsor two children," James said. "But there's more…" He ran into their bedroom and came back a few minutes later with a colorful Caribbean shirt and a straw hat. He started to hum salsa music and grabbed Ginny to dance. "Guess what else."

Ginny laughed. "Too late to skip Christmas and go on a cruise!"

"We're going there to visit our sponsored kids, and we can see Aidan," James blurted.

"What?" Ginny screamed.

"We're going to see Aidan for two weeks or more. The date is up to you. Pick a month when sales are low."

Ginny put her head on his to help take the shock. How long had she wanted to go on a missionary trip…to see Aidan's work in Dominican Republic? She looked up at James. "Can we afford this?"

"Yes, now that we're debt free and it's just you and me. No kids to take."

Ginny put her hands over her heart. "I guess there are advantages to an empty nest? No more empty bank account! Oh, I can't wait...Thank you James." She jumped up on him and gave him a hug

Judah went over and got the big red box with green ribbon, hidden in the spare room. "Here, Ginny. It's from Joseph and me. Merry Christmas."

"*Mom,* if you don't mind," Ginny corrected Judah with a hug and then hugged her brother. "Thank you both. You didn't have to buy me anything." She ripped off the paper and saw the box. "No way!" she gasped. The box had a Jim Shore logo on it. Ginny sat down and opened the box to find the nativity set she's always wanted. She stared at the colorful painted figures. She held the baby Jesus in her hand and stared. "Thank you so much."

"We wanted you to have it since you didn't want to decorate this year, everything reminding you of Mom," Joseph said. "So we thought we'd get you some new things."

"And it's the nativity set, of all things, the real meaning of Christmas. Oh, I love it," Ginny whispered, looking at each figurine carefully. "I love the Ukrainian style artwork. It's so beautiful. Thank you my boys."

Ginny cradled the baby Jesus figurine in her hands. She thanked Jesus for coming into this world for her.

~*~

Katie could tell the children had practiced hard for the annual Christmas Eve program. They sang the Christmas songs with confidence and smiled out at their parents. She looked at her nieces and nephews and pride filled her heart. How they must miss Sadie, but they bravely moved on with their lives. They sang songs in English and German, all praise songs to God, thanking him for sending His son to the earth. She breathed in the smell of freshly cut pine, and looked at the greenery around the windows with a single candle on each pane.

Katie tried to push a thought out of her mind, but it kept returning; she should be watching children of her own sing. She was thirty-one now and an old *maedel*. Levi was right. She was deceiving herself, thinking she was content being single. But Katie could never leave the People for Joseph, though she'd thought of it. She loved the simplicity of her faith and the community, even though living in the Gmay was hard at times; so much submission for the common good.

Her niece got up to recite Ten Little Candles.

"*Ten little candles, Jesus bade them shine,*
But selfishness just snuffed one out, and there were nine.
Nine little candles, one without a mate,
Bad companions came along, and then there were eight.
Eight little candles, doing work for heaven,
'I Forgot' sat down on one, and then there were seven.
Seven little candles, all with blazing wicks,
Someone cried out, 'Goody Boy,' and there were six.
Six little candles, all of them alive,
But one was tired of playing, and then there were five.
Five little candles, once there were more,
Sunday baseball fanned one out, and then there were four.
Four little candles, bright as bright could be,
But one of them just didn't have time, so then there were three.
Three little candles, could one of them be you?
That one gave up going to church, and then there were two.
Two little candles, our story's almost done;
'I'm too small, no use,' one cried, and then there was one.
One little candle, left all alone,
It kept on burning by itself, and oh how bright it shown.
Brave and steady burned the flame, until the other nine,

Fired by its example, once again began to shine."

Katie thought of the words and she got a knot in her stomach. Was she taking time to feed her faith, like she fed her plants in the greenhouse? No, she was consumed with thoughts of Joseph. When she prayed, it was all about her pleading with God to be with him. She was becoming so self-absorbed.

She looked over at Reuben and he was all aglow. He accepted his loss and was moving on. He was living out the Serenity Prayer he so often said. Enjoying one moment at a time: Accept the things he could not change. She turned her attention toward her nieces and nephews again, who were moving forward in life with smiles on their faces. They inspired her. She needed to move on, too.

~*~

Ginny gripped her acoustic guitar and struck a chord and felt her heart go up into throat. She couldn't talk or sing. She tried again, but she felt numb; all she could think of was that her Mom was in the audience last year when she sang with the choir. She stared at Suzy sitting in the front row. Suzy got up and went to her friend and embraced her and. Ginny sat down.

Suzy got the music on the stand. "Our little knitting circle's been praying about Ginny singing this song she wrote. She was afraid she wouldn't be able to do it. But we're all family here, right? We try to be transparent so we know when someone needs a burden carried. Ginny wrote this while her mom was in the hospital years ago when she suffered a stroke, a week before Christmas.

"She sits in the hospital, awake in the silent night,

People don't say 'Merry Christmas,' they ask, "Will you be alright?

It is so sad   you can't be home at this special time",
But as she reads her Bible, tears come to her eyes,

She is reminded of why Christ was born,
He came to comfort those who mourn,
And He came to die that we might have life
His light is so much brighter than all of the Christmas lights.

So if you're alone in the silent night,
And you feel you've gone too far and things can't be made right,
If holiday cheer, makes your sadness clear,
Remember why we celebrate this time of year,

And be reminded of why Christ was born
He came to comfort those who mourn,
He came to die that we might have life
Oh His light is so much brighter than all of the Christmas lights.

She lies in the hospital, wrapped with love in the silent night,
For she is not alone, Jesus is by her side.
He didn't come for all the holly and all of the mistletoe,
He came for us so we will never be alone.

So be reminded of why Christ was born
He came to comfort those who mourn,
And He came to die that we might have life
His light is so much brighter than all of the Christmas lights."

~*~

A woman sitting in the back row ran outside the church and Joseph followed her. She kicked at the snow that drifted up on the walkway and clenched her fists.

"What's wrong? Can I help you?" Joseph asked.

"That song was about me...the part about feeling alone and things never being right again."

Joseph took her hands. "I felt that way once. I was homeless, living on the streets. God rescued me...from myself, and he can rescue you, too. My name's Joseph. What's yours?"

"Maria. I live at Forget-Me-Not. The little girl sitting next to me is Lilly. We've been homeless for a while."

"So, if you don't mind me asking, how did you become homeless?" Joseph gently asked, releasing her hand. "We all have a story, don't we?"

"Well...when I got pregnant, my parents were disgraced and kicked me out. I was seventeen. I lived with my boyfriend for a few years, but then Lilly and I left because of domestic violence."

"I'm sorry," Joseph said. "Where did you go after that?"

"Being a single mom with a child, I got lots of student grants for college. I got my LPN and was a nurse, but then they cut back a lot at the hospital. I lost my job."

"So you're a Licensed Practical Nurse, then?"

"Yes. I wanted to go the extra year to be a registered nurse, but with no work and a child to feed, I got a job at the grocery store, and then I got laid off. That's when we became homeless."

"So how long have you been homeless?"

"Since this past spring. It wasn't hard living in the car when the weather was nice. But when this bone chilling weather hit, I knew I needed some help."

"I had some friends help me, even though they weren't the best people to get involved with," Joseph said.

"I worked too many hours to have friends, even bad ones." She managed a smile.

Joseph took Maria's hands. "I'd like to pray for you." He bowed his head to pray, but looked up to see a buggy going past, and he looked into Katie's pain-filled eyes.

~*~

Dear Mom and Dad,

MERRY CHRISTMAS! I miss you both! I miss Grandma today, but she'd be happy I'm seeing Italy; she talked about Riccia so much.

I checked out the schools in Rome, but there's a French chef who owns the Riccia Bakery. He's agreed to keep me on as an apprentice, so I can learn French baking from him, and Italian cooking from Angelina.

There are other things keeping me here, too. I love having all the family around and the mountains are magnificent. I've made several friends my age and they're patiently teaching me more Italian.

Angelina, Carmine, Silvia and the familia say ciao and Buon Natale!

Love you both!
PS…give Noah my love…
Kirsten

~*~

Joseph gripped the steering wheel. He could barely see a foot in front of him; the snow was coming down like an avalanche. He didn't know whether to turn back and stay with Jerry and Janice or continue to his place. Only two miles to get home. He shifted the Jeep in second gear and didn't dare go faster than ten miles per hour. Joseph flipped the defrost switch up to high, but it didn't help his visibility.

He crawled along for the next mile, and then saw something black on the road. Joseph wasn't sure what it was but he had time to slow down and glide to a stop. When he got out of the car, he saw a buggy, smashed and on its side. He slid over to see who was inside. It was Eli! Joseph grabbed his cell phone from his pocket and dialed 911, and then looked to see if he could help Eli in any way, but he was unconscious. Joseph knelt beside him and prayed. He looked up at the black night sky, not a star in sight. A chill went through his body as he looked again at Eli's bloody body...was he even alive?

~*~

An ambulance came and a paramedic jumped out. He checked Eli's vitals. "We'll need to life flight him to Pittsburgh and quick. His injuries are too massive for Indiana Hospital. You can tell the family he'll be at UPMC." He turned from Joseph and talked into his phone to coordinate the flight.

"Can I go with him?" Joseph asked.

"Are you related?"

"No, but he's like a brother."

"Sorry, Bud, you can't come. Go break the news to his family."

Joseph waited until the helicopter came and he watched as they put Eli's bloody body on a stretcher, and all too soon the helicopter went up and was out of sight. Joseph put his head between his knees and couldn't stop shaking. He dialed Ginny's number. "Eli's buggy's been hit. They're life flighting him down to Pittsburgh. I don't know what to do. Should we arrange drivers to take Lottie to the hospital? There's black ice out here."

"Where are you?" Ginny asked.

"Only a mile from home."

"Go to the Weavers and have them tell Lottie. She needs her woman friends around her. They'll know what to do. Let them make the decision," Ginny said with a broken voice. "Lord, I hope Eli makes it. He was out in this weather to help put out a fire, can you believe it? The whole Amish community's in an uproar. One of the Coblentz houses caught fire and Eli's helps the fire department…"

"How will we know he's OK?" Joseph asked, sobbing now.

"I'll call Mike Lee. He's working for Medevac. I'll call you back…Oh, and stay with Moses. He'll take this hard."

~*~

Joseph threw a log in Moses' woodstove. He paced across the small living room, then pulled out his cell phone and called 911 again.

"I need to talk to the Smicksburg Fire Department," he said.

His call was redirected, and he soon heard someone say, "Hello, this is the Fire Department. Is this an emergency?"

"Well….kind of. Did you know one of your own was badly hurt trying to get the Coblentz's house fire? Eli Hershberger. They flew him to Pittsburgh." He cleared his throat. "The fire trucks can get through anything, right? Can you take Lottie to be with her husband?"

There was a long pause on the other end of the line. "I'll take the Fire Chief's Jeep. It has chains on the wheels and he can get anywhere. Tell Eli's wife to pack her things and we'll be over. I have room for three people, besides myself."

"Thank you!" Joseph yelled. He turned to Moses and put his thumb up. "Mission accomplished." He walked outside to get to the front of the house and knocked on the door. "I need to talk to Lottie," he told Leah.

"We're grateful you called the paramedics. You probably saved his life, but Lottie isn't up for company."

"I understand. I heard her crying through Moses' door, so I came in this way. Tell her to pack her things and the Smicksburg Fire Department will take her and two others to Pittsburgh to be with Eli."

Leah ran over to Joseph and hugged him. "Danki, Joseph. You are so kind."

Joseph's cell phone rang. It was Mike Lee. "Your sister gave me your number. It appears your friend's legs were badly damaged and he may have a spinal cord injury, but he'll make it. He'll have full use of his upper body."

"What are you saying, Mike?" Joseph asked.

"He's alive and will make it. Time will tell concerning the extent of permanent damage done. It's a good thing you found him; he lost a lot of blood. Take care, Pal."

Leah looked at him with concern. "What is it?"

"Tell Lottie a medic from Pittsburgh just called and said Eli will live, but she needs to go to the hospital to be with him."

Joseph went back to be with Moses, who was in his rocker, eyes closed, mouth moving. Joseph sat in the other rocker. "I talked to a medic in Pittsburgh. Eli will live."

Moses gasped and tears spilt down his cheeks. He clapped his hands, and thanked the Lord over and over.

"He may have some damage, though," Joseph said, not knowing if he should mention that the battle wasn't over. "He may have a hard time walking."

"He's alive. It's a gift to live, whether my son is walking or not, he's alive, *jah*? That's what matters." Moses got up and kept thanking the Lord. He stopped and turned to Joseph. "You think I don't know what this means. I do. I'm sad and afraid, but don't you see? He's alive! Thank you Lord!"

Joseph felt his understanding of the Bible was lacking. He'd seen lots of Christians react differently to a crisis. They shook their fists at God and some fell away from their faith, but here Moses was praising God.

Lottie walked in from the main house. "*Daed*, the Fire Captain is here, and I'll be leaving to go be with Eli. The baby will be across the street with Leah, so she's not too far from you."

Moses got up and embraced Lottie and they sobbed. "The Lord go with you, my child."

Lottie brushed the tears from her cheeks and looked over at Joseph. "Can I have a word with you?"

Joseph followed her into the main house. She looked at him evenly. "There's ice everywhere, I hear a quarter inch on the trees. Moses will try to go out and cut off the branches on the apple trees to save them; a broken limb can kill a tree and they need sawed off. Do not let Moses go out and do it. He may get hurt. I'd rather lose the whole orchard than to see that happen. In a few days when things thaw, helpers will come. When they ask how to help, tell them to saw off the tree limbs that are broken. Understand?"

"But what if no helpers show up? What should I do?"

"I don't understand your meaning, Joseph," Lottie said.

"These helpers, have they been contacted and agreed to come?"

"Oh…our Gmay will come. We depend on each other. When men arrive, have them saw off the branches, but only when the ice thaws."

"Lottie, are you ready to go?" the Fire Chief called from the living room. "Your friends are in the car and we're ready."

"*Jah*," Lottie said, turning back to Joseph. "I trust you to manage here. Do you hear me? You're my trusted *English* friend." She broke down crying and leaned forward to embrace Joseph.

"I'm here for you and your family."

Lottie buried her head in Joseph's chest and sobbed. "A buggy accident took my mother-in-law, but not my husband...Miriam died on that road not far from Eli's accident." She wiped her eyes with her hanky. "This is so emotional for us all; I worry about Moses. Stay with him and let him talk. He needs to."

CHAPTER 17

$Lottie$, Katie, and Granny Weaver sat in the waiting room. A lady with a gray two piece suit came in. "Hello, I'm Karen, the social worker. Can you come into my office? It's right around the corner."

The three women followed Karen and they took seats in her office.

"Which one of you is the spouse of Eli Hershberger?"

Lottie nodded and Karen shook her head. "So sorry you're going through such a tragedy, but I need to ask you some questions. Do you mind if your friends are here? These questions are confidential."

"My friends will be helping me make any decisions," Lottie said.

"You do realize the hospital expenses will be large, but if you sue the person who hit your husband, you won't have to pay anything. I wanted to reassure you of that."

Granny Weaver's eyes grew round. "Sue? We don't sue, and we're praying the police find the person who hit Eli so we can comfort him."

Karen clasped her hands on her desk. "I, ah, read about Amish forgiveness, and it's really a wonderful thing. I admire it, truly. But the cost of medical care needs to be understood. This could be over a million dollars. Eli won't be going straight home. He'll be in the hospital for a few weeks and then a rehabilitation center for several."

"Can we do the rehabilitation in the home?" Katie asked. "We'll have enough people to be with Eli around the clock, and we can learn what we need to do."

"How do you know he'll have consistent care?" Karen asked.

"We're Amish," Katie said. "We take care of each other all the time."

Karen sat back and fidgeted with her red, shoulder-length hair. "I've never had anyone ask me that question. I suppose we could have a home health care worker stop in to monitor his progress."

"Danki. When can I see my husband?" Lottie asked.

"They'll send for you. Most likely they're changing bandages and will let you in when they're done."

Lottie broke down and cried. Katie and Granny Weaver took her hands, lending her their strength.

~*~

Joseph peered over at the mammoth book Moses was reading, *The Martyr's Mirror.* He thought over the past two days and how much he'd learned. Moses went over with him *1001 Questions and Answers on the Christian Life and The Dordrecht Confession of Faith.* Joseph was consumed by the rich theology in the books. The cracking apple tree branches outside hadn't broken their concentration. He heard the sound of several buggies pull in the driveway. He opened the side door and saw a couple dozen men outside carrying hand saws. "We've come to try and save the orchard," Roman said.

"Lottie doesn't want anyone climbing trees that are still icy."

"We understand, but the ice is real thin now. It's safe," Roman said. "We have the big icehouse to store any meals that'll be coming, if you run out of room in the icebox. I'll bring over the ice blocks for the icebox, too." Roman scratched his beard. "I have a request. I need a driver to go pick up my mom and Katie. I got word Lottie will be staying for three weeks in the hospital, in a special room, and needs more clothes. Joseph, can you help?"

"I'll go if someone stays with Moses. Lottie doesn't want him climbing the trees."

"Danki," Roman said. "I'll fetch Leah."

~*~

Joseph walked down the hall of the hospital, but hesitated to knock when he got to Eli's room. He still saw Eli's mangled body in bad dreams, and bowed for a moment to say a prayer for strength. The door opened and he saw Lottie and embraced her. "How's Eli?"

"He's in and out with all the pain medicines." She motioned for him to come in. "You can sit with him if you'd like. He may wake up, and if so, he needs to hit the morphine pump. I'll be right back."

Joseph sat on the chair next to Eli. The smell of blood mixed with antiseptics made his stomach turn. He sat for a while by his sleeping friend, thinking of how spry Eli used to be. He heard a man with a sing-song type of voice and soon saw an Indian man come in the room.

"Hello, I'm Doctor Pal." He shook Joseph's hand. "Your friend is lucky to be alive. He's fortunate to have such a nice family. It's most unusual."

"Nice to meet you, Doc, but I don't know what you mean. What's unusual?" Joseph asked.

"The Amish and how they care for their families. I come from India, and when someone needs ongoing care, the family takes on the task, no matter the inconvenience. I don't see it much here in the U.S."

Joseph straightened himself in his chair. "We had my Mom in a rehabilitation center to get the best care, after her stroke. We felt it was the best thing. She learned to walk and talk again."

"Oh, I did not mean to say rehabilitation centers are bad. I have many patients there. What I'm trying to say it that the Amish care for their own with cheerfulness. Many folks in India do it out of obligation, but no one is really happy about it. The Amish are a mystery to me, but in a good way."

Katie walked in. "I couldn't help but overhear you, Dr. Pal. We look at taking care of our own as an act of worship to God. We find joy in that."

Dr. Pal smiled at her. "Very interesting, Katie. There needs to be more Amish in the world, then?"

Katie took the doctor's hand. "Dr. Pal, since we met three days ago, you've given us compliments we're not so used to. It's the only way of life we've known, but thank you for such kind words. I'm going to leave now. It's been very nice talking to you and I feel so much better knowing Eli's in your care."

Dr. Pal put both his hands over Katie's. "I'll look in on your friend often." The doctor looked at Eli's monitors and wrote something in his chart and then said good-bye.

"Katie, you look so tired," Joseph said, getting up. "Have a seat."

"Granny's anxious to leave. This has been hard on her and she's developed a bad cough. When will you be ready to go?"

"Now," Joseph said. He wanted to take the pain he saw in Katie's eyes. She was heartbroken over Eli.

"Did you tell Moses?" she asked.

"He'll be a paraplegic...yes, I told him."

"I'll be staying at the house over the next few weeks to keep an eye on things," she said.

"We'll be neighbors again..." Joseph said, fondly.

"I'll meet your new girlfriend then."

"What? I don't have a girlfriend."

"Joseph, you can be honest with me. I saw you outside your church holding a woman's hand."

Joseph thought she looked cute when she tried to look well poised. "That girl is your new neighbor, Maria. She'd just come to Forget-Me-Not Manor. She was touched by the Christmas Eve service; it made her cry. I was only trying to calm her down."

Katie looked at him with suspicion and he held her gaze. "You were just holding hands with the doctor. Is he your boyfriend?" Joseph saw a grin spread across her face. "I miss you, Katie, more than you know. I'm learning all kinds of things from Moses about the Amish faith. It's fascinating."

Katie's eyes widened. "Maybe that's the crossroads you're to take. Maybe you're to be Amish."

"I can't say for sure. I need to be convinced in my own mind. If I say I want to be Amish right now, it would be for you."

Katie's eyes grew dark and she put her head down. "Other outsiders have turned Amish because of love. Why can't you?"

"I'd have to make a vow that's more a commitment than marriage. If I have doubts down the road, I'd be shunned." He searched her eyes for understanding.

"I'm sorry, Joseph. I don't mean to hurt you. Maybe Ginny's right. I'm Amish and you're not," Katie said. "Levi's asking me for an answer to his proposal. He deserves an answer."

Joseph clenched his fists and wanted to punch the wall. How could Katie give up so easily? Was she really falling in love with Levi? He had Jeremiah 6:16 on sticky notes on his bathroom mirror and icebox so he wouldn't forget to pray for their future...to wait at the crossroads and pray. He grabbed her hands. "You don't love Levi. Don't give up." He heard someone loudly clear their throat and he turned to see Granny Weaver in the doorway.

~*~

"We put up thirty cords of wood in New York," Leah said to Levi as he chopped wood.

"That's a lot of wood. We only put up fifteen." He swung the ax and the log split in two. "Better stand back; these little logs can fly."

"I know. I can chop wood, too. We New York girls split and stack wood like the men."

"Really?" Levi asked. "Can I see you split a piece?"

"Be happy to." Leah took the ax and hit the log in the middle, breaking it in two.

"That's *goot*, but maybe a lucky strike." Levi grinned.

"I'll quarter it then." Leah took half of the log she just split and laid it on the tree stump. She hit it again, perfectly in the center. One piece of the log came close to landing on Levi. "Better stand back," she said, laughing.

"Okay, I believe you. Eli may need your help when he gets back, if you stay long. Do you like Pennsylvania?"

"I do. People are friendly. You have many more *English* friends than we did in New York."

"Why is that?" Levi asked.

"Well, there are levels of Old Order strictness as you know. Our community was very strict. *Oma* said she's had *English* friends stay at her house overnight for a visit. That would never happen in my old community. I couldn't even write to an outsider."

"Were you *Swartzentruber* Amish?" Levi asked. "They're too strict for me."

"No, but our community was very strict concerning outsiders. I've never really heard of a trusted *English* friend once. Here you seem to trust many."

"Well, we've lived among them for a long while and the shop owners respect us. They help us sell lots of stuff."

"So how is Katie? Are *yinz* courting?" Leah asked out of the blue. "Rumor has it you'll be wed in the spring."

"We're courting as friends," Levi said, hitting the wood a little too hard. "She's not sure of her feelings just yet."

"So you just started courting, *jah*?"

"It's been eight months," Levi mumbled.

"That's unusual, but people move at their own pace, *jah*?" she asked.

"Suppose so," Levi said as he split a log so hard, a piece bounced a few times before it landed.

Joseph pulled into the driveway and Katie jumped out of the car. Levi smiled at Katie and she smiled back, and Joseph felt his heart sink. He got out of the car and headed toward the back of the house but stopped when he saw the orchard. He walked back to the apple trees, amazed. All the broken limbs were sawed off and neatly piled. The apple farm was saved, but as he looked at all the trees missing their limbs, he thought of Katie. He didn't feel whole without her, but was that right? He could turn Amish for her, but what if he changed his mind? He'd been prone to making impulsive decisions in the past, and learned to tread carefully when making a decision. No, he needed to know beyond a doubt if he could make such an oath.

~*~

Dear Mom and Dad,

Hope you are both well. I miss you and everyone in Smicksburg, but I'm learning so much about cooking, baking, and life. I'm still shocked that Italians don't have clothes dryers. They hang up their clothes like the Amish. They're so down to earth, too. The girls don't wear gobs of make-up and don't have a ton of clothes. Being outside America, I see we have too much.

I'm glad you love living in town and seeing Suzy and David every day. I was worried at first, thinking you'd regret giving up the old house. I looked online and see your new store listed among the Smicksburg merchants. Serenity Book Nook....I love it. I think it's great you have the complete Serenity Prayer on the wall. It's awesome. I pray it, too. I'm glad you'll have a section for used and antique books as well as Amish books in the store. Mom, you need to sell the Pathway Readers we used for homeschooling. The stories are so good. The store can be for the Amish and English. I'm guessing there's a Jane Austen section now that you're carrying classics.

Speaking of Jane Austen, I met my Mr. Darcy. Although he's short and dark haired and is from Riccia. He's the love of my life. More on that later.

Miss you. Hope January in Smicksburg isn't too cold. It's freezing in these mountains.

Xoxo
Kirsten

~*~

Katie looked at the women washing down Lottie's kitchen wall. A work frolic was something she needed. Over the past week, seeing a lot of Levi and Joseph had her nerves completely shot. The men seemed like they had quills like porcupines around each other, no matter how nice they tried to be.

Katie smelt the hot gingerbread cookies set out on the table. Other women started to arrive carrying pound cakes, fried dough, and more pies. She loved to mix work with good fellowship, taking breaks for goodies. They planned to work all day, scrubbing and painting the walls and floors, stocking the pantry with canned chili, stew, and soup. Lottie wouldn't have to cook for months when she returned.

Men started arriving. Reuben came with a wagon of lumber for the new ramp to be installed up to the front porch. An *English* truck pulled up and Katie was puzzled. She saw Levi motioning for the driver to back up on the side of the house. She grabbed her cape and went out to see what was going on. "So much commotion today, my work frolic has been successful, *jah*?"

Levi beamed at her. "It was *goot* of you to organize it."

"But what's this truck here for?" she asked.

"Our Gmay raised enough money to build a variety store on the side of the house. We plan to break ground in February and build when the weather warms. I got a cement block at a *goot* price and it's being delivered."

Katie felt love well up in her heart for this dear man. She jumped up on Levi to give him a hug. "You organized this!"

"The whole Gmay agreed. It wasn't me."

"You're so modest, Levi. So *goot* of you." She remained in his arms. She saw Moses watching them on the front porch and quickly withdrew her arms from Levi and put them under her cape.

She returned to the house and saw her *mamm* and went over to embrace her. "*Mamm*, I didn't see you come in. I've missed you these two weeks."

"I've missed you, too," Millie said.

"But I'll be home next week," Katie said.

Millie pursed her lips. "Didn't you hear? Lottie talked to Joseph and said Eli won't be back for three more weeks, at least. His injuries really do need expert care and the money that came in from the card shower will cover it all. Granny Weaver put a notice of what happened in the Die Botschaf. She gave an address to send cards. There was so much mail; it couldn't fit in a mailbox. The post office put them in boxes and delivered them that way Granny Weaver and I kept track of the states the letters came from and we counted twenty-four."

"And the cards had money?" Katie asked.

"Enough to cover most medical bills. The money from the auction helped, too, but the card shower was a miracle of sorts."

Katie's eyes were wide. "What a day for surprises. Did you hear about the store to be built on the side of the house? It will be income for Eli and lots of company, too. Levi organized it."

"Levi is plain *wunderbar*. He comes here to chop the apple branches into firewood, and then he goes over to the Weavers to make sure they have enough wood, too. I hear Leah helps him and can swing an ax like a man."

"I didn't know that…" Katie said.

"Ach, he only has eyes for you, dear one. Have you answered his proposal yet?"

"Not yet, but I think I know what I'll be saying." Katie grinned.

CHAPTER 18

*J*udah walked the fieldstone path to the Rowlands' old house, now Forget-Me-Not Manor. He turned and looked across the street to see Katie's old house. Memories of her flooded his mind, but he needed to move on. He wasn't returning to the Amish and Maria was such a nice girl.

"Hi lover-boy," Janice teased, as she answered the door. "Sit here and talk to me while Maria gets ready." She placed a cup of coffee in front of him.

Judah looked around the house. It seemed strange that the Rowlands weren't there.

"Did you hear Maria's going to finish college and be a registered nurse? I'm so happy I could just burst open! She'll make a wonderful nurse, don't you think?" Janice asked.

"She sure would. She has a heart like no other."

"Even Katie Byler?" Janice asked.

"Well, Katie's a sweet girl and I loved her once. I think sometimes I wanted to be a part of the whole Byler family and marrying Katie would give me that family I've always wanted. I think Joseph is making the same mistake. He's so taken with Katie because he lacks family, like I do."

"He has Ginny and James and their family." Janice sat at the table with a mug of coffee.

"But not a huge clan like the Bylers."

"So you really think you only loved Katie Byler for her family and think Joseph's doing the same?"

"No, I'm sure I did love her. Can't say about Joseph."

Janice laughed. "Something changed around the same time Maria moved here."

"I guess so," Judah grinned. "She's a gem, Janice."

"I know. But she has a lot of baggage. She's carried around a lot of pain for a long time, rejection from the people who should have loved her the most."

"Maybe that's what we have in common; two people with families who didn't care for them. We understand each other."

"That reminds me," Janice said. "Did you write to your brothers? When Jerry counsels, he expects follow-up."

"No, I haven't. I've been so busy working on the Rowland's bookstore."

"And spending time with Maria, too. Jerry's going to kill you." Janice winked. "You know you've made a splash on everyone in church. We love you like a son as do Ginny and James, and now Suzy talks about Judah this and Judah that. Everybody loves Judah."

"Maybe I'm in a clan as big as the Bylers," Judah mused.

Maria came out of her room with Lilly. Judah held his breath when he saw Maria's long brown, wavy hair. It was so shiny. Did she spray something on it to get it to shine like that? She looked stunning in her purple dress.

"Hi Judah," Maria said, glowing. She looked at Janice. "Lilly and I went over the rules again and she understands the warning system and the time-out chair."

"Thank you, Maria," Janice said.

Judah went over to Lilly and pulled one of her curls straight. "I wish I had some of your curls," he said. "Can I have some?"

"Judah's losing his hair, Lilly. How can we help him?" Janice laughed.

"He can have some of mine. I'll share," Lilly said.

Judah looked at the little girl fondly. "I'll take you up on your offer."

Maria hugged Lilly good-bye and took Judah's hand. "I'll be back soon."

"Not if I can help it," Judah said.

~*~

Judah helped Maria out of the sleigh and thanked his friend again. Maria always wanted a horse-drawn sleigh ride. He helped her into the car and rubbed his hands together briskly. "I say we head back to Smicksburg and go it at the Country Junction and get some hot chocolate." Judah noticed Maria looked nervous. "What's wrong?"

"I can't remember when I had such a nice date. Doesn't seem real. You really *are* a nice guy."

"Well, tell the Amish that. When we go into the restaurant you'll see what a shunning feels like."

"Then why do you stay? You don't have to be here and be treated like dirt."

"They don't treat me like dirt, really. They'll say hello but that's about it. I'm an outsider to them. I stay here because I've found a family with Ginny and James and all the folks at church. James is like my Dad now." Judah pulled out and headed back to Smicksburg.

"The Amish are friendly with Ginny and James. Aren't they outsiders?" Maria asked.

"They're trusted *English* friends. They've befriended quite a few Amish, but have had to earn their respect over time. If they do something to break that trust, they'd be treated like outsiders again."

"Sounds to me like a friendship. Once the trust is gone, it's hard to get back."

"You're right. It's something like that."

"I hope we can be good, trusting friends," Maria said.

Judah took her hand and held it until they got to the Country Junction. The place was packed; several Amish families he knew were in the restaurant. The look on their faces was more like pity than a shunning. He said hello to a few people and most smiled and nodded their heads. An elderly Amish man came over to Judah and extended his hand. "We forgive you."

Judah was puzzled. Were they lifting the ban...the shunning? "Thank you," Judah said.

The other Amish in turn shook his hand, saying they forgave him, too. Some embraced him and patted him on the back. Judah thanked them, but didn't know why they had done this, and why they acted so sad while shaking his hand.

~*~

Katie heard the door creak open and turned to see Moses walking nimbly out of his *dawdyhaus*. "*Guder mariye*, Moses. Are you hungry for apple pancakes? I have plenty here."

"Good morning, dear girl. *Danki*. I'd like some coffee, too."

Katie took a plate full of pancakes drizzled with their homemade maple syrup and a cup of coffee over to him and sat down. "Looks like another cold day."

"*Jah*, it does. I was wondering what Joseph's doing today. Would you be knowing?"

"No, I haven't seen him in a few days."

"He's what I call good medicine. Hangs on every word I teach him and always studying one of the books from my little library."

Katie tried to hide her hope. "What's he reading now?"

"Oh, the *Dordrecht Confession of Faith*, mainly."

"And what does he think about it? Is he in agreement with it?

"*Jah*, he said it's backed up by so many scripture. I think he'd be Amish if the *goot* Lord proved to him he should be." Moses shifted in his chair. "I'd like him to come over. Could you run over and see if he's busy?"

"Ach, Moses. You know we're not to be alone," Katie said. "The ice has all melted, it might do you *goot* to get out and walk a spell."

"Must be arthritis that makes walking tough." He rubbed his right knee. "I'm a Senior Bishop and I say go ahead over and see Joseph. It's okay. You'll only be there a minute."

Arthritis? He almost skipped to the breakfast table and could easily go over himself. "Are you sure?"

"Go ahead over. Tell him to come over and see Old Moses."

She was living in a different church district for a while and Moses' words carried a lot of weight. Katie looked at him and nodded in agreement. She got her black bonnet, and headed over to Joseph's. She noticed his bird feeders were full and birds were everywhere. Katie sighed when she saw the mourning dove; birds that mated for life. She wished she and Joseph could be those two birds and fly away. She knocked on the door but there was no answer. She knocked again and saw Joseph come to the door.

"Katie, come in," Joseph said with a yawn.

"I can't come in, Joseph, you know that. Moses wants you to come over and visit him. We can talk over there."

"I've missed our talks...I've been busy. Come in and see all I've done to the house."

She pondered a few seconds, and then stepped inside. "For just a minute." She looked around and was surprised the he'd refinished the oak floors. The walls were white with white curtains in the windows. "Looks Amish," Katie said.

"I didn't mean for it to. White looks clean. Leah made the curtains."

Katie clenched her fists. Leah? Leah made him curtains? That was a wife's job. "What'd she do that for?"

"She's neighborly. All the Weavers are. I miss the Byler's, though."

"Seems like the Weavers have filled the void."

He drew close to her, but this time she needed to stand her ground. She was on a path that was firm, and she'd stick with it. "Katie, you know I miss you, right?"

"*Jah*, but Moses will be expecting us."

"Katie, have I done something wrong? You're not your sweet self."

"Nothing. It's nothing," she said. "Moses wants to see you and I've delivered the message. I'll be getting back now."

Joseph grabbed her arms. "We need to talk, Katie. I still love you. Don't you feel the same for me?"

"Did you have fun on your double date? Ginny mentioned it to me…"

"I didn't go. My sister's attempts at being a matchmaker are failing. I think you know why. I love you."

She didn't know what to say, but soon felt Joseph's hand on her chin to make her look at him. "What's wrong? Tell me."

"I have a lot on my mind."

"Do you want to talk about it?"

She turned her head and stared aimlessly out the window.

"Katie, I can't stand seeing you like this."

She stiffened, trying not to show emotion. "I need to get back to Moses," she said softly.

Joseph continued to try to hold her. "You know I'm praying here for an answer to our dilemma. I think I'm finding some answers."

She wanted to look at him but didn't dare; afraid she'd want to kiss him. If she lingered too long she might just fall into that temptation again. Katie tore herself from his arms, and ran across the small living room, and slammed the door.

~*~

Joseph got on his boots and threw on his coat to walk over to see Moses. Patches of grass peeped through the snow, the rest laid buried. Just like Katie's heart, he thought. Most of her feelings toward him were under thick blankets of snow. When he reached the house he saw Moses, eager to talk. "Can we chat in my little house?" he said. "More private," he whispered so Katie wouldn't hear.

Joseph followed Moses through the door into his private domain. They took their usual chairs by the wood burning stove. "Son, I want to warn you about something. The woman folk don't know I can hear through that door." He pointed to the door leading to the main house. "Now I'm not spying, just overhearing things. They're all encouraging Katie to marry Levi."

Joseph felt his heart thump. "It's not their place to tell her who to marry. What does she say?"

"Oh, she doesn't love him. I do have eyes. He's over here a lot, working on the store. But something's not right. Levi's pressuring her for an answer, but it's like his heart isn't in the asking, like a man who's in love." He leaned forward and pointed his long crooked finger at him. "She loves you and is torn apart."

"But she's Amish and I may not be," Joseph said, exasperated.

"But you *might* be. We believe the same things. We've gone around the mulberry bush a few times over certain issues. My head aches after we talk about being saved by grace and how you hammer in how important that is to you. We're in agreement, and you have what it takes. You love the slower pace with no electricity. You love Katie, too, and she'd be helping you stay true to the Amish way; she's Amish to the core."

Joseph put his head back on the Amish rocker. Moses handed him the book, A *Devoted Christian's Prayer Book*. "Just got this in the mail yesterday and want you to be using it. You said you were at a crossroads, so best be praying which way to go, and quick."

"Thank you, Moses. I will be praying mighty hard." The thought of Katie being pressured to marry Levi appalled him and he didn't want to talk about it further. "What's the latest on Eli?"

"Well, he has full use of his upper body but he can't seem to feel anything below the waist. He'll be home soon with a list of exercises he needs to do to keep up his strength."

"So he'll have no use of his legs for sure? Even after all the physical therapy? I know there was hope of slight movement."

Tears formed in Moses' eyes. "Eli wrote me a letter and it warmed my heart more than a blazing fire." He got up and went to the basket that hung on the wall to retrieve the letter "It's short, but to the point." He sat down, got on his glasses and read:

Dear Daed,

I know my accident must be doubly hard for you, since we lost Mamm to a buggy accident. I'm so grateful to be alive and will find a way to serve my Lord in a wheelchair. We're pilgrims on this earth and if I can bring glory to God in my weakness, I find it an honor. I'm going to look at every customer who comes into my new store as a person I can touch with His love and goodness. I figure I'm a blessed man. Hope to be home soon.

Love you Daed.

Eli

Moses held the letter to his heart. "It hits me right here. I'm so proud of my boy."

Joseph stopped his rocking chair. "You lost your wife in a buggy accident? How do you feel now that Eli was hit in a buggy?"

"I don't understand your meaning."

"Maybe the Amish should stop using the horse and buggy. It's too dangerous."

"No, the car's dangerous. We've seen what it's done, making life too fast and you depend less on the community." Moses shifted in his chair. "I have something else to talk to you about. Your friend, Judah Yoder, is under suspicion for hitting Eli's buggy. The police were here last night. They're investigating Eli's accident and asked me if anyone showed hostility toward the Amish. I had to be honest and tell them about Judah's behavior toward the Bylers last summer. They're going to question Judah today."

"So that's what's really bothering Katie? Did the police ask her questions, too?"

"No," Moses shook his head. "Maybe I didn't make it clear. Levi wants to marry her and wants an answer to his proposal *now!*"

Joseph shot out of his rocker. "She can't do that! I need to go and talk to her."

"Don't forget the prayer book. I'll be praying for you, Son."

"Danki, I mean thank you," Joseph said as he grabbed the book and went into the main part of the house. Levi Miller was at the kitchen table having coffee and cookies with Katie.

Katie looked up at him. "Do you want some snicker doodles? I just got them out of the oven."

"C-can I talk to you... alone?" Joseph wanted to throw Levi out in the snow, but held his flaring temper in check.

Levi looked evenly at him. "She's not to be with you...alone."

"I'm talking to Katie."

"You know what the Bishop said." Katie looked up at him, her eyes pleading.

Levi cleared his throat. "Will you be willing to help with the foundation next week? It's February and the ground is softened enough for the *English* to dig the foundation with their trucks. We'll need help laying the bricks."

Joseph tightened his fists. Levi saw the tension between them and was making an attempt to dissolve the air in the room, so thick it was suffocating.

Katie got up and went to the red hand pump to get Joseph a drink. "Here. You don't look *goot*. Drink this."

Joseph looked into Katie's distressed eyes. "Thank you. I'll stop over later to see Moses."

"I'm going back home next week to start the seeds in the greenhouse. I won't be next door anymore," she said. "Will you be coming over to visit *Mamm* and me? Reuben's *kinner* ask about you. You're always welcome."

Levi glared at Katie. Joseph looked at her and smiled faintly. He admired her courage. Was she asking him to visit so they could talk alone?

~*~

"No, Officer. I was home the night of the accident," Judah said.

"Was someone with you?" the officer asked.

"The roads were treacherous. No one was out in them."

"How do you know the roads were treacherous if you weren't out on them?" The officer kept pushing for a confession, but Judah gave none.

"Black ice has a dull look to it. I was going to go out but when I saw the ice I stayed home."

"The accident wasn't far from here. You didn't see any car or hear anything?"

"I remember hearing the wind. When it howls that loud you know you might have a tree down somewhere and lose power."

"We understand you acted hostile toward the Amish this past summer? Is that true?"

Judah looked steadily into the officer's eyes. "Yes. My sister died and I was upset."

"Are you still upset with the Amish? I understand you're a shunned man."

"Yes, I am, but I have nothing against them."

"You're lucky the Amish only want this investigation to extend forgiveness to the person who hit Eli. We're calling it a hit and run and you're our only suspect. They won't be pressing charges, though."

"But I didn't do it."

"What proof do you have? None."

Judah thought hard. "My friend found Eli and said there weren't any cars on the road."

"We have a statement from Joseph Hummel at the scene of the accident. Is that who you're talking about?"

"Yes. He told me he could barely see a foot in front of him that day. White-out conditions."

"We know, but someone hit that poor Amish man and we intend to find out who it was."

"Aren't I innocent until proven guilty?" Judah asked.

"Yes, but you remain our prime suspect. The Amish know that."

Judah thought about the Amish saying they forgave him at the Country Junction. They must be forgiving him of hitting Eli. Despite the helpless feeling of not being able to clear his name, he was touched that the Amish would forgive a shunned man.

~*~

Ginny looked at Suzy and then all the new yarn she'd spun, neatly placed on the shop shelves. "I love to knit. I also love walking to classes."

Suzy smiled. "It's been fun having you and James next door. We have to watch the clock, though. We were playing Scrabble until two in the morning. James is so competitive."

"You'll be afraid when we play Monopoly. He acts like a dictator, trying to conquer the world." Ginny laughed. "Kirsten's the same way."

The little gold bell on the door rang. It was two Amish ladies. "Can I help you?" Suzy asked.

"We're looking for wool yarn. Best for making nice warm socks," the older lady said.

"Well, everything is wool, since I spin all the yarn from my sheep. I just started spinning alpaca too. Take a look around."

Suzy went back to her chair to knit. "Any news from Kirsten?"

"Actually, yes, and big news, too. She said she met the love of her life in Riccia. Now she wants to bring him home in May. He wants to live in America. He apparently got a green card with no problems."

"I thought it was harder to get into the States…How odd," Suzy said.

"We figured he could live with Judah or Joseph, depending on how much he likes electricity."

"What's his name?"

"Romeo, can you believe it? Romeo, of all things," Ginny said.

Suzy put her yarn in her lap and laughed. The two Amish women in the store bought some yarn and left.

"They don't look familiar. Do you know them?" Ginny asked.

"They're from the Mast clan, I believe," Suzy said.

"Noah's a Mast. You think they'll tell Noah about Romeo?"

"If they do, it's better to hear it from a family member."

Ginny said a prayer for Noah. She really liked him and felt bad Kirsten's affections were with someone else now.

CHAPTER 19

Noah felt nauseous and went over the sink to get a glass of water, and then returned to the kitchen table. "I don't believe it, *Daed*," he said. "Kirsten isn't that fickle. It's country gossip, is all."

"Your Aunt Maryann heard it with her own ears. An Italian man Kirsten met will be coming to live in Smicksburg." Jacob Mast leaned forward. "I'm so sorry, Son, but maybe this will open your eyes to all the nice Amish girls around you. You might be thinking harder about being baptized into the church in April, too."

"I told Kirsten I wouldn't make my vow unless she was there with me," Noah said, bewildered.

"You aren't hearing me, are you? She's in love with another. You need to move on. We can have baptism class right here, since I'm your *Daed*."

Noah couldn't believe Kirsten would fall for another. But then, they were always able to write to each other before, when they were apart. Could she fall for someone else so quickly? He knew he still loved her. "No, *Daed*. When Kirsten gets back I'll talk to her. We can't write so now everything looks real confusing; if I get baptized it will be with Kirsten."

"Well, there's a singing tomorrow night. Why don't you go? You haven't been to one in years and I always wondered why, thought you had a secret romance going on. Now I know that girl has kept you back."

"Don't talk about her like that. I held myself back because I already found the right girl."

"I must admit, I admire your loyalty," Jacob said. "Maybe it just hasn't sunk in yet that she loves some Italian fellow. You may not go to a singing tomorrow, but

I bet you will in two weeks' time, when reality's sets in." He got up and went to the icebox. "Want some peach pie? I can heat a piece up for you?"

"No *danki, Daed.* I need to milk the cows and get ready for bed. I'm tired."

"You've never passed up a piece of pie in your life…are you sick?"

~*~

Eli looked at the weights in the rehab room, and then rolled his eyes.

Lottie cheered him on. "You can do a hundred, like they asked."

"I'm tired," he moaned.

"You need to keep your upper body strength now. You'll need to use it more to compensate for your legs."

"So I can swing like a monkey around the house, *jah*?" Eli asked.

Lottie looked fondly at her husband. "Yes, like a caveman swinging around the jungle. The exercises will make you able to walk on your hands. You'll be able to walk over to the neighbors and back on your hands."

Eli laughed and pulled his wife closer. "At least I can still give you a hug. I may have lost my ability to be a man to you, but…"

Lottie hugged her husband. "You're all the man I need." She kissed him.

"No PDA in here, Hershberger," Eddie, the physical therapist said.

"What's that? Another rule I don't understand?"

Eddie laughed. "PDA stands for public display of affection. I'm kidding, though." He looked at his chart. "Did you hit a hundred yet?"

"No, I'm tired today."

"We've been working you hard so you can go home. I have good news. With the encouragement of your wife, you can go home and continue all the exercises there. Have your buddies come over and arm wrestle. You'll win, hands down."

"Ach," Lottie said, "go home? We haven't been there in months. I can't wait!"

"You'll be here a few more days but after that, you are free to roam the country. I'm off for the next few days so I'll be saying good-bye now. I must say I'm going to miss you both."

"It was *goot* having you for an instructor," Eli said, reaching out to shake his hand.

"There's something very different about you Eli. Most people who have gone down your path are very depressed. You have will power."

"I have God power," Eli said.

"Well, I'm not too religious, but I must say, you have something I don't have."

"Jesus in your heart?" Eli asked. "He can live in you, too. He loves you."

Eddie's eyes grew cold. "Jesus never did me any favors. Why would I want Him in my life?"

"We live in a fallen, dark world. Don't you think I felt depressed when my accident happened? I thought I was drowning in darkness, but then I cried to the Lord and His light chased away the darkness. Now I can walk in the light…and so can you."

Eddie's eyes softened. "You really believe that?"

"*Jah*, cry out to the Lord and ask for help. It's easy. Our daughter cries out to us and we go right to her. God's a loving father. If you call out to Him, He'll come to you."

"I have another group coming in for therapy. Can I come by your room before I leave and talk about this some more?"

"You know my room number," Eli smiled.

~*~

Katie looked into Levi's eyes. He was serious. He wanted an answer to his proposal now or he wanted to break off their courtship. "Why the impatience all of a sudden?"

Levi shifted in his chair. "When you look at Joseph like you do, it confuses me. I need to know where I stand."

"I look at Joseph like any other man," Katie said. She walked over to the coffee pot and poured more of the hot liquid in her mug. "Do you want more?"

"No, Katie. I came over here to talk and get some answers. Why did you encourage Joseph to come and visit you?"

"The kids miss him. They want him to bring over his telescope and watch the winter stars. *Mamm* misses him, too."

"And you?"

"He's a *goot* friend." Katie sat down and looked into her coffee.

"Why can't you give me an answer?" Levi said, loudly. "Forgive me. I don't mean to shout."

There was a knock on the door and Moses walked in. "Someone call for me?"

"No, Moses. Levi and I were just having a loud discussion."

"You mean a fight?" Moses said, trying to hide a grin.

"No, not a fight. I just raised my voice a little, is all," Levi said. "You look tired, Moses. Best be getting back to bed."

"No. I'm wide awake. I say we play Dutch Blitz."

"Katie and I are having a private conversation, Moses. Do you mind giving us some privacy?"

"What could you possibly be talking to this girl about that I can't hear?" Moses said, his eyes twinkling.

Katie cocked one eyebrow. "You said you were going to bed an hour ago and that you were tired."

"I got a second wind. You know what that's like. A burst of energy that needs worked out."

"Why don't you go visit your *goot* friend, Joseph?" Levi asked, exasperated.

"Why don't we ask Joseph over here to play cards? It's better with four players."

Katie went to look through the side door. She could see an oil lamp was on and Joseph was sitting in a chair reading. She wished she could go over and spend time with him. "He's awake and reading a book. Maybe he'd like to play."

Levi looked at Moses sternly. "Can you hear our conversations through that door?"

"What makes you ask such a question? Are you accusing me of spying?" Moses put his hand over his heart.

"Levi and I do have important things to discuss, Moses," Katie said.

"Oh, I'll leave in a bit, after a nice cup of coffee."

Levi looked up at the ceiling in disbelief.

~*~

Granny Weaver beamed. "Ach, it's so *goot* to be back here again, in our little knitting circle. We're strong together, and I'm sure we'll all be able to help Lottie."

"I'd do anything for that woman," Ginny said. "Is that why you called the knitting circle meeting, Granny?"

"Well, I missed everyone, too. I've been down with the flu and it's the mercy of the *goot* Lord I'm still alive."

Millie put her hand over her mouth to hide a giggle. Ginny narrowed her eyes. "What's so funny, Millie?"

"Ach, you know. Granny can be so dramatic at times."

"She was really sick," Sarah said, seriously.

"How many pairs of mittens have we sent to Christian Aid?" Katie asked.

"Over a hundred pairs, so far," Suzy said. "Winter is for knitting and I've been putting any spare yarn into those mittens. Can you imagine how cold it is in Romania with no gloves?"

Ginny looked around the room, studying each woman. Something was wrong. They acted strangely. She knew Noah found out about Kirsten and her new boyfriend. Was Sarah nervous to talk about it? Most likely happy and relieved and didn't want to show it. "I heard from Kirsten today," she ventured. "She called to wish me a happy Big 5-0."

Sarah looked at her and grinned. "Bet you never thought you'd be in your fifties like me?"

"I don't see you as old, Sarah. Anyhow, fifty is the new thirty."

Millie started to giggle uncontrollably and Ginny became concerned. Was she in her right mind? Was she ill? "Millie, can we talk, private like?"

"*Jah*, how about we go over to your house?"

"We can go into the store and talk there."

"You go on over to your place," Granny said. "It's awfully stuffy in here...so crowded."

Ginny gasped. "Have I done something wrong? I know there's this fine line between Amish and *English* but — "

Millie laughed so hard she doubled over. "I best be taking her to my place," Ginny said.

She helped Millie, who was crying now, over to her house. She stopped at the bottom of the steps. "Are you alright to walk? You really are scaring me. I've read about personality changes with aging. You need to take Gingko Biloba."

Millie looked at her, tears running down her cheeks. "Do you have any?"

"Yes, and I'll get you some right now."

Ginny and Millie walked upstairs and when she opened the door she heard, "Surprise!" She was bombarded with hugs from women in red and pink hats. She looked at Millie, eyes wide.

Millie hugged her tight. "The harder I tried to keep a straight face, the more I laughed. I've never been to a surprise party. *Goot* idea!"

Ginny heard footsteps behind her and saw her knitting circle, all pointing at her, laughing. She hugged them one by one, and then heard James behind her. She leaned on his chest too stunned to talk. He walked with her over to where there was a big chocolate cake on one table and another table filled with lovely hors d'oeuvres. "The cake's from the Oakmont Bakery. Your Red Hat friends from Pittsburgh brought it up."

Suddenly she was whisked away by her Red Hat friends, Jesse, Kathy, and Suzanne. They held out a hideously huge, broad-rimmed red hat with a purple plume on the side. They crowned her as a member of their Red Hat Society. She was now fifty and had to turn in her pink hat and boa and wear a red one. The women with red hats cheered, "You're one of us now!" The women in pink hats, yelled, "Poor Ginny."

After greeting everyone, James asked if he could show her one of her surprises. They walked downstairs and put a blind fold over her eyes and they walked into the bookstore. He made her guess what the present was, but she couldn't think of anything to say, still in shock. He took off the blind fold and when she opened her eyes, she had to hold on to James for support.

Beautiful cherry shelves in all four rooms, just the way she wanted them. The windows had cherry molding and the floor were also stained a shiny red. The walls were painted mint green. A sofa, red and green checked, was in a sitting area. A stained glass lamp hung from the center of each room. Oriental rugs covered the floors. Antique lace hung from the windows. She was breathless. It looked like a high class library out of an old-fashioned movie.

"Do you like it?" James asked.

"I'm speechless. This is a bookstore beyond my wildest dreams." She walked around each room. "Are we still within our budget?"

"With the help of family and friends, yes," James said.

Ginny ran into James' arms. "Thank you so much. I can't believe it." Judah walked in and stopped mid-stride and spun around. Ginny yelled, "Wait, Judah! You can come in. Can you believe this?"

"He helped make this happen. He and Joseph did most of the work. The three of us make quite a team." James patted Judah's back.

Ginny kissed Judah on the cheek. "Thank you." She looked down though and pursed her lips. "I am confused, though. Oriental rugs of this quality aren't cheap. Are they a gift from someone?"

"You don't miss a beat," James laughed. "Your Aunt Winnie and Uncle Slavie bought them. They couldn't be here, too cold to make the trip at their ages, but the rugs are from them."

"I need to drive to Jeannette and thank them in person. How sweet..."

"Right now we should get back to the party. Your friends have lots of old age jokes to play on you. Your cousin Tom looks mighty determined to embarrass you."

~*~

Joseph made his way through the crowd to reach Katie, Millie, and Moses. "Ginny sure looked surprised, huh? I still can't believe we pulled it off. Ginny's hard to keep a secret from."

"It's so funny about the hat colors. I always wondered about the tourist and their red hats," Millie chuckled. "Eli and Lottie would be here for sure if they could. They'll be home tomorrow, though."

"*Wunderbar goot* news," Joseph said looking at Moses with a chuckle.

"*Wunderbar goot* German, Joseph," Moses grinned. "Er muss auf seinen Akzent aber funktionieren."

Katie nodded in agreement.

"What did he say?" Joseph asked, turning to Katie.

"He says you need to work on your accent," Katie said, biting her lower lip.

"*Jah*, I do," he said, looking at Katie. "Want to go see Ginny's new store downstairs? It's James' gift to her. I did a lot of the work"

She nodded in agreement and followed Joseph across the room and down the long staircase. Millie and Moses followed but when they got to the bottom of the stairs, they bumped into Ginny, James, and Judah. Ginny hugged Millie again and dragged her into her shop and the two went about chatting. Moses stuck his head in to see the store, and then went back upstairs with James. Katie found herself standing in between Joseph and Judah.

"Hello, Katie," Judah said. "Go inside and see all the cabinets Joseph and I made. I need to get back up to Maria."

Katie's eyebrows went up. She nodded and went inside. Joseph followed her into the store.

"It's so fancy," Katie said, looking stunned.

"You think that's wrong?" Joseph asked.

"No, I mean, pretty. You helped build this? I didn't know you were a carpenter."

"I love working with wood and James needed the help. I've been here for weeks working on the place."

"I wondered where you were over these past weeks," Katie said, rubbing her hand against a shelf. "Ginny said she was ordering books from Pathway Publishing. They're Amish. She's going to have classics, too. Maybe I'll read a Jane Austen book."

"Are you allowed?" Joseph asked.

"Granny Weaver says it best. She said when she was young you could read most things the *English* read, even the newspaper, but today, you can't. The stories are immoral and there's so much violence. Jane Austen lived in the early 1800's, so I bet she's safe to read."

"How'd you learn all this?"

"Ginny told me."

"Are you going to read *Persuasion*?" Joseph asked, with a crooked grin.

"You think I need to read it, *jah*? You think I let other people persuade me to do things I don't want to?"

"No… Well, maybe yes. Moses told me people were persuading you to marry Levi."

"Ach, Moses can hear from behind his door. He's always trying to interrupt my conversations with Levi."

"He can tell you don't love Levi," Joseph said, wanting to take Katie's hand but not daring to.

Katie sat on the checkered sofa and Joseph sat next to her. "It's so difficult not being able to talk to you. We haven't had a *goot* talk in months. I get confused. Levi wants an answer to his proposal." She sighed deeply. "So many people are telling me I should accept so I can have an Amish family."

Joseph slumped back on the couch. "Moses was a bishop and understands human emotions, unlike Bishop Mast. Keeping us apart…to not be able to talk, is mean."

"Word has it Noah won't be baptized this spring unless Kirsten's by his side, and he's blaming himself for not properly instructing him. We can tell in the church service he looks more concerned than ever that someone will leave the Amish."

"I see. He thinks Kirsten's leading Noah astray, and I'm leading you astray." Joseph looked up. "I pray the Lord gives me an answer soon…I wonder if He's listening sometimes."

"No direction at all?" Katie's eyes plead for any information. "I don't know how long I can be in this limbo. I do love you, Joseph, but we're not getting any answers. Maybe we're praying for the wrong thing."

"What do you mean?"

"Maybe the answer is before us but we don't like the way God is answering it." She sighed. "It's all confusing."

Joseph sighed. "I'm not giving up hope. I love you, Katie."

~*~

Noah got into the red sports car. "Thanks for the ride to church, Roger."

"Not a problem. You said you already went to my church. I never saw you there."

"Kirsten and I only went once. Met Pastor Sheldon; real nice guy, but I didn't like the music."

"I bet the music was a shock, coming from an Amish church. I know I was floored at first."

Noah stared at Roger. "You were Amish?"

"Yep, I came from a settlement near Volant, about an hour from here. It's near the Ohio border."

"Were you baptized into the Amish church?"

"No, during my rumspringa days, I knew I couldn't be Amish. I went to libraries and read a lot. I knew I wanted a higher education and went to college and got my teaching degree."

"So how'd I meet you working construction?" Noah asked.

"I got laid off," he said.

"How'd your parents take it when you didn't join the Amish church?"

"Hard, very hard. They were such good parents and didn't do anything wrong at all in bringing me up. I just had to have an education. I got my GED and went on to college at seventeen."

Noah felt Kirsten was worth more than a college education. When they arrived at the church, he prayed the Lord would open his eyes to learn what he was supposed to learn from the Mennonites, even though they played guitars in church.

~*~

Judah looked as Pastor Jerry hit the top of his desk, and yelled, "Praise God". He grinned and nodded in agreement.

"God works in mysterious ways, but this takes the cake. You've felt rejected by the Amish all your life, and now you have the Amish coming up to you saying they forgive you and love you, for something you didn't even do." He leaned back in his swivel chair. "How do you feel now toward these people, and more importantly, how do you feel about yourself?"

"I don't know. I guess I feel more accepted by them." Judah pursed his lips. "I don't know what you're getting at."

"Son, I grew up in the deep south in the white section of town. I had people turn their nose up at me all my life. I had to forgive them and they never asked me to. Here the Amish are coming up to you practically welcoming you back into the church. Don't you feel less rejection, almost a freedom that you're their equal?"

Judah slowly looked up at Jerry with a smile. "You're right. God works in mysterious ways. That was what we've been working on all along: my feelings of rejection. I blamed all the Amish, even the Bylers, for not helping when my dad was drunk."

"Were you mad at Katie Byler as well? Did you run from her because you were mad?"

Judah thought of Katie and stiffened. Yes, he was mad at her. She knew the kind of home he lived in, yet wouldn't leave with him for a better life. "Yes, I was mad at her, too."

"Are you still mad?" Jerry probed.

He knew every time he saw her that he got knots in his stomach. "I don't know," he admitted.

"If you don't know, you still are. Emotions are either yes or no. Do you still have some feelings for her?"

Judah sighed. This was a tough counseling session, talking about the Amish and then Katie. He felt wiped out and wished Jerry would stop with all the questions.

"How do you feel when you see her?" he continued.

"I, ah, feel regret," he finally said. "I also feel mad because if I came from a normal family, we'd be married and have children by now."

"But you're still young. What's holding you back?"

Judah shrugged his shoulders. "Don't know. Just don't know."

~*~

Katie lit the gas stove in her small greenhouse where she started plants. Soon it warmed up the tiny place and she began to pour black soil into the shallow trays she laid on the wooden shelves. When she filled twenty trays, she had to sit down. Katie had never felt tired working with plants, especially in February; it always reminded her that spring was around the corner. So could her wedding, if she accepted Levi's proposal.

Would Levi approve of her running a business as a married woman? She'd be tied down with raising little Mica and having children of her own. The more Katie thought, the more fatigued she felt. She looked at all the seed packets. *Turn around so I can take your picture.* She could almost hear Joseph's voice. *What's your favorite flower? Yellow tea roses*, she had said. Katie thought of Joseph's green eyes...eyes as warm as the light from the oil lamps. Then his arms...arms that saved her life. She got a knot in her stomach. If she was going to marry Levi, she'd lose Joseph forever. Did remaining Amish mean more to her than him? She stared at the plant seeds and threw them back in the box. She'd start the seeds tomorrow. Since there was no snow on the road, and it wasn't too chilly, she was going to visit Ginny, and ask to borrow a copy of *Persuasion*.

~*~

Ginny heard a knock on her door and went to answer it. "Katie. Come in."

"*Danki*. I came over to borrow your copy of *Persuasion*? Joseph thinks I need to read it."

Ginny looked at her eyes and knew she'd been crying. "Come sit down and have some hot chocolate and tell me what's troubling you." Ginny led her into the kitchen and put some water in the teapot. "Is it my brother, again?"

"*Jah*," Katie admitted. "I almost accepted Levi's proposal of marriage the other day and it scared me. I could never talk to Joseph again. Levi wouldn't have it; I'm sure."

"You'd have no future at all with Joseph; it would be with Levi. Think about it Katie."

"I could learn to love him, don't you think?"

"I guess it's possible. James and I have had tough years, especially when he worked such long hours; we barely saw each other, but I knew I was in love when I married him." Ginny got up to make the hot chocolate. "If I had my way, I'd make the cultural divide between the Amish and *English* disappear, but we need to live in reality. If you would marry Joseph, you'd be shunned. Would you rather live being a shunned woman and have a life with Joseph? Are you willing to make that sacrifice?" She stirred the hot chocolate and sat it in front of Katie.

"*Danki*, Ginny, but I feel too hot to drink that."

"You don't look good. Are you feeling sick?" Ginny went to the bathroom to get a thermometer. "Here, let me take your temperature."

Katie put her head on the table. "Okay, *jah*."

After a minute Ginny read the thermometer and gasped. "You have a temperature of 103 degrees. I'm putting you in the guest bedroom." She put her arm around Katie to help lift her up and led her to the bed. She ran to the kitchen and returned with a bowl of water and vinegar. Ginny placed a cloth in the solution and put it on her forehead. She ran to get more towels from the bathroom and wet a large one and put it under Katie's neck and cupped it around her cheeks. Katie started to shiver. "That's good, the chills make the fever go down," Ginny said, sitting next to her.

"My head hurts..." Katie said.

Ginny heard someone come in. "Joseph, I need help."

"What's wrong, Sis?" Joseph ran into the bedroom. He knelt down and took Katie's hand. "She's as cold as ice. We need to wrap her up."

"Go get some blankets. I have them in the ottoman. The top flips up."

Joseph ran and got the blankets and laid them on her and sat next to her, cradling her head. "It'll be Okay, my girl."

Katie's teeth were chattering. "My head hurts..."

Joseph kissed her on the forehead. "Now she's burning up. We need to get her to the emergency room."

"My horse..." Katie whispered.

"Don't worry about it. We'll have someone take it home. We're headed to the ER," Ginny said.

~*~

Joseph held Katie in his arms as they waited in the emergency room of the Indiana Memorial Hospital. A nurse called them back and Joseph carried her back into the ER and placed her on the bed. A doctor pulled the curtain around them and examined Katie. After taking her temperature, he called for a nurse. The nurse took her temperature again while the doctor did some blood work. Katie looked scared, but Joseph held her hand. After the exam, the doctor told them she needed to stay overnight, just in case she had H1N1.

"I'm staying with her," Joseph said. "Don't even try to talk me out of it, Sis."

Ginny looked at the way Joseph hovered over Katie and was touched. *He really loves this girl.* "Where will you sleep?"

"In the recliner next to the bed or in the waiting room. I stayed overnight on park benches, remember?"

She hugged her brother. "Call me if there's any change. I'll pick you up in the morning."

~*~

Joseph was startled in the middle of the night. He got up from the recliner and heard Katie mumbling something over and over. He couldn't make out what she said, but she looked so afraid. He rang for the nurse.

After a few minutes the nurse came in. "She's delirious. Side effect of a high fever. The doctor ordered meds in case her fever spiked. I'll get them"

Katie turned to Joseph. "They can't make me," she said in terror.

Joseph got up and sat on the bed next to her. He held her and rocked her back and forth, trying to sooth her. "No one's going to make you do anything, now try to relax."

"But they will and I'll die if they do.–I won't do it. I won't. I love Joseph."

Joseph held her tighter. The nurse walked in and put a pill in Katie's mouth and then some water. "That should bring down her fever."

~*~

Katie noticed through the dark that the walls were white, just like home, but it smelled different. And the blankets felt so heavy she felt like they were suffocating her. When she grabbed them to pull them off, she turned to see Joseph, and tried not to panic. "What are you doing here? Where am I?"

Joseph yawned and rubbed his eyes. "Sorry. I fell asleep. You don't remember coming to the hospital?"

"No. Why am I here? And I'm not in Amish clothes." She touched her head. "Ach, my prayer *kapp* is off."

"I'm sure the Amish won't mind if you're in a hospital gown. You were really sick. Ginny and I brought you here, but I couldn't leave. You were so sick."

Katie looked at Joseph. "I feel so weak. As limp as a wet dish rag."

"You have the flu. They kept you overnight to make sure your temperature went down. Let me feel your forehead." Joseph put his lips on her forehead. "You're still warm, but not like last night, thank God."

Katie tried to keep her eyes from closing, but soon fell back to sleep, and Joseph continued to hold her.

~*~

The lights went on in the hospital room and Joseph shot out of the recliner. "Is her fever up again?"

A man in white came into the hospital room and turned to Katie. "Is this man your husband?" the doctor asked.

"No, he's my friend. He can hear what you have to say."

The doctor leaned against the wall. "You haven't been eating right, young lady. You're blood work shows mild malnourishment. Have you been eating at all?"

"My appetite hasn't been too *goot* for a few months...I have a stressful decision to make.

"Anyone you can talk to? Someone who can give you advice?"

She yawned. " I have lots of advice at home; that's for sure." Katie laid her head back on her pillow. "Just an impossible problem, it seems."

"Well, my advice is to get yourself out of perpetual stress. When you are in constant stress you are continually firing up your adrenal glands. You know, fight or flight. Your body simply can't handle this ongoing situation. Your immune system is shot." He tapped her medical chart with his pen. "Stress can be dangerous. I'll discharge you with a prescription for iron, and a list of vitamins I recommend. See your family doctor to follow-up in two weeks."

After the doctor left, Joseph looked at Katie in disbelief. "You haven't eaten right in months? No appetite? What's going on?"

"Our dilemma..."

CHAPTER 20

Katie laid *Persuasion* on her nightstand and stared at the ceiling. Two days out of the hospital and still so weak; when would her strength return? Lottie and Eli were back home and she longed to visit, but fear that she had a contagious flu kept her inside. She was so grateful for her *mamm's* kindness, bringing her hot soup in bed, and heaping blankets on her when she had the chills.

She looked at the vase of flowers that were on her dresser: beautiful yellow tea roses from Joseph. Next to it was a lavender-scented candle from Ginny. Her friend always said lavender was good for stress. Her *mamm* had it lit and lavender filled the room and she was feeling calmer. A large stack of cards sent by friends was tied with string and sitting on her nightstand.

Her door creaked open and her *mamm* appeared. "Here's more soup, Katie, but you need to eat more real food." Millie put the tray on her nightstand and tried to fluff the pillow behind Katie. "I've added every strengthening herb to the soup, especially oregano and garlic, but you need to eat solid food soon." She reached into her pocket. "More cards came in the mail."

"*Danki*. The doctor said I need to take stressful decisions out of my life, and I believe I have one out of the way." She looked at her *mamm* evenly. "I'll be telling Levi I can't marry him. I don't love him."

Millie put her hands on her hips. "Ach, Katie. I thought things were *goot* between *yinz*. I saw moments of such tenderness, or should I say, romance. Don't be saying no when you're too ill for such a decision."

Katie fidgeted with her long braid of hair. "I may have tricked myself into thinking I cared for him, but I don't."

"That doesn't sound like my Katie, to not know her own mind. What are you reading? Is that book putting notions about romance in your head that aren't true?"

"It's a book of Ginny's." Katie handed the book to her. "It's from her favorite author."

"She's mentioned this Jane Austen to me. She gave me a book by Charles Dickens; A Christmas Carol, and it's *goot*. She's able to open her store sooner than she thought. When you get better, we'll go over and pick out some books. Maybe one that will make you look more fondly on Levi?"

"I do think fondly of Levi, I just don't love him."

"You mean how you loved Judah all those years ago, and now Joseph?" Millie reached over for Katie's hand. "Levi is a fine man for sure and for certain."

"I need to rest, *Mamm*. I have a headache. Can you pull down the shade? The light hurts my eyes..."

~*~

Katie woke up in the middle of the night. Although her hands shook from fatigue, she lit a candle and saw the unread mail. After opening several cards, she came to one that made her heart stop. It was from Levi.

Dear Katie,

I hope you're feeling better. I'd come over to visit, but we all fear it's a contagious flu. I'm sure you understand. I hope you've been thinking kindly of me and will be able to answer my marriage proposal soon. I hope we can wed in early April, before planting time. With his card I send all my love.

Levi.

Katie threw the card on the floor. *Joseph stayed with me in the hospital when I was contagious, and Levi can't even come over to visit?* She felt strength run out of her and prayed for wisdom, to accept the things she could not change; she knew she couldn't change her feelings about Levi. She needed the courage to do the right thing.

~*~

Eli looked at amazement at his new store. It was a miracle to have such a beautiful store stocked full of goods, paid for by the Amish across the country. The new fifteen by thirty foot structure had wooden shelves on three walls and a peg board to hang little gadgets for sale on the other. In the middle were two aisles, wide enough for his wheelchair to get through. Coloring books, toys, and games were on a bottom shelf so the children could easily get to them. Baking and canning supplies lined an entire wall: pots and pans, canning jars, pressure cookers, mixing bowls and hand held gadgets. Hunting and fishing equipment lined another. Looks like church, Eli thought. Men's things on one side, women's on the other. A line of cleaning supplies also took up a row. Hardware store items such as screw drivers, hammers, levels, and even moth and fly traps would save the people a trip to Dayton.

He looked at the big window that Levi put in so Eli could have a desk under it, spending much of his day in the sunlight. The entrance door was beside the window, so he could see customers come in. He thought of his dear friends, Ginny and James, and how they now had a store they lived on top of, making their commute a flight of stairs. He couldn't climb stairs, but he had two arms to move his chair around, and he was thankful.

He heard a knock at the store entrance; it was Joseph.

"Welcome home neighbor," Joseph said, beaming.

Eli lifted his arms out to Joseph and they embraced. "You saved my life," Eli said.-"Gilbert just couldn't keep from slipping. I'm so glad no one put him down."

Joseph scratched his chin. "Who's Gilbert?"

"My oldest horse and friend. He slid on the road and we both went down. He struggled to get up and the buggy took quite a banging up...along with me." Eli looked down at his paralyzed legs. "My memory is back to normal and I remember it as clear as day now."

Joseph leaned up against the shelf. "So a car didn't hit you? The Amish have been forgiving Judah Yoder. He's their prime suspect, since he gave Reuben a shiner last summer."

Eli grinned. "The Lord works in mysterious ways. I'm glad for Judah." Eli looked out the window. "A shunning is a hard thing to get through. My *bruder* was shunned years ago and we haven't heard from him in almost fifteen years. Married an outsider. My *Daed's* taken quite a likin' to you, calling you 'Son' and all. I think you've helped him not miss his own son so much."

Joseph's jaw dropped. "Moses never told me he had a shunned son...."

"Well, we don't talk about it." Eli looked to turn the conversation. "I really like this store. All the more special since it was built by loving hands. The project went out well beyond our Gmay.-It's times like these when I'm so blessed to be Amish."

"I've never seen anything like it. Such generosity. Is it common for Amish people to do this or are you just really well liked?"

"The Amish would have done this for anyone in need. It's not common to have a farmer become a paraplegic and so they know I needed some type of income."

"You talk so freely about being a paraplegic. Isn't it hard for you?"

" 'Accepting hardships as the pathway to peace.' Ginny put the whole prayer in calligraphy for me. I pray it many times a day. I also don't look back and turn to salt, like Lot's wife. Granny Weaver keeps warning me about that. Lot's wife couldn't move, but I'm looking forward and moving."

"I'm praying hard the first two lines; God grant me the serenity to accept the things I cannot change; courage to change the things I can; and wisdom to know the difference." Joseph looked down as he said the prayer.

"You're talking about Katie? *Daed's* kept me posted on all the happenings in Smicksburg. His letters were like books. *Daed's* real happy with Katie's decision, since he's on your side."

"Katie's decision? What do you mean, Eli?"

"She turned down his marriage proposal."

Joseph couldn't hide his smile. "I was worried at times, only able to talk with her in groups, something I find hard to accept."

"You can make it right, you know. Why not become Amish and marry the girl? It's not *goot* for man to be alone, the Good Book says.

Joseph pulled at his goatee and sat on a stool by the wall. "I believe everything you believe, but the whole church district has to agree for me to be a member and with Bishop Mast against me, they might reject me."

Eli grinned. "Oh, go talk to *Daed*. He has something up his sleeve."

~*~

Joseph walked into Bylers Herbs Shop, and saw shelves lined from top to bottom with herbs, tinctures, vitamins and strengthening juices. An older man was checking out an *English* customer; Ginny had told him customers traveled as far as thirty miles to get their homeopathic remedies from the tiny store. Ginny and James were regular customers, saying that Goji juice was making James's hair grow back. Joseph chuckled to himself. What a pair Ginny and James were, never a dull moment.

The owner waved hello to Joseph. "Hey, you're Ginny's *bruder* aren't you? We never had the chance to meet. I'm Reed Byler, owner of this big establishment." He winked as he smiled.

"Yes, I'm the infamous Joseph. Nice to meet you. I've come for a good vitamin or mineral for my friend. She's a little deficient; the doctor called it mild malnutrition."

"You talking about Katie Byler? I did hear she was sick and you and Ginny took her to the hospital. You say the doctor told you this information? How odd."

"I was with her in the hospital. I talked to the doctor when she was being discharged and asked a bunch of questions. He said she needed liquid minerals and vitamins. Can you recommend any?" Out of Joseph's eyes, he spied another Amish man, glaring at him. It was Bishop Mast.

"You were told not to be alone with Katie Byler. She didn't respect my wishes." The Bishop's eyes were ablaze. "Now I have to give a second warning to Katie."

Joseph slammed the jar of vitamins he was looking at on the counter. "What's wrong with you? My sister and I took her to the hospital."

"Did your sister stay with *yinz* at all times?"

Joseph knew this was the straw that broke the camel's back. He felt a tight band form around his forehead, like he used to get before fighting someone in his former days. He took a deep breath. "Ginny needed to get home. I stayed. I refused to leave Katie. She was too sick."

"Your sister didn't see anything immoral with a man staying with a woman overnight?"

Joseph stepped toward the bishop and backed him into the corner. Then he thought of all that Moses told him about the vote being taken. If he slugged the Bishop, the People would never let him in and once Amish, he needed to be a pacifist and turn the other cheek. He backed away and put his head down. "You know my sister is a moral woman and I did nothing immoral."

"Your sister knew you were not to be left alone with Katie. She also gave Katie a book that made her not accept a *goot* Amish man as her husband. She's leading people astray."

Reed Byler looked as shocked as Joseph was. "Bishop Mast, we're allowed to read books that aren't immoral. Classic books are allowed. Actually, I bought *Moby Dick* at Ginny's store the other day. What a whale of a story."

Reed's' attempt at a joke fell on deaf ears. "I'm going to talk to Millie and Katie about being too close with the Rowland's. They may be trusted by some Amish, but not me. My wife said her store is quite fancy inside, too. She's proud."

Joseph didn't know if he could keep his composure any longer. "Many things were gifts for her birthday. She has Amish books in the store, too."

"That's so she can lure them in to the store and talk to them about becoming Baptist, like Judah Yoder. If Judah didn't fall into the Rowlands trap, he'd have come back and repented of his sin and be Amish again." The bishop took off this hat and ran his fingers through his gray hair, and then he pointed his finger in Joseph's face. "Their store exists to trick Amish into leaving their faith."

Joseph felt nauseous. No one had talked to him like this since he was a kid; his dad. Feelings of guilt welled up inside him. Had he done something wrong again? Was he stupid to stay in the hospital with Katie? Emotions he hadn't experienced in a long time overpowered him until he felt like he was drowning. Then he prayed to his Father in heaven. The Bishop kept up his rant but Joseph kept his head down thinking of all the scripture about God's love. He thought of them over and over and didn't notice the Bishop brush past him in disgust.

~*~

The one claim I shall make for my own sex is that we love longest, when all hope is gone. Katie held the little copy of *Persuasion* to her heart. What a beautiful thought. All hope is gone for a life with Joseph, but she wouldn't marry another. Her love for Joseph was something no one could take from her. Even though they couldn't be together, she would love him and not marry, like Jane Austen. Making the decision to turn down Levi's proposal hurt her, because she did care about him, as a dear friend. She loved him almost as much as her brothers, but it went no further than friendship. She'd loved Judah long ago but something was missing: the spiritual element. She couldn't talk freely about her faith with him like she did with Joseph. Judah lacked spiritual depth, if he had any faith at all.

She heard voices in the living room. Bishop Mast! Why was he shouting at *Mamm*? Did he feel she did something wrong again? Katie got out of bed and put on her robe. She wrapped her hair up, and though still shaky, managed to get it in a bun and put on her prayer *kapp*. Katie walked down the hall into the kitchen and saw her mother crying at the oak table and the bishop towering over her. "What's wrong, *Mamm*?"

Millie motioned for Katie to come over and take a seat, but she stood dumbfounded.

The front door open and Reuben appeared. "I saw your buggy, Bishop. What's wrong?" He guided Katie over to the table and sat by his *mamm*.

"I don't want you going into the Rowland's new store, and they are not to be trusted *English* friends. They're bad apples allowed to come in our bushel and are making others rotten. Do you know they encouraged my son to leave the Amish and become Mennonite?"

Reuben looked at his *mamm* in disbelief. "He hasn't been baptized and has that right. We've known the Rowlands for ages and they admire the Amish. They've never once done anything to challenge our way of life; they encourage it." Reuben's voice shook. "My *daed* and James went coon hunting together, and me and my *brieder* tagged along. He's a *goot* man."

"Do you know Ginny encouraged Joseph to spend the night with Katie in the hospital? Even though she knew they were not to be alone. 'Avoid all appearances of evil,' my Bibles says, and an unmarried couple does not stay in the same room overnight. On top of that, Katie has turned Levi Miller's marriage proposal down." He held up his hand. "She has the right to, but I think they planned for Joseph to be alone with Katie to woo her." He looked sternly at Katie. "You were told to never be alone with him; yet you ignored my command."

The room was swirling now and Katie couldn't think. "I-I was sick. I don't remember much. Hardly anything. Joseph said he could bring a fever down with vinegar. Ginny taught him and he sponged my forehead with it."

"Only your forehead?" the Bishop said, suspicious.

"I was too sick to know. I was on medicine that knocked me out." Fatigue swept over her, but something deep inside snapped. Why was she sitting like a dumb lamb, afraid to say anything? She would not remain silent. She would not let the bishop make innuendos about her morality. "Enough! Where is your compassion? I did nothing wrong and I will confess to nothing. Do you hear me? Nothing!"

The bishop's face was beet red. His eyes were blazing with anger. "You did not listen to me. You were alone with this man, and I give you a second warning. I'll give you six weeks to repent, or I'll put you under the ban."

"I don't need six weeks. I won't repent. I did nothing wrong. *You're* doing something wrong. You're upset Noah loves Kirsten and are taking it out on the Rowlands."

"I'll give you six week to repent." He turned to Reuben and Millie. "Will you agree not to enter the Rowland's store and not be so cozy with them as friends?"

Millie stood up and stood tall. "It would be like losing a sister. Ginny's been through so much over the past year, losing her *mamm*, and she was here for me when we lost Sadie. They sold their house real cheap to their church to house homeless women and children. What's so evil about them? I find them inspiring."

"Are you reading one of her novels, too? Is she trying to contaminate your mind as well?"

Reuben stiffened and put his hand on his *mamm's* shoulder. "I think I can speak for all the Byler's. We'll not go into the store, but if the Rowland's need any help from us, we'll be here for them."

"Do not go into that store, do you hear? It's a trap to pull you out of the Amish." The Bishop spun around and left, slamming the door.

~*~

Katie heard footsteps on the porch. Exhausted after the Bishop's warning, she'd fallen asleep on the couch and could see the image of a tall man through the dim light. The bishop again? She lit the oil lamp and saw she was alone in the room. Katie opened the door; it was Joseph. As soon as she saw him, she ran into his arms. "The Bishop won't let us go into Ginny's store. He said you're all rotten apples, and he wanted me to repent of being alone with you in the hospital." Katie put her arms around Joseph's neck and clung to him. "But I won't repent. I did nothing wrong."

Joseph led Katie to the couch. "I heard through the Amish grapevine. Bishop Mast needs help." He kissed her forehead. "No more fever. That's good." Joseph held her close. "I came to ask you something. I hear you rejected Levi's marriage proposal. How did you come to make such a decision?"

" 'We love longest, when all hope is gone.' That's in *Persuasion*, the book you wanted me to read." She cupped Joseph's face in her hands. "I'll always love you. I mean forever. I just won't marry anyone, like Jane Austen." She kissed him tenderly and hugged him around his neck.

Joseph held her tight. "No one's ever loved me like you, Katie. You risk everything for me, even a chance at having an Amish family. I believe what the Amish do, but it could take years of testing before the church will let me in, and they may never let me in, now that Bishop Mast has gone around telling everyone I'm an immoral man leading you astray…I doubt they'll ever let me in."

She turned her head to kiss Joseph on the cheek, but their lips met. "You'd turn Amish for me?"

"I believe it's the path to take...no more crossroads, only a road block. Bishop Mast. I talked to Moses and he said the People in his *Gmay* won't vote me in. Bishop Mast's word carries lots of weight."

She felt his breath on hers, the warmth of his body on such a cold winter night. The memory of him was all she needed...

CHAPTER 21

$\mathcal{M}$illie looked in disbelief at Katie. She put her fork down on the table and couldn't continue eating her peach pie. "You want to move to Colorado? Katie, can't you just not see Joseph?"

Katie took a bite of pie. "I'll be shunned if I continue to be seen with him. Smicksburg's so tiny and we're always bumping into each other." Katie got up to get the coffee off the stove and poured more in her cup, then her *mamm's*. "I had a *goot* time visiting the cousins in Colorado. I know I'm welcome there."

"But it's so far. Two days by train and you'd be traveling alone. You went out west with a group before."

Katie reached across the table to hold her *mamm's* hand. "There's no other solution. Where else could I go?"

Millie sighed. "In *Die Botschaft* a few weeks ago they said they needed a teacher. Their teacher got pneumonia and had to quit. It's in the same settlement as Eli's *bruder*."

"Is it in the place where the Weavers moved to?"

"No, it's an old settlement." Millie moved her spoon in her coffee. "You know, Katie, you can't run from the *Gmay*. You need to make things right. It's part of your baptismal vow. The Bishop is being unreasonable, I'll admit, but I'm trusting the Lord will change his heart."

"What am I to confess, *Mamm*? Confess to being an immoral woman? I can't do that. It would be a lie," Katie snapped.

Millie looked at her evenly. "You've always treasured the *Gmay* more than anything, but when living in community gets hard, we don't see the beauty in it. If you go away for a while, you may see things differently. A change of scenery sometimes gives us a change of heart." Millie squeezed Katie's hand. "You love Joseph more than the community?"

"I don't know."

"*Ach*, you don't know? You do need to get away from him then. When you're away you'll come to your senses and make things right, I'm sure."

"The Bishop's insulted me in front of the entire town. He's gone crazy. Maybe New York is where I'm supposed to be permanently. If I change church districts, I'll be under a new bishop…maybe a sane one." She bit her lip and stared into her coffee. "I'll need to inquire of the job and leave as soon as possible."

"So you have no intention of making things right with Bishop Mast? It's not the Christian way. Peace needs to be made. Remember when John Miller had a fall out with his bishop and built a house on the other end of his property to get into another *Gmay*? Somehow, I always thought he lacked Christian character for that."

Katie rolled her eyes. "Bishop Mast, in time, I pray calms down, but until he does, I won't be subject to the man. He's the one with no *goot* Christian character."

"I fear sometimes you're turning from the Amish ways in your heart. Joseph is pulling you away…. you better be careful."

"*Mamm*, he is not. I'm a stronger Christian being around him. Isn't that what it's all about, being a Christian, not so much as being Amish?"

Millie put both hands over her face and groaned as if in pain. Katie went around the table to sit by her. "*Mamm*, what's wrong?"

"You don't sound Amish the way you speak. Maybe the Bishop is right. Joseph is a bad apple and it's spoiling you."

~*~

Ginny heard the little gold bell ring, announcing another customer was coming into the store. She was glad Suzy bought it for her as her birthday present; it was nice to know when to go from the back office to the front door. She told Joseph she'd be back in a minute.

"Hi Mrs. Rowland," Noah said, stomping the snow off his boots.

Ginny looked down. She was glad Suzy got her the big entry rug for people to wipe their feet, too. "How are you, Noah? I haven't seen you in so long." She hugged him. "Where have you been hiding?"

He looked at her with determined eyes. "I'd like Kirsten's address. I need to write to her."

Ginny put both hands on his shoulders. "You know I can't. Your dad won't allow it. Come on in and have some coffee. I serve it free." She led him to the cappuccino bar. "Do you want cream and sugar?"

"*Jah. Danki.*" He took off his black wool hat and brushed some snowflakes off the wide brim. "My *daed* isn't himself. He's angry I've been attending a Mennonite Church."

Ginny put the coffee on one of the little round tables and motioned for him to sit down. "You're going to the Old Order Mennonite Church in Homer City?"

"No, the one in Punxsy. It's not Old Order. Kirsten and I went there once and she liked it. When I heard about this new guy in Italy, I was literally sick." Noah hit the brim of his hat as if to get more snowflakes off, but there were none. "I looked back and felt I didn't try hard enough to make a bridge between our two…"

"Cultures?" Ginny asked. "Aidan has this problem in Dominican Republic. He tells me his struggles, and I see similarities with the Amish and us *English*. We do have a completely different culture."

"You know my *daed* thinks you crossed the line; he knows I read some of your kids' homeschooling books and you didn't stop me. He said you should have known better and you were leading me astray from my faith. He's talking to some of your closest Amish friends, asking them not to come here to the store." Noah put his head down in embarrassment. "I'm sorry, Mrs. Rowland.

"You're Dad thinks I encouraged your leaving then…" Ginny whispered. "But in your rumspringa years you could have read anything, and you're not baptized, so you're free to choose to leave." She sighed. "Millie came into Suzy's store and signed up for knitting lessons the same time as mine. She said she couldn't come to my house but she could take knitting when I did." Ginny leaned her elbows on the table. "Eli and Lottie and the Weavers are in another church district, so I don't need to worry about them…Does your Dad know you're here?"

"No, but Mrs. Rowland, I need to get Kirsten's address before it's too late. I was being bull-headed and she needs to know that, before this Romeo…I can't even say his name; it's bitter in my mouth. I really don't believe she'd be so fickle, but I need to hear it from her. There's some kind of mistake."

"I won't go against your dad's wishes. If it makes you feel better, Kirsten hasn't mentioned this Romeo again in an email. Maybe the whole thing's over. I, too, have a hard time believing Kirsten would fall for some Italian guy she hardly knows. It's just not like her."

"If you can't give me her address, can you tell her I love her in an email? I'd appreciate that. Tell her I'm becoming Mennonite."

"I'm not telling her that until I know for sure you are. It's a big jump going fancy."

Noah looked at Ginny with his big brown eyes twinkling. "She's worth the jump."

Joseph emerged from the back room. "Well put, Noah. Well, put."

~*~

Katie looked through the bus window at the snow laden mountains that were across the icy Allegheny River. She thought of the Rocky Mountains on her trip to Colorado. The Allegheny's were softer, like white feathers. Covered with trees and not rocks, she was in awe of their beauty. Ice chunks floating south, the route she wished she was taking; back home to Smicksburg. But she couldn't stay. She needed time away to make some decisions.

She hoped her letter to Joseph was clear and he saw the love in it. She couldn't live in the same small town as him, but he would live in her heart always. She looked up at the mountains; *I will lift up mine eyes unto the hills, from whence cometh my help. My help cometh from the LORD, which made heaven and earth.* Katie always felt strengthened when she saw the mountains. They showed her the magnificence of God, her creator, and that He had everything in control.

She dosed off and two hours later heard the bus driver announce their arrival in Warren. She saw stately Victorian homes, and thought of the Rowland's new house and bookstore. She missed them already. Katie gazed at the houses; some were painted in several colors. She preferred the simple white farmhouse of the Amish. Larger houses began to appear as the bus moved on, heading north. She wondered how one family lived in such big homes. Amish farms were big but they housed a dozen people.

Soon she'd be crossing the border to New York. A lump formed in her throat and tears threatened to brim over; Katie loved Pennsylvania. Even though she had no reason to dislike New York, it was just unfamiliar. She'd be living with John Hershberger and his family, but even though he was Eli's brother, they were all strangers. The further north she traveled, the colder it felt.

Katie opened her prayer book and turned to the *Rules of a Godly Life*. Her eyes fell on Rule Six:

If anyone wrongs you, bear it patiently. For if you take the wrong to heart or become angry, you hurt no one but yourself and are only doing what your enemy would like for you to do, giving him the satisfaction of seeing how annoyed you are. If you can be patient, God will in His time judge rightly and bring your innocence to light.

She closed her eyes and prayed the Lord would give her strength to forgive the Bishop. She started to pray for him, knowing you couldn't be angry with someone you're praying for.

~*~

Joseph stomped the snow off his boots and went to his Amish rocker to read the letter he got in the mail:

My Dear Joseph,

When you read this I'll be most likely be in a new state, having accepted a teaching position in New York. I hope you understand why I left without saying good-bye. When I'm with you I never want to leave. I've asked Mamm to not give you my address and this is nothing against you. You've had your time alone at your little house and I believe this time in NY will be my time to find some solitude, because I'm at a crossroads now, too. I'm confused. I feel torn from my Amish roots; maybe God wants me to leave to be with you. Maybe I should just remain single. I don't know. I just believe there's something in NY he wants to show me.

I love you Joseph....I'm standing at the crossroads and looking for direction. Jeremiah 6:16

Katie

He gasped for air, not realizing he'd been holding his breath. Katie felt too far away. He reread the letter. '*...maybe God wants me to leave to be with you*'? Joseph banged his head up against the back of his rocker. She couldn't leave the Amish. Her Amish ways are what he loved about her. Joseph ran and grabbed his down jacket and headed over to see Eli and Moses. He needed to try to be Amish, even though Bishop Mast made his name as good as mud.

~*~

Anna poured coffee into Levi's cup. "Son, I'm glad you found out what kind of girl Katie Byler is before you married her. She was seen more than one time with that outsider. Someone saw them kissing at her place, right on that fancy couch the Rowlands gave Millie."

"What are you talking about, *Mamm*?"

"Someone walking down the road saw through the window. They were kissing late at night, most likely when Millie went to bed. Sins are done in darkness, you know."

Levi was stunned. "Leah said Katie went to visit Joseph even though she wasn't supposed to. No one wanted to say anything, since Katie's a nice girl."

"Was a nice girl until she got tangled in with an *Englisher*. I'm glad she won't be mothering any of my grandchildren," Anna said, bitterly.

"*Mamm*, it's not like you to talk so," Levi said. "I know full well you hoped Katie and I would be wed come spring. But I have to say, since she rejected my proposal, I'm free to be with another."

Anna's eyebrows shot up. "Leah?"

"The first time I met her I was taken, but I was courting Katie. I thought it was just infatuation, but the more time I spent chopping wood with her, I started to see she had qualities Katie didn't have. She's more my type, so spunky, bringing me out of my shyness. We've laughed so much during our wood chopping competitions; I can't even remember when I had so much fun." He took a swig of coffee and smiled. "She's a gem. I pushed Katie for an answer, thinking if she said yes, I'd forget Leah. Maybe Katie knew deep down I only felt friendship toward her."

"So you'll be courting Leah?" Anna clasped her hands and sighed.

"*Jah*, I told her everything about me trying to hold back my feelings for her. It was so easy to talk to her. She fits me like a shoe."

"Well, the garden was twice as big this past year and we have plenty put up to feed everyone a nice spring wedding dinner."

"Hold on, *Mamm*. I didn't say we're getting married this spring. Please don't be telling everyone about Leah and me. It's too close to my courtship with Katie."

"A courtship I'm sure glad is over," Anna muttered.

~*~

Ginny sat down so she wouldn't faint. "You're going to try to be Amish? What does that mean? How do you try to be Amish?"

"I have to prove myself over time that I can live without modern conveniences," Joseph said. "I didn't even know that when I went into my Walden Pond, no electricity experiment. I need to go without a car now and see if I can handle it."

"Honey, I know you love Katie, but are you serious? Be Amish!"

"She's worth the jump, just like Noah said about Kirsten. He's young and met the right girl. I'm thirty-six, but it isn't too late to have what I want: a family with the girl I love. I don't know if this makes any sense." Joseph shifted in his chair. "I see something in Noah I've been lacking. He's young and daring and I'm getting old and set in my ways."

James leaned forward. "Bishop Mast has practically banned the Amish from having any contact with us. Could you submit to authority like that? You can't go church hopping in the Amish."

"As far as not talking to you, only the people in Bishop Mast's church district are affected. If over time, a person, even the Bishop is out of line, he'll be asked to repent by a member and from what Moses told me, it's common. The leaders are supposed to be servants, not dictators. Moses is talking to Bishop Mast about his behavior." Joseph grinned. "Moses is going around to all the people in his church district asking for their vote; he said he feels like a politician."

"Okay, so you need to make a baptismal vow and the People have to vote you in. Is that all?" Ginny asked.

"Well, I'll be giving up my Jeep, cell phone, and computer. I can't work on your online store anymore, but I can still do construction with you, James."

"March is a slow month, so don't worry...but no phone?" James asked in disbelief. "How will we contact you?"

"Drive over in your car. Most likely I'll be home studying for my baptism classes, even though Moses said

I know most of the material since he's been teaching me without me knowing it," Joseph grinned again.

Ginny's eyes misted. "You've found a real dad in him, huh?"

"Yes. I'm surprised what a difference it makes; it's a bond I've never known. Maybe I understand how much you two mean to Judah."

James looked at Ginny and put his arm around her. "He is like a son to us. God's been healing his heart in the oddest ways, too; Amish forgiving him of something he didn't do, and a relationship with a single mom whose little girl loves him like a daddy."

"He's had a lot to work through, getting over Katie, of all things. I know I never could," Joseph said. "I'm sure hoping to marry Katie as soon as I'm Amish. Don't mention to Millie or any of the Bylers about me crossing over to the Amish. Most likely they'd be writing to Katie and I don't want her upset if I'm not accepted. The Hershberger's and Weavers know the whole plan and said they won't be saying anything to her either."

James got up and shook Joseph's hand. "I bet you never guessed all this would happen when you came here to Smicksburg. Crossing over to the Amish, as you put it."

Ginny got up and hugged her brother. "I know from my friendships with the Amish, nothing will change between us, *jah*?"

Joseph squeezed Ginny tight. "*Jah.*"

CHAPTER 22

Katie wore two pairs of black wool stockings and was still cold. She put on her new boots that went up to her knees, and slowly stomped though the deep snow to get to the outhouse. On this freezing March night, she wished she was back home in Smicksburg; she'd never seen so much snow and the wind blew the chilly air right through her. When she returned to the house, she went immediately to the large woodstove, rubbing her hands against each other to get warm. She thought about her new students. The children were all so eager to learn and accepted her immediately, even though they talked about their former teacher fondly.

Katie thought of little Timmy. A little five year old who lost his *mamm* in a house fire last year. His father, Matthew, was such a loving, doting father. They looked so much alike; both having blonde hair and blue eyes. Timmy was so attached to his teacher and now he wouldn't be seeing her as much. She bowed her head and prayed for the little student who captured her heart.

She went back up to bed and climbed under the heavy quilts. She loved the Hershberger family already; all five children were adorable. Katie was glad to be of help cooking supper after school, since Deborah was so busy with a new baby. John told her she was working too hard, but it was good to work; it kept her mind off of home…and Joseph.

She tried to sleep, but images of Bishop Mast kept coming to her, shaking his finger at her, calling her an immoral woman. The clock on her nightstand ticked away as did the night and still no sleep. Katie reached for the stationary and pen she kept in the nightstand drawer to write a letter to the Bishop.

Bishop Mast,

I'm settling in here at Cherry Creek. I am praying to see if there is anything in me that needs repenting. I left my home to be away from the man I know I can't marry. This has been difficult to say the least. The charge of me being alone with Joseph multiple times is true but I've don't nothing sinful. If I was courting an Amish man, it would be considered wonderful, at my age, to find love. I just fell for an outsider. Ginny is a good woman and I hope in time, your pain of Noah leaving the Amish will be over and you'll be able to see clearly it wasn't the Rowlands who made him cross the line and go behind your back to the Mennonites; it was for love.

I pray for you daily,
Katie

She bowed her head and prayed for the bishop. Bitter thoughts toward him were giving her sleepless nights, and she knew she'd only overcome these feeling by praying for, and being nice to, the man who was making her life miserable.

~*~

Bishop Mast looked at the clock on his nightstand. He just couldn't sleep lately. He looked over at his wife of forty years. He loved Sarah with his whole heart. They'd been through so much together, raising the four boys. Gideon's rumspringa days were hard on them both. When Gideon told his *mamm* of the *English* girlfriend, Sarah cried all night, and nothing comforted her, yet she slept soundly now. They both liked Kirsten, but his son being Mennonite and driving a car? Gideon's old girlfriend was not like Kirsten in morals. Isabelle was what the *English* called a loose goose. Oh, how he'd worried about Gideon and Isabelle having a child out of wedlock. He remembered Gideon's face when he threatened him with excommunication, even though he wasn't baptized, and it worked. He couldn't help but think Gideon had married a girl he truly didn't love, but he was Amish and that's what mattered. He thought of Katie. He only wanted the same for her. He prayed she'd find a good Amish man in New York to love. Now he had to pray for Millie and what he needed to do tomorrow.

~*~

"*Goot* morning, Bishop," Millie said. "Would you like some coffee?"

"I'm not here on a pleasant task," he said as he stepped inside the little *dawdyhaus*. "I hear you're going to the Rowland's. Your buggy's been seen outside their store."

"Well, I go to the knitting circle at SuzyB Knits," Millie said, evenly.

"*Jah*, I know. My Sarah won't be going anymore. Too much *English* influence. I'm asking you to do the same. Quit going to that knitting circle."

Millie sat down in her Amish rocker and gripped the hand rest. Fury rose within her, and she bit her bottom lip, afraid of losing control.

"Are you reading any more of those trashy novels?" the Bishop continued.

"I read only *goot* things...Bishop. *Goot* novels are allowed."

Bishop Mast leaned over her. "Have you heard from your wayward daughter?"

Millie thought of all the times Katie was with her to comfort her in distressing times, and her stomach tightened. She swallowed a large lump forming in her throat. The Bishop was calling her dear daughter wayward. How much could she take before she told the bishop what she really thought? "Yes, I've heard from my dear daughter. She's adjusting to New York. She loves the children in the school."

"I wrote the Hershberger's about her lack of morals and to warn them to keep an eye on her. Of course Eli told his brother the opposite!" the Bishop fumed. "I just came from their place and Moses told me to my face I was acting like a heathen, of all things. If he was in my church district, he'd be getting a warning, Senior Bishop or not."

"Moses is concerned for my daughter's reputation. Being her *mamm*, I am, too. She is not a worldly girl and you know it. She's not like that *English* lady that almost won Gideon's heart long ago."

The Bishop glared at her and then grew quiet.

"I remember it well. Sarah was afraid he'd get his old girlfriend pregnant because Gideon was immoral in those days. How many times were they caught kissing and the Lord knows what else…?"

"This has nothing to do with Gideon, and my son isn't immoral now."

"Katie never was…"

The Bishop's eyes were ablaze with fury. "Katie loving an *Englisher* could cause other young Amish girls to do the same! Satan can come as an angel of light, as the Bible says."

Millie stood up and stomped her foot. "I'll be asking you kindly to leave, Bishop. Your past with your son Gideon, and now Noah wanting to be Mennonite, has made a bitter root spring up in you again. You're hurt, and hurt people need someone to blame. But, you've targeted my daughter to take out your rage and I'll be praying the Lord forgives you."

To her surprise the bishop stopped talking and slowly walked outside and gently closed the door. She could see as he walked down to his buggy his head was down, bowed in shame?

~*~

Judah and Maria each took one of Lilly's hands to swing her across the mud puddle. She begged them to do it again when they got to another one. "Wee, there she flies." Judah said and they helped her over the many mud puddles along the road. Amish buggies were out with the nice change in temperature, and they all waved at Judah fondly. Even though they all knew now he didn't hit Eli, they were all friendly toward him again. Maybe it was the change in him they liked, or maybe his Christian faith made him see them differently.

"Judah, lift me up," Lilly chimed.

"Okay, Sweetie Pie. This puddle's as big as a pond." He looked over at Maria. Even though he'd only dated her a little over two months, he loved her. Her countenance had completely changed. Her eyes no longer were filled with fear and rejection. He wanted to tell her he loved her, but didn't want to scare her. No, he'd be patient and wait until she was more comfortable in the relationship.

"Are we there yet?" Lilly asked.

"It's right ahead, honey." Judah said, pointing to the Old Smicksburg Park. "Lots of dry land there to fly kites." He winked at Maria, who winked back. They entered the playground and saw the cement floor already had hopscotch marks on it with chalk. Lilly ran to the swing and asked to be pushed. Maria pushed her while

Judah worked at untangling the string; all three strings had gotten tied up in a knot.

Maria walked over to Judah and saw the mess. "A three strand cord is not easily broken."

Judah turned and encircled her in his arms. "Sounds like words of wisdom."

"It's from the Bible. Granny Weaver shared it with me. She said I need more steady relationships in my life because on my own, I'm easily broken. But a cord is made of at least three strings, woven together. It's strong and can't be broken." She leaned forward to kiss Judah. "Granny's teaching me to knit… and said I need to be knit together in love…"

Judah leaned to kiss her and whispered, "I think I love you." As soon as he said it, shock registered on his face. "I'm sorry. I'm impulsive."

"I love you, too…" she said.

~*~

Katie looked out the window at the sparkling snow on the ground. "This is unbelievable," she said, turning to Deborah. "How can there be this much snow in March?"

"It's lake effect snow. So much moisture off Lake Erie comes swooping over us and we get dumped on with snow. Sit down, Katie. You look so tired." Deborah motioned for her to sit on the Amish bench across from her. She continued to nurse her baby. "Do you know the Bible calls the snow a treasure? 'Hast thou entered into the treasures of the snow?'"

Katie curled her toes in her black leather boots. "A cold treasure. How about buggy accidents? Are they common?"

"Not really. We don't get much ice, only snow on top of snow. I have to admit, after Eli's accident I was a bit nervous, but I won't let it hold me back." She smiled at her *boppli*. "Think you'll ever settle down and marry and have children?"

Katie looked into Deborah's light blue eyes. Such a pool of tranquility. She was so content and happy being a *mamm*. "I doubt I'll ever marry."

"Well, I think Matthew's taken a liking to you. His dear wife dying in that house fire was enough to threaten any man's faith, but not Matthew's. He and Timmy are coming over for dinner tonight." She lifted up the *boplli* to pat her back.

"They only need a *goot* Amish *mamm, jah*?" Katie said, surprising herself at her cynicism. "I'm sorry, Deborah, really I am. I'm just so tired of widowed men who want a wife to raise their children."

"The Bishop wrote us quite a long letter about you, how you turned down a proposal of a *goot* Amish widower…." Deborah said hesitantly. "Look at it like God's given you a new start here. Don't let the past hold you back."

"But I love Joseph," Katie said as she picked up the yarn in the basket next to her and started to knit.

"Yes, the Bishop also mentioned Joseph, the *Englisher*. There can be no future with this Joseph since he's not Amish. Matthew loved his wife, but he's moving on." She raised her brow. "You know that, right?"

"*Jah*, I suppose."

"Ach, enough talk about this. I haven't cooked in the weeks you've been here and I'm grateful. I'd like to cook tonight, though."

"*Danki*," Katie said as she continued to knit. She thought of Ginny coming over to learn to knit to get over her grief. She needed to knit now more than ever.

~*~

Matthew and Timmy arrived at six sharp. Their cheeks were red from the cold and they got warmed up by the stove in the living room. Katie had lost track of time knitting and was embarrassed to be doing a craft while Deborah set the table. "What're you making?" Matthew asked.

"Scarves for friends back home. They're for Christmas presents," she said.

"You're a bit late," Matthew said, blue eyes sparkling at her.

"Oh, they're for next year," Katie laughed. "They wouldn't need scarves now anyhow because it's too warm in Smicksburg."

"Seriously?" Matthew asked. "March is one of our hardest months. We'll see spring in late May and plant in early July."

"We plant in April with covers over the plants." Katie sighed. "Right now it's kite-flying time."

"Living so close to the lake makes our winters longer. *Goot* for us, *jah*? More snowmen, ice skating, and sleigh rides." He paused. "Have you ever gone on a sleigh ride before?"

"*Jah*, I have, a few times. Not many have sleighs, so it was a treat."

"I'd be happy to take you out on a ride. We'll have snow like this for a while…What do you say, a sleigh ride sometime this weekend?"

Katie was embarrassed because she knew she was blushing profusely. She opened her mouth, but nothing came out. She was glad when Deborah yelled that dinner was ready.

They all took their places at the long oak trundle table. John was at the head and Deborah was to his right. The children filed in and Katie, Matthew and Timmy sat at the far end. Deborah brought out a large pot and sat it on the table. The children licked their lips as she ladled the rabbit stew into each person's bowl. Then she turned to get the biscuits out of her woodstove.

"It feels so *goot* to be back in the kitchen," Deborah said, smiling contently.

Sadness washed over Katie. This is what she wanted, a family. Well, maybe she would have to have an *English* one, if she left the Amish.

John cleared his throat. "I got a letter from my *bruder* today. He's adjusting well to being a paraplegic. We should go down and visit Smicksburg in the spring. You *kinner* can learn a lot from your Uncle Eli."

"I have a second uncle who lived down there, but he's long gone," Matthew said. "He had three boys who all left the Amish. It's a sad story."

Katie turned to him in disbelief. "I thought you looked like someone I know. Is Judah Yoder your cousin?"

"I only know my uncle's name was Hezekiah. Never met him, have you?"

"*Jah*, I have. I grew up with his kids, and one of them married my *bruder*. I thought you reminded me of someone and now I know who: Judah Yoder."

"They were engaged," John piped in, grinning. "We know everything through Eli and the circle letters."

Katie pursed her lips. "It was long ago. I do know Judah's tormented about his family, though. Any information about his *brieder* would be helpful."

"How would you know, Katie?" Deborah asked. "Judah is shunned so you don't talk to him, *jah*?"

"We have trusted *English* friends who are friends with him. He's a changed man. Gave his heart to the Lord, saying his parents never taught him about the Bible in the home. So when he came to Smicksburg, my friends started teaching him. He's Baptist now."

"That's unusual," Matthew said. "We Amish take that as our highest responsibility to teach our young the ways of God. Uncle Hezekiah failed miserably at his most important job."

Katie was stunned by his comment. He was a man who took God's Word seriously. A man not bitter by tragedy.

After dinner, Matthew asked Katie if she'd like to go on a sleigh ride and then ice skating. She said yes.

~*~

Dear Mom,

I can't hide it anymore in my emails. I'm homesick. I love Italy, but there's no place like home. I was going to stay until May but I'd like to come home sooner. I've learned all I can at the Riccia bakery and from Angelina. I've changed my flight without charge for April 1st. This is not an April Fool's Day joke, so please pick me up at the airport…haha. I know April Fool's is huge at our house and I want to be home for this one. I think you'll see hands down, that I tricked everyone the best this year.

Mom, I'll be bringing Romeo home with me if it's okay. He already bought his ticket, actually. I know we lack room now, so maybe he can live with Uncle Joseph if he's alright with it. Is he still living with no electricity? I bet he isn't. If he can come to the airport with you and Dad, it would be great.

Love you more than you love me!
Kirsten

Ginny squealed from the back office and she heard a customer gasp. She poked her head through the velvet curtain. "Sorry everyone! I just got an email from my daughter. She's coming home sooner than I thought." James smiled broadly at her and then rang up a customer.

CHAPTER 23

*J*acob and Sarah Mast walked into SuzyB Knits, the little gold bell announcing their arrival. The store was empty, except for one customer. "Hello there. Sarah. Bishop." She turned to Sarah. "I haven't seen you in two weeks."

"I'm *goot*, Suzy. Spring is in the air and Jacob and I were over getting some fudge at the Sampler." Sarah attempted to smile. "Is everyone coming to the knitting circle?"

"All but you and we miss you."

"Ginny is in the group and I won't have Sarah keeping company with a deceitful woman," Jacob said evenly.

Suzy gawked at the Bishop. "Ginny Rowland? Immoral?"

"She hasn't told you about my warning to my flock?"

Suzy took her knitting and sat down. "No. She's not a gossip."

The little gold bell rang again and it was Ginny. Suzy took in a deep breath. Ginny said hello to Jacob and Sarah, and excused herself for interrupting. "Suzy, I have good news, but I'll sit here and wait until you're done." She looked at Sarah. "We've missed you at knitting circle. Where've you been?"

"Come Sarah," Jacob said. "She'll fill your head with nonsense, too."

Sarah looked at Jacob firmly. "I know my own mind and it's not Ginny's fault Noah doesn't want to be Amish."

Jacob took off his black hat and picked at lint that wasn't there. "She does it subtly, luring people away, like Satan, and I won't have it."

Ginny got up. "I'm a Christian, Jacob, and you know that I love the Amish. You're taking your anger out on me. When my mom had her stroke years ago, I blamed the doctors and yelled at them. I needed to blame someone. Give your pain to God."

"Who are you to talk about God?" Jacob said, belligerently. "You stay away from my family."

Sarah looked at Jacob in disbelief. "We'll be talking at home about this. Suzy and Ginny, I hope to see you next knitting circle."

~*~

Judah put his arm around Maria at the movies. The scent of her perfume was intoxicating. He kissed her on the cheek. She turned her head and kissed him back.

"Sitting in the back row has its advantages, huh?" Judah said. He leaned over to kiss her again. "I never meant to tell you I loved you so soon," he whispered in her ear. "It just came out, so natural like."

"What's surprising is I'm not afraid. There's something so different in this relationship." She leaned over to kiss him.

"I've never loved anyone like the way I love you. I know I was engaged twice, but I'm serious. Something was lacking in me, I suppose. The Lord's given me a great love for you, Maria. I was selfish in other relationships. It was all about me."

"Remember, a three strand cord isn't broken. We have three in this relationship, and I don't mean Lilly. It's you, me and God. He's the glue holding us together maybe?"

Judah cupped her cheeks in his hands and kissed her. "I'd be honored to have four in the relationship. Me, you, Lilly, and God. We could be a family."

"What are you saying, Judah?"

"Marry me." He searched her eyes for fear, but found none, only tears.

"We'll need to run this past Jerry and Janice first, to get the right timing. But yes, Judah, I could marry no other. I love you so much."

~*~

Jerry and Janice sat on the blue checkered couch in shock. "Say that again," Jerry said.

"We're engaged," Judah said, nervously "I know I'm full of surprises, but I asked Maria to marry me and she said yes."

"So where's the ring?" Janice asked.

"I didn't buy it yet. But I will." He planted a big kiss on Maria's cheek and pulled her close.

Jerry's eyes bulged. "Are you saying you proposed on impulse? I mean to not have a ring?"

"You don't approve, do you?" Maria asked.

Jerry put his hand up. "It's not that at all. You're both great people, but you both have baggage from the past. Unpacking that baggage takes time, or you bring it right into your marriage. Are you willing to give this engagement at least a year to have time to unload?"

"You think it's necessary?" Judah asked. "A year's a long time."

"No, being married is a long time," Janice said. "You need time to prepare, too. Maria, you deserve a nice wedding. Going to nursing school and planning a wedding will keep you so busy the time will fly right by."

"Judah, you need to establish yourself further, too. You decided against college and are doing construction and remodeling with James and Joseph, correct? No change in plans?" Jerry asked.

"No change. We're the Three Musketeers."

"Okay, sounds like we have a plan. So you're getting married next spring?"

"Next March, one year from today," Judah said, grinning.

Jerry and Janice got up and hugged the beaming couple.

~*~

Katie was bundled up, waiting inside for Matthew. "I'm so afraid," she admitted to Deborah.

"Afraid you might fall in love again and get hurt?" she asked.

She pointed to her heart. "Joseph will be here forever."

Deborah stopped rolling pie dough and turned to Katie. "Please don't take this wrong, but isn't that the place where God should be, not a man? I love John, but it's the Lord who gives me love for John in the first place."

Katie's brow furrowed. "I don't think I've put Joseph before the Lord. I hope not." She heard Matthew's sleigh pull in. "I'll be thinking about what you just said…." She walked outside to greet Matthew.

"Hello Katie. We have a *goot* sunny day today."

"*Jah*," Katie said. "But I'm not up to ice skating, so I won't be bringing my skates, if that's alright."

"That's fine." He took her hand and helped her into the sleigh and then hopped in on his side. He brought up the fur buggy robe. "Are you warmer now?"

"Very. This fur is so warm."

"*Jah*, it is, but I put a bag of hot potatoes under the seat, too."

"This is amazing. Now I think I can enjoy myself. I get cold so easily." She put the buggy robe up to her chin and they were off. They pulled onto Meyers Road and turned left onto County Road 40.

"What do you think?" Matthew asked.

"It's so smooth. We have too many stones sticking through the snow back home, but I don't see a rock in sight. And with fewer houses, you see the snow all the more. People live so far apart here."

"We're dairy farmers, so we need more land. I have five hundred acres. I almost sold it all last year but decided to stay. A new house was built last summer by the People and I have *goot* help on the farm."

"You must have lots of cows to milk with that much land."

"It keeps me busy and I like that," Matthew said with a smile. "So why don't you want to ice skate? I'm on the ice all the time."

She thought of Joseph saving her life, but willed him out of her mind. "I fell through the ice the last time I went and I haven't skated since." She looked down. "I'm afraid and don't care to skate."

"Well, I have another set of skates at home if you change your mind and I won't let you fall in," he said. "I fell in as a kid and it took me a while to overcome my fear. But I did and I went ice fishing a year later on Chautauqua Lake. My *daed* always told me never to let my fears hold me back. I'll always remember him saying, 'Don't look back like Lot's wife.'" He chuckled. "As a kid I was always afraid of turning into salt."

Katie laughed. "My *daed* used to say the same. He's been gone almost six years now."

"My Dead's been gone five. My *mamm* passed on when I was a wee kid, so I was especially close to my *daed*."

"I'm sorry," Katie said. "So you understand Timmy like no one else can. Didn't your *daed* ever remarry?"

"He did, but my *step-mamm* didn't want much to do with me. She couldn't have children and I suppose she thought I was in the way." Katie noticed shadows darken his eyes, but he quickly cheered up. "So, do you like the snow or wish you were flying kites back home?"

"The snow is magical, actually. I've never seen snow drifts in pasture land before. The wind swirling across it makes it look like sand along a beach. It would make some wonderful pictures."

"That's an odd thing for an Amish woman to say," Matthew teased. "Can you take pictures in your *Gmay*?"

Katie thought of her first time out with Joseph. The fear that gripped him at the schoolhouse, how he thought of the Nickel Back school shootings and his post-traumatic stress made him panic. He'd overcome his fears since he moved to Smicksburg. Again, she willed him out of her mind. "I have an English friend who's a photographer. He's working on a calendar. He takes Amish farm scenes."

"The *English* world is so fast paced. They don't seem to have much community and I think they look at the Amish and admire our barn raisings and whatnot...I wish everyone could live on a farm, where life is nice and slow."

Katie felt anger rise within her. She loved the Amish community as long as it was led by a loving bishop. But you could have no peace, even on a farm, with a harsh bishop. She prayed for Bishop Mast as soon as the bitter thought came. Katie took a deep breath and turned to look at the farmhouses along the way.

She wasn't nervous at all out on the roads since they were straight. The land was flat between the mountains, unlike Smicksburg with its rolling hills and ever bending roads. In Cherry Creek, a car could see a buggy in plenty of time to stop.

They turned right onto Seeger Road. When they came to the crest of the hill, she gasped. Large farms dotted the landscape as far as she could see. Smoke coming from their chimneys reaching for the blue sky. Black and Red Angus cows threw snow into the air with their heads as they plodded along. No cars were on the roads, unlike Smicksburg. She thought of her favorite view from her pond; this one, she had to admit was prettier.

"Where's the town?" Katie asked. "Where do the tourists shop?"

"Ellington is seven miles to the west and Randolph is seven miles to the south. Folks drive down from Buffalo, but we don't see many tourists out in the country."

They continued on Seeger Road and soon Matthew glided right onto Snow Hill Road. He pulled into the first farm in sight, on the right. "This is my place," he said, beaming.

Katie saw a large white house; dark blue curtains peeked out from each window. Across the street was a red barn close to the road. Beyond it was a vast fence enclosed with barbwire that extended to a ridge. "Is this all yours?"

"I have twenty acres around the house and five hundred across the street," he said. "Want to see the barn?" Without waiting for an answer, he took her hand to help her out of the sleigh and they walked across the street to the barn. She slipped, but he caught her. When they entered the barn, he took in a deep breath and sighed. "I'm more at home in this barn than in my house."

"The barns back home are similar in shape, but not this big."

"I guess most Amish barns are the same. I haven't traveled much," he said. "I just know the beams up above come from some tall trees; each beam is a tree." He rubbed his hands together. "Let's go in and get warmed up. The pond is in the back, just waiting for us to skate on it, if you change your mind." He helped Katie across the street and up the long flight of stairs to his house.

When he opened the door, Katie saw that everything was blue, white or black: white walls, blue curtains, and a huge black wood burning stove. A large oak trundle table was in the dining room along with a matching china closet. "It's such a beautiful room. It still smells of fresh oak."

"I just got done making the table and china closet, that's why."

"You made this? I thought you were a dairy farmer, not a carpenter." She put her hand on the table to feel the smooth surface. "You could make a living selling dining room sets like this."

"I'm a farmer, though. This table comes with its dreams, but selling furniture is not one of them." He put the black kettle of water on the woodstove. "*Goot*, I still have a fire going. Just need to go out back and get more wood. Sit down and I'll be right back."

Katie looked around the house. It was so clean for a man living without a wife. She wondered how he did it all; work, be a father, cook and clean. He entered the room with several logs in his arms. The stove was big enough to put four in easily. "So, how does a man keep such a big house clean?" she asked.

"Well, I'm alone a lot. It's only Timmy and me. Not much to mess up the place. I can *redd* up the rooms in a few minutes."

"But it gets dusty, especially with using a woodstove. Ashes need swept up and taken out. Windows need cleaning. You're a modest man."

"I'm a lonely man," Matthew said as he stacked the extra logs by the woodstove for future use. "I suppose I have nothing better to do."

Katie felt for this kind, gentle man. He'd lost so much, yet he didn't carry an ounce of self-pity. "No family nearby?"

"An uncle and some cousins…"

"I have eight *brieder*. I'm smack dab in the middle and have felt like a second *mamm* to them all my life, until they married. I have over seventy nieces and nephews last count."

"Why'd you never marry?"

"Well, I was engaged to Judah Yoder, like you know. After that I just felt comfortable being single."

"So for ten years you never thought of marrying? A pretty girl like you should have been snatched up by now."

Katie felt her cheeks grow warm. "Well, I've turned down a few fellas. I really enjoy living with my *mamm*. We're best friends…"

Matthew got up to get the hot water off the stove, and then went into the kitchen to get the sandwiches he'd made out of the icebox. "Do you want black tea or herbal?"

"Black tea is fine."

He came out with the sandwiches and a mug of tea. "*Danki*, Matthew," she said. When he handed her the mug, their hands met, then their eyes, but Katie quickly looked away. They ate the ham and cheese sandwiches and drank enough tea to warm up.

"So, do we skate or not?" he asked. "I have ice skates that would probably fit you."

"Your wife's skates, *jah*?" Katie asked, sympathetically.

"She loved to skate. I have *goot* memories of us skating but I don't want to turn to salt."

Katie grinned. "Me neither. Let's see if the skates fit."

Matthew ran up the stairs to get them. Katie felt nervous to skate though. She remembered how cold she was when she regained consciousness; she remembered Joseph warming her up in his arms too. The tug on her heart for Joseph was painful. Would this ever go away? Was it right to love someone this much? Did she love Joseph more than God? What if she was married to Joseph, and he died; would she be able to go on living, like Matthew? She could see in him something she didn't have: the Lord first place in her life.

Matthew ran down the steps with his wife's white skates. He took off her boots and put the skates on. They fit her perfectly. They headed out to the pond behind the house. She was plowing her way through the deep the snow, and Matthew picked her up as if she were a feather and carried her to the pond. She was glad it wasn't far from the house, being in the arms of a stranger, but a nice one, nevertheless. They joined hands and skated around the pond.

~*~

Joseph slouched as he sat on the log near his fishing hole. He looked over at the barn and wondered if he should use the original farmhouse's foundation. He thought of Katie's greenhouses. They could be moved further back on the property.

Dread about their future together gripped him. Moses got a letter saying she was friends with Judah's cousin, of all things. And he looked like Judah, too. A widower with a little boy living on a big dairy farm. What Amish girl wouldn't want that? He promised not to tell Katie of his plan to be Amish until the *Gmay* took the vote, next month. Maybe he should have Moses write to tell her, but what if they didn't vote him in? He had a reputation of being immoral with Katie.

Joseph learned to bow his head in prayer when life seemed to overwhelm him. He closed his eyes, praying until he felt peace in his soul. He prayed for the Lord to direct Katie's heart, hopefully, toward him and not Matthew Yoder.

~*~

Matthew tried to twirl Katie on the ice, but she tripped over her skates and started to fall. He caught her and their eyes met and held. "You're a *wunderbar goot* girl, Katie. So easy to talk to." He leaned in close to her. "I haven't had this much fun in months."

Katie couldn't believe what a nice man Matthew was, and his blue eyes showed warmth she hadn't seen in a man since she briefly saw Joseph a month ago. The closer he drew near, the more she thought of Joseph, and then Deborah saying no man should have the throne of her heart except the Lord. His hands warmed her cheeks and before she knew it their lips were almost touching, but she pushed him back, and thought of Joseph.

"I'm sorry for being too forward," Matthew said, releasing her.

Katie burst into tears. "I'm confused. I'm not on *goot* terms with my *Gmay* over...." She couldn't talk, she just sobbed.

"Over an *Englisher* who won your heart, *jah*? Deborah told me all about it." He drew Katie to himself like a child and held her head against his chest. "You're Amish and need to move on, as painful as life is. There's not future with an outsider."

CHAPTER 24

G̲inny looked across the knitting circle at Granny Weaver. "Your so-called 'casting off prayers' seem to be getting answered. I know how worried you were about Judah and Maria, and things are really working out."

"I can make myself sick with worry. I used to say I loved people too much, but then I had to call it for what is was: not trusting God. It was like I was saying to God, 'I love them more than you and I know what's best.'" She chuckled. "Ach, when Judah came back, I had his and Katie's wedding all planned, and I'm not even her *mamm*."

Millie nodded. "I felt the same way. Was hoping Judah would repent and come back to the Amish way."

"Well, he's in the Baptist way now, and we're both Christian, *jah*?" Ginny grinned.

"*Jah*," Millie said, nudging Ginny.

Suzy got up and looked out the window. "Seems like Sarah won't be making it; Jacob Mast needs a good spanking."

Granny Weaver slowly looked up at Suzy. "I won't be hearing slander about a bishop, even though he's not my own."

"*Ach*, you have to admit he's lost his mind," Millie said.

"Does he know Joseph is trying to be Amish?"

"*Jah*, and is asking the People to not let him in. He's jaded by the past."

Ginny thought of Katie so far away, but she could easily drive up to see her. Tell her how hard Joseph was trying to be Amish, but she promised her brother not to interfere. She thought of all the rejection her brother received at her father's hand, and now he might feel totally rejected by an entire community. The more she thought, the faster she knit. She thought of Noah and how devastated he'd be to see Kirsten with Romeo.

"Cast all your cares on the Lord, Ginny. He cares for you," Granny Weaver said. "I see worry in those eyes of yours."

"Can we pray for Joseph and Kirsten? They're both at such crossroads in their life and I'm afraid they'll take the wrong turn."

"Let's join hands," Suzy said. "We can pray about this, and Sarah, too. It would be so hard to live with such a miserable, nasty husband."

Granny Weaver cleared her throat. "Let's pray, shall we?"

~*~

Jacob gawked as Noah came into his house with his fancy clothes. Sarah patted his hand and he remembered their talk and tried to calm down. He wiped his sweaty palms on his pants and put his elbows on the table. "So, ah, what did you learn at church today?"

"The Golden Rule."

"Therefore all things whatsoever ye would that men should do to you, do ye even so to them: for this is the law and the prophets. Matthew 7:12. I know it well, though I've been a poor example of it lately," he said, taking a swig of coffee. "I've confessed my sin of pride to the People today. It's the beginning of our five week communion preparation, and I need to lead by example. Confession is *goot* for the soul." He reached over to put his hand on Sarah's. "When you find a *goot* wife to keep you in line, it's a *goot* thing." He felt a knot in his stomach. "If you find that in a nice Mennonite girl like Kirsten, I'll not be threatening you like I have been. It was wrong of me, since you're not baptized into the church. Forgive me son."

"I forgive you, *Daed*," Noah said. "Forgive me of my anger toward you over these past months." He got up and went over to his *daed* to shake hands and give him a holy kiss. "I'm thankful for my Amish upbringing; you know that, don't you *Mamm* and *Daed*?"

"It's the best way to live, but if you're choosing another, I'll love you either way. You're always welcome to eat at the table with us," Jacob said, then bent over to cough.

"*Danki, Daed.* It means a lot." He went back to his seat. "Are things better with the Rowland's and Katie Byler, too?"

"I was wrong to blame the Rowlands and I'll be apologizing. Ginny was right; I was taking my pain out on her. She's a nice lady. Like mother, like daughter," he said. "But the issue with Katie Byler is not resolved. The way I approached it was severe and I wrote her to know she can come and confess to her bishop who isn't so...hostile. But she's been a bad example to the young girls, putting an *Englisher* over the *Gmay*."

"*Daed*, you do know Joseph is trying to be Amish, *jah*?"

Jacob clasped his hand on the table. "Moses mentioned this to me, but the old rascal's always up to something. He encouraged Katie to refuse Levi's marriage proposal, something I find hard to forgive. I know Moses lost his wife and sees love as a more precious gift now, but he encouraged Katie to visit Joseph at his place." Jacob struggled to hide his grin. "Do you know he dumped out all the coffee in the compost pit one night so they wouldn't have coffee in the morning? He asked Katie to go over and borrow some from Joseph." He cleared his throat. "If Joseph is a candidate for baptism, I can't believe Moses would teach him right."

"Moses sees they're in love," Noah said, boldly.

"Let's not go there, son. It's New Birth Sunday and it was hard to not see you up there being baptized; I must admit. But it was a *goot* day, nonetheless, and let's keep it that way."

~*~

Joseph passed the cinnamon rolls to Eli. "Thank you for having me over for breakfast. What was it that you wanted to talk to me about?"

Eli looked up to the ceiling, praying for strength. Lottie took his hand. "We need to sell the apple farm and we wanted to offer it to you first." He forced a smile in Lottie's direction. "I've done all I can with my physical therapy and the movement I have now is what I can expect for the rest of my life, for sure and for certain."

"We were hoping, by some miracle, maybe Eli would walk again. We were in denial. But we're not denying the reality of it anymore," Lottie said.

"I love my store, for sure, too. Looking at all the catalogs of items to stock the walls with, I'm a natural at it. I meet all kinds of folks, too. I may like it as much as the apple farm."

Emotions caught in Moses' throat. "I planted this apple farm in 1962 when we first settled here. We've pruned, cut down useless trees and replanted so many times over the years, all sixty acres. I look at it like this, some of us branches will be breaking off from this world someday and we need to replace it with other young ones, like you, Joseph." He cleared his throat loudly. "My tree out back that has four different kinds of apples coming out is a perfect picture of my family tree here, no pun intended. That tree has Granny Smith, Macintosh,

Delicious and Gala apples on it. It's not natural all those different types of apples would come out of one tree. I grafted them in and the *goot* Lord has grafted you into our family, Joseph. Understand?"

Joseph didn't try to hide the tears streaming down his face. He got up and embraced Moses. "When I see that tree I'll always think of you...You're like the dad I never had."

"You took the place of my shunned son. My heart ached for him until I met you. Your love for the Amish ways is something my son lacked greatly."

Lottie handed a box of tissues to them, and Joseph grabbed a few and then took his seat again. "I am more than honored to be asked first to buy the farm, but they cost money, and I'm not too sure about my future right now."

"I am," Moses piped in. He grabbed another cinnamon roll and took a bite. "Things look mighty *goot* for you to be Amish. The *Gmay* hasn't come to an agreement yet, but it's leaning in your favor. Since Jacob Mast confessed his sin of pride, word's gotten out, and not everyone believes everything he's said about you and Katie. He knows he overreacted about the hospital stay." Moses chuckled. "He can act ridiculous at times."

"*Daed*," Eli said. "Jacob is a *goot* man, even though *yinz* don't see eye to eye much."

"Well he practically said I was incompetent to teach Joseph baptism classes when he came over here asking you to oversee things. I turned the other cheek."

Joseph couldn't help but laugh. Moses was a pistol. "I'm learning from both of you, and Moses, you're the Bishop, and your word has great weight here. As far as the farm, how much would you be asking?"

"A thousand an acre," Eli said. "The land comes with the cider press and all the equipment you'll need to run it like we did. All the business contact, too."

"A thousand dollars an acre isn't enough," Joseph said. "I wouldn't feel right. It's worth a lot more than that!"

Eli leaned toward Joseph and slapped his arm. "How much did my store cost you? I wish I could give you the farm, but I have ongoing medical expenses with my condition. It'll be a thirty year land contract with no interest."

"It's your time now, my boy. Buy the land and go get the girl. That Yoder fella's pursuing her something fierce."

"*Daed*," Eli said. "You're not to be telling anyone what's in those letters, and the vote needs to be taken in two weeks. It does look *goot*, but he can't propose until he's baptized."

"You're right, Son. I'm getting impatient in my old age."

"Eli, you've h-heard more about the Y-Yoder guy?" Joseph stuttered. "Tell me."

"Well, Matthew Yoder lost his wife last winter in a house fire. He's moving forward in life and helping Katie do the same," Eli said. "He's one of my *bruder's* best friends, so he's a *goot* man."

Joseph's heart sank. He couldn't believe Katie would care for another so soon. She wasn't like that. "What do I do?"

"John and the family are coming down to visit and I've invited Katie, too." Lottie said. "She needs to make things right with her *Gmay*. I'm encouraging her to confess her sin and ask for forgiveness."

"But we didn't do anything wrong," Joseph said, incredulous.

"Don't worry so much, Joseph. I'm on your side and working on a plan."

Eli smiled at his wife. "Her plans always work. Do you want to think about the apple orchard or shake on it now?"

Joseph reached out to Eli with his hand. "I'll take it. Thank you, friend."

~*~

Ginny felt Kirsten was near and the thought made her heart leap. But what will Noah feel when he meets Romeo? She tried to push the thought out of her mind.

"She'll never believe this is not an April Fool's Day joke. Look at the two of you, dressed as you are," Ginny said, wringing her hands. "And, Noah, no matter what this Romeo looks like, remember, Mennonites are against violence just as much as the Amish." She put her hand on her heart. "That's her flight coming in now," she squealed. "I can't wait to see my baby girl." She looked at Noah. "We need to sit here until they come to meet us. Are you sure you're up for this. Do you want to sit on the other side, out of sight, and see Romeo from a distance and take time to cool off?"

"No, I'm ready. I've been waiting to see Kirsten for months."

"When she sees you in fancy clothes, she'll be in shock. You look good in your new red flannel-checked shirt; always the farm boy." Ginny grinned. "Kirsten will faint when she sees her Uncle Joseph in Amish clothes."

Soon luggage was coming in from Delta Airlines from Rome. Ginny saw Kirsten's pink floral luggage come around the belt and she knew her daughter would soon be arriving with her friend. She shot a "casting off prayer". God was in control of this situation, not her.

She saw Kirsten come into the baggage claim area; she was alone. They all yelled and waved to her through the growing crowd, and she ran to them. She hugged her mom and dad together. "I've missed *yinz* so much." She clung on to them and wouldn't let go.

Joseph tapped her on the shoulder. "Hey, aren't you going to say hello to your Uncle Joseph?"

Kirsten turned around and laughed. "Uncle Joseph? I didn't recognize you. Oh, Happy April Fool's Day."

Her eyes grew big and then she went straight to Noah and hugged and kissed him. She looked at him and laughed. "This is so funny. When your Dad finds out you're wearing fancy clothes as a joke, he'll have a fit." She doubled over in laughter. "This is too much. Thanks for the laughs."

Noah smiled at her. "We dress like this every day now. You've missed a lot while you were gone."

"No, you cannot get me on this one. I'm not falling for this joke. I'd never hear the end of it." She giggled. "Speaking of, I forgot about Romeo. I need to get him."

Kirsten ran off to talk to a man who gave her a package with a handle on the top. She told her mom to close her eyes for effect. "Mom, open your eyes and meet Romeo. Happy Birthday!"

Ginny stared into the eyes of a black pug, and then stomped her feet as she laughed. "He's a dog?"

"Ha-ha. I gotcha! You never guessed once. I win the big April Fool's Day Competition. You guys never fooled me by exchanging clothes. Kind of lame. Must be Uncle Joseph's idea." She poked her uncle in the ribs. Everyone was somber and quiet. "Hey, what's going on?"

~*~

Katie pulled up the log cabin quilt, then the crazy quilt, and finally the flower applique quilt. She was finally tucked into bed. It was still so cold in early April. She thought of her day and thanked the Lord for coming to New York. She loved the children in her class so much. Every day some little delight happened that warmed her heart, a child giving her a daffodil that popped up through the snow, a poem about spring, and as always, an apple or other gift for the teacher.

Katie opened her Bible to the Psalms to read five, as she did every night. She remembered Ginny reading five a day and how much it helped her. In one month, she'd get through with all of them, and start again next month. So many emotions in the Psalms helped her express her own in prayer.

When she was finished, she reread the letter she got from the Bishop.

Dear Katie,

On this New Birth Sunday, we had several young folk baptized and it was a happy day. I also confessed before the People my sin of pride. I was upset with Noah not being Amish, and took it out on the Rowlands. I was wrong and I admitted it. Confession is good for the soul. Please consider your need. I speak this not in my old harsh tone, but in a gentle one, as a shepherd does his sheep. We all love you and want you back in good standing in the Gmay.

I hear we're to be blessed with a visit from Eli's bruder and family. Would you consider coming down with them to confess? I'm anxious to hear from you, my child.

In Christian Love,
Jacob Mast

Katie was touched by the Bishop confessing his sin and gentle tone, but what was she to confess? That she behaved immorally? How could she?

She saw an unopened letter on the nightstand. It had a beautiful purple flowered envelope and it smelled like lavender. When she opened it, she could see it was from Lottie.

My Dearest Friend,

I miss you so much. In your last letter we talked about this Matthew Yoder. He sounds nice, but please don't make any rash decisions in your distress over all that's happened between you and the People. Things need to be made right. Would you please come down with John and Deborah in a few weeks? Your Mamm looks good, but sad. She misses you. Why not come down just to see her? Confess before your Gmay who loves you and move back to where you belong.

Always remember to never move in haste.

I love you like a sister,

Lottie

PS. Joseph bought our apple farm, and Eli couldn't be happier about it. He loves his store.

Homesickness flooded Katie. *Mamm looks sad?* Was she ill? The Bishop said he apologized for his harsh words. Joseph bought the farm? Too much news to absorb; all about the place and people she loved…

But she knew now she couldn't go back. Joseph would be permanently beside her best friend and it would be hard. Move back to where she belonged? Lottie wasn't making sense. She'd encouraged her to move to New York in the first place and live with her relatives. She'd be missed if she left in the middle of April since school wasn't out until May.

Katie took a deep breath and exhaled slowly. How would she react to seeing Joseph again? Would it set her back? She was moving forward and making progress. Katie realized she had put Joseph above God himself. Matthew had shared how the heart was always restless, until it rested in Christ, and it pierced her to the core. She had been so restless trying to let one person be the source of her happiness. Like Matthew said, when his wife died, he didn't stop living. She was learning so much from this kind man and was thankful for him.

She thought of her new *Gmay*. The bishop was firm, but so gentle. She'd become fond of his family and the others in the church. As far as strictness, she liked the rule of only blue and black for clothing. The more she was in Cherry Creek, Katie realized she was more plain than she ever thought. To think she'd leave the Amish for Joseph scared her. She could have ruined her life. No, she would not go home to visit as Lottie asked.

CHAPTER 25

Kirsten and Noah walked hand in hand down Trillium Trail. The white three-petal wildflowers were out in full bloom, carpeting the woods on both sides of the dirt road. The sun's rays through the woods made the setting dreamlike for a romantic walk. They approached a huge boulder that doubled as a seat, and sat down. Noah pulled something out of his jean pocket, and then got down on one knee. "Kirsten, will you marry me?"

Kirsten looked at the red garnet ring with its gold, old-fashioned filigree. Noah remembered this was her favorite gemstone. She felt her heart race, but her love for Noah overcame all her fears. "Yes!"

He put the ring on her finger. "I love you so much…." He stood up and pulled her to himself and kissed her like he never had. "Let's not wait for years like the *English*, let get married soon."

Kirsten put her head on his chest. "I'd love that. We need to discuss some important things, though," she said. She was afraid of breaking such a magical moment, but she needed to share her heart. "I learned a lot about myself in Italy and it may shock you. I'm more like my Great Grandma Grassi than I thought."

They sat back down on the boulder and Noah took her hand. "Don't be afraid Kirsten…tell me everything."

"Well, my great grandma worked harder than any Amish person alive. I saw in the Riccia Museum how ladies used a common woodstove, like a community bakery. They made their bread together and took it home. She didn't have indoor plumbing and had to go out to break ice early in the morning to heat in a big kettle to wash clothes. Today in Italy, everyone has their own gardens and makes their own wine. I felt right at home there. I think I inherited her earthiness." Kirsten sighed. "The women weren't as vain either. Most women didn't wear make-up. I didn't put on any for days and it felt good."

Noah eyes narrowed. "You want to go back to Italy?"

"No, I'm saying it all made me appreciate the Amish way of living. I think I could be Amish." She looked at Noah, expecting to see him glad, but he wasn't. "What's wrong?"

"I know you, Kirsten. You're not plain. My family accepts you for who you are, too. Are you afraid they don't approve?"

"No, I guess they live so simply in Italy and I'm afraid that all the materialism in America will choke out all the things I learned." She leaned her head on his shoulder. "I don't know if I like seeing you look so modern, with your new haircut and blue jeans. You being plain kept me that way, too, to a degree." She put her hand on his heart. "I just don't want you to change at all. I love everything about you."

Noah pulled her close to him and held her. "Nothing will change. I promise. Let's pray and see where the good Lord leads us, OK?"

"The *goot* Lord, Noah, jah?" she said. "Talk like my old Noah. Don't try to change your accent."

Noah looked at her and tilted her chin up. "This is a happy day, *jah*? I'm engaged to my *liebe, jah*?"

"What's that?" she asked, grinning.

"I'm engaged to my love," he said, leaning forward to kiss her, but she pushed him back.

"*Tu sei il mio amore*," Kirsten said, then drew near to kiss him. "It means you're my love, too, in Italian," she said, then leaned forward to kiss her fiancé.

~*~

Millie looked out her front window. Another police car at Forget-Me-Not Manor. The poor girl living there was so afraid of her husband showing up. She said a silent prayer for Dawn and her daughter, who just moved in a few days ago. So far, all her suspicions of seeing her husband in town were unfounded and she hoped it stayed that way.

She liked meeting the girls who came in and out of the house, going over with Granny Weaver to teach them how to knit. But she missed the Rowlands. Ginny and James lived three miles away, not close for horse and buggy. Now Katie was in New York, not wanting to come home. Too much change, she thought and sighed. Millie loved her whole family dearly, but she had a special bond with Katie. As much as she sounded brave in her letters, she missed home and Joseph. Millie couldn't wait for Joseph to be baptized so he could propose in a proper Amish way. Only two weeks to go and if all went well, Eli said he'd be one of the People.

She remembered when he first came to Smicksburg, only a year ago. He was nervous living in the country, and at times it made her laugh out loud; he said it was too quiet and it was spooky. She thought of the time he called the police when he saw lights in the backyard; it was some of her grandkids coon hunting. Millie giggled and then remembered how their black lab, Duke, went up to him at night while he was watching the stars and he ran for his life, thinking it was a black bear. Now he was living alone, without a car and eating up all the nature he could get.

Millie reread the letter Katie sent:

Dear Mamm,

How I wish you could move to New York. The wildflowers aren't up yet, only daffodils, but they come through the snow. There's a little blue flower called bluegrass. It's so small and dainty, yet it pushes up through the snow. It's amazing. Matthew has them all over his yard. It's a sight to behold. It looks like blue polka dots on white fabric.

Mamm, I won't be coming back until late May since school is let out later here. Right now I'm busy making a quilt for the school auction. It's an applique yellow rose pattern with an all-white background. I missed my greenhouse and all its flowers, so a flower quilt's the next best thing. The auction's in two weeks, April 16th. Pray we make enough money to put a new roof on our school.

Love you much,

Katie

~*~

Ginny was snuggled up in bed, reading *Pride and Prejudice,* her favorite Jane Austen book. James lay next to her reading, *Freedom of Simplicity* by Richard Foster. He turned to his wife. "Foster says simplicity makes you live in the moment." James said. "You don't have to have ten voices screaming at you inside that you should be doing what they say to do...go clean the garage, and when cleaning the garage, another voice says, spend time with your kids, and when you're with your kids, another voice says you should be feeding the homeless and on and on...it's exhausting. Since we have less, I can see so much better what I should be doing."

"So you don't miss your big garden, the farm animals, cutting all that grass...our old life?"

"Not one bit. I like this slower pace. Like I said, I feel settled inside."

Ginny put a bookmark in her book and snuggled next to James. "I do, too. I've learned to relax. When I'm at Suzy's knitting, I'm totally there. No guilt trip over anything, like I should be home cleaning or whatever." She kissed James on the cheek. "I'm going to start giving knitting lessons over at Suzy's... plus crocheting."

"So you can crochet again?"

"Yes. Knitting has made me sit down and work through my grief. It's really addicting, and I love it, but I miss crocheting now. Suzy said some knitters want to learn to crochet, so I'll be teaching them."

She squeezed his arm and noticed it was stiff. "I have the time, you know."

"It's not that. I think Kirsten's losing it, talking about being Amish."

"She's in culture shock after being in Italy. We know Kirsten and she's not plain. I'm not worried at all."

James put his head on hers. "You're right. Life's too short to worry, and besides, it doesn't work."

"My worrying days are over. I'm so glad we cut back with Mom's inheritance money and didn't buy some big house to 'keep up with the Jones'."

"Me too," James said. "Living with no debt is a load off my shoulders." He sighed.

"I hope Joseph didn't get himself into something he'll regret. Eli made him a generous offer, but sometimes I'm afraid his secret plan won't work out."

James reached over to set the alarm clock. "I didn't know he had a secret plan. Do tell."

"Well, Millie and I are working on it. No one knows, since we just thought of it today. Eli, Lottie, and Moses want Katie to come home, hoping Joseph will be accepted into the Amish. They feel she should know, but of course, Joseph being a gentleman, doesn't want anything said until after his baptism, when he can give her a proper Amish proposal. John and Deborah in New York don't want her to see Joseph. They think their friend, this Matthew guy, is perfect for her."

James snickered. "I take it you don't like this 'Matthew guy'?'" He hugged her. "How did we go from talking about never worrying to, well, worrying about Joseph?"

"Okay, let's pray some 'casting off prayers'," she said. "Let's pray for Dawn too. I just love that girl and I'm afraid her husband will find her."

Concern creased James' brow. "I must admit I'm really concerned about Judah and Maria. Judah's impulsive and I think they got engaged too soon."

"Well, I'm glad we have these people in our lives to be concerned about. If we didn't sell the house, we wouldn't be praying for Dawn and Maria." Ginny took James' hand to pray.

~*~

Katie picked up one of the buckets in the schoolhouse and stepped outside to empty it. She hoped her quilt could bring in enough money to get a new roof on the school. She looked at the expanse of flat land that jutted out to the mountains a few miles away. She was finding strength in these mountains. The snow was melting, and to her surprise, she missed it. The greenest grass she'd seen was now covering the schoolyard. The harsh winters gave way to such vivid colors. Katie looked at the bluegrass flowers that edged the two outhouses; one for boys and one for girls. She bent down to pick some daffodils to take home, when Matthew pulled into the schoolyard.

He was smiling broadly and lifted something out of the back of the buggy and walked over to her; he sat a yellow teacup rose bush at her feet. "This is for you," he said. "I figured you made a yellow rose quilt because they're your favorite flower." Katie was amazed. Most men didn't notice such things. "*Danki*, Matthew, very much." She bent down to touch the little buds, aching to bloom. "We can plant it in the front of the school."

"It's a present for you, to plant wherever you want," Matthew said. "Deborah mentioned you missed your greenhouse. Why not have one up here? We need one."

"I couldn't ask John and Deborah to put one on their property."

"How about my property? We could own it together, if you'll marry me." He drew near, putting his hands on her shoulders. "I know we haven't known each other long, but there's a freshness, a purity of spirit in you that I haven't seen in many women. I've come to love you in a short time."

Katie looked at him, eyes misting. She thought of the Bishop accusing her of being an immoral woman. How embarrassing it was. Now, Matthew said he saw purity. She thought of Joseph and their impossible situation.

"You don't have to answer now. I know this is shocking to you. I'm shocked I could care for someone so soon after Lydia's death. But I do." He took Katie's hand and kissed it.

Katie couldn't talk; so much emotion in one year: Levi's proposal, Judah returning, Joseph and their forbidden love, now Matthew's proposal.

"Give me an answer when you're ready. There's no rush." He looked at her fondly. "We'll put the roses in the schoolhouse until you decide where they're going. I have to admit, it'd make me happy to see them planted at my place."

"You're so sweet, Matthew. I-I can hardly talk. I am surprised."

"Since the kids had a half day of school, I had Timmy go home with the Hershberger kids, hoping you'd take a ride with me. It's a beautiful spring day."

"I should clean the school. All those buckets need dumped. I should stay and work."

"Hop in the buggy and I'll dump the buckets. We wait all year for these spring days, and I want to show you the best spots in Cherry Creek. Now do as you're told, teacher."

Katie laughed. "Alright."

~*~

"Easter's my favorite holiday," Maria said to Judah as they walked up to the church with Lilly. "No fussing about presents and the focus is all on the Lord."

Judah looked at Maria in her mint green two-piece suit. Lilly had on a mint green dress, too. "You ladies both look beautiful. You're like twins, wearing the same color."

"I saw Mommy's dress and wanted one, too," Lilly said. "I wove green."

Judah bent over to pinch her cheek. "I wove you, Little Princess."

Lilly smiled. "And Mommy, too. I saw you kiss her."

Judah scooped Lilly into his arms. "Like this?" He planted a kiss on her cheek.

"I wove you. I'm your girl, too, right?" She hugged him around her neck.

"Yes," Judah whispered in her ear. "You're my girl, too."

He walked into the church. White calla lilies were in tall vases on the altar. He knew Ginny put them there in remembrance of her mom; they were her favorite flower.

Now Ginny was like a mom to him. He smiled over at her and noticed Dawn sitting next to her with her daughter. They both looked much better. Maria and Lilly sat on either side of him and they naturally all held hands.

Kirsten came out with her acoustic guitar to lead worship. "Open your Hymnal to number twelve," she said. She strummed her guitar and the church sang along. Judah closed his eyes and smiled. James must have asked Kirsten to play this song to celebrate his new birth. He remembered how the song bothered him, but now he could sing along, knowing he had a loving heavenly father.

> *This is my Father's world, the birds their carols raise,*
> *The morning light, the lily white, declare their Maker's praise.*
> *This is my Father's world: He shines in all that's fair;*
> *In the rustling grass I hear Him pass;*
> *He speaks to me everywhere.*

God had spoken to Judah so much over his life, but he hadn't recognized his voice. Happy childhood memories had come back. The Lord saw him through cancer, and had put people in his life to help him, even though he felt alone. He almost made the mistake of his life and married Elizabeth, but God spoke to him when he saw Katie again. Her goodness was something Elizabeth lacked. Now here he was with a new life completely formed by God's hand: a church family, and a new family with Maria and Lilly, Lord willing, next spring. Judah raised his hands in worship.

~*~

The barn was packed with more benches than normal; it was the baptismal service and many came to witness this special event. After two hours of singing and preaching, the four male candidates were taken to a private corner, where the Bishop asked them if they were willing to accept the role of minister, if the lot should fall on them. They all affirmed by shaking their heads yes.

One by one they were called forward to make their baptismal vow. Moses looked down at Joseph kneeling before him. How he loved him like a son.

"Can you confess that you believe Jesus Christ is the Son of God?"

"Yes," Joseph said.

"Do you recognize this to be a Christian order, church, and fellowship under which you now submit yourself?"

"Yes," he said.

Moses took a deep breath and smiled at Joseph. "Do you renounce the world, the devil with all his subtle ways, as well as your own flesh, and desire to serve Jesus Christ alone, who died on the cross for you?"

"Yes."

"Do you also promise before God and his church that you will support these teachings and regulations with the Lord's help, faithfully attend the services of the church, and help to counsel and work in it, and not forsake it?"

"Yes."

Moses heard a noise of a car pulling up to the barn. Ginny, James, Kirsten, and Noah tip toed into the back of the barn and stood. Moses remembered Joseph saying they'd be at his baptism after their church service. Moses looked at them and grinned.

The deacon came over to Moses with a wooden bucket of water. Moses cupped his hands over Joseph's head and the deacon filled them with water. Moses released the water over Joseph's head and said, "They that believe and are baptized are saved." He placed his hands on Joseph's head and prayed a special prayer. "Oh, heavenly Father, receive Joseph in Thy grace, forgive all his sins, and set him apart as Thy child and heir. In Thy name, Oh God, this work is begun; complete it through Thy grace and power. This I pray in the name of the Father, Son, and Holy Spirit. Amen.

Moses felt the hot tears streaming down his cheeks. When Joseph stood up, he embraced him and continued to cry. He kissed his cheek, and shook his hand. He'd lost a son to the world but the Lord had given him another one.

Karen Anna Vogel

CHAPTER 26

Ginny looked at Millie in disbelief. "Katie's considering this Matthew guy? I could ring the Casanova's neck!"

Millie's eyes were as round as saucers. "Sit down and have a cup of coffee." She turned to her stove to get the coffeepot and put a mug on the table. "His name is Yoder, not Casa...whatever you said, and he's a respectable Amish man."

"Oh, you know me, Millie. I'm just so upset. We all thought she'd be coming home with John and Deborah so Joseph could propose, but this Mr. Darcy wannabe is now standing in the way. Ugh."

"She made a quilt for the auction. I thought I told you. I did, didn't I?"

"I heard about the auction, but I thought she was coming home next weekend."

"School's not out until the end of May, and Katie doesn't feel right leaving until her duties are over. She has a lot to think about, too." Millie cleared her throat. "Matthew proposed last week."

"What?" Ginny snapped.

"She doesn't know a thing about Joseph being Amish. It happened only today."

Ginny grabbed her purse. "I need to go. I need to tell Joseph. Let me see, the mail goes out tomorrow. If he sends the letter priority..." She started toward the door, then spun on her heel and looked at Millie. "If an Amish woman accepts a proposal, she can undo it right? I mean, she can change her mind without being shunned, right?"

"She can undo it, but it would be highly unlikely, as it's like breaking a promise. That's why it took her so long to accept or reject Levi. We take the spoken word seriously."

"But she broke off her engagement to Judah," Ginny said.

"For a *goot* reason. There's no reason to break a commitment to a *goot* Amish man."

Ginny spun around to leave and Millie collapsed on the green couch and started to knit.

~*~

Katie spread her finished quilt on her bed. She put her hands over the appliqued roses. She thought of the rose bush Matthew gave her, still sitting in the schoolhouse. Where should it be planted? She thought again of Matthew's proposal. It was sudden, but she did feel like she knew him forever. Did she love him though? Katie loved his farm and little boy. She had to admit he was the most handsome Amish man she'd ever met, even better looking than Judah.

She thought of her future alone. She was growing weaker by the day to remain single. She was lonely and longed more than ever for children. Katie remembered her bold prayer shortly after Sadie's death...Bring the right man into my life or take away the desire to have children... Matthew built a new house, believing God would bring the right girl into his life to fill it with *kinner*. Wasn't the writing on the wall? But, was it right to marry someone when her heart was still full of Joseph? She remembered Deborah's admonition of putting Joseph before God himself. She'd spent many hours praying to make sure her heart was right with God, and that he sat on the throne of her heart.

~*~

Matthew pulled up to the auction site and got Katie's quilt out of the back. They hung it up with clothes pins on the rope strung across the front of the little platform. Katie looked at all the items up for auction: jellies of all sorts, baskets, knitted scarves and shawls, hooked rugs, Amish dolls, and several quilts. They should easily make enough money to have a new roof and windows on all the schoolhouses in the district. She was so happy to be contributing to this worthy cause.

The church benches were spread out on the grass. She was surprised to see two hundred in attendance, many wearing sunglasses due to the blaring sun. A student waved to Katie for her to sit by him. There was enough room for Matthew, too. She was a bit embarrassed to be late, but Matthew needed to drop Timmy off at the babysitter and then they had important matters to discuss.

The auctioneer began with the jellies. He sold them in lots of five. Katie always thought the way the auctioneer talked was funny enough to laugh out loud. She looked to see the beautiful farm that offered to host this event. The auction was across the street from the big white house with dark blue curtains peeking out. She also saw little children playing on the porch while the older sisters watched them. Katie hoped to have a brood like that. She listened as the auctioneer continued and the prices went higher.

One of her students collecting money motioned for her to come over to the payment booth. The poor girls looked nervous, even though they were in the eighth grade and should be able to give cash back easily. She got up and crossed over to sit with them. Someone had given them a hundred dollar bill and they didn't have enough change. Katie wrote an IOU out to the man, telling him to collect his change after the auction. The bidding went fast for the smaller items. Now it was time for the quilts.

Katie was nervous about her quilt. She knew the quality was good, but would it fetch a good price? Hers was the first being auctioned off and it would set the price for the other ones. If no one bid high, the others wouldn't go as high either. She held her breath as the auctioneer started the bidding on her beloved yellow tea rose quilt.

"Do I hear one-hundred dollars?"

Twenty or more red number went up, including Matthew's. He smiled at her.

"Let's move this along faster," said the auctioneer. "Do I hear five-hundred?"

Five red numbers went up, including Matthew's. Katie was shocked. She didn't know he wanted the quilt. She could easily make him one much cheaper.

"Do I hear seven hundred dollars?"

Three numbers went up: Matthew, another Amish man and an *Englisher.*

"Do I hear one-thousand dollars?"

Two numbers went up: Matthew and another Amish man.

"Do I hear one-thousand-three hundred?"

Both red numbers went up. Katie looked at Matthew, motioning for him to stop.

"Do I hear one-thousand-five hundred?"

Again, both numbers went up. Katie held her breath.

"Do I hear two-thousand dollars?"

One red number went up.

"Going, going, gone, to number fifteen. Please take your ticket to the ladies here at the booth for payment, and thank you for your generous offer," the auctioneer said.

The tall Amish man went over to pay for the quilt. He took off his sunglasses.

"Joseph!" Katie squealed. "How can this be? Y-You can't w-wear Amish clothes." She looked at him and laughed and then starting crying. She fled and hid behind some quilts hanging on the clothesline.

Joseph followed her. "Katie, I'm Amish now. I was baptized last week." He turned her toward him. "Katie, look at me. It's Joseph."

Katie could not stop shaking and crying. She couldn't even talk.

"Will you marry me?"

Katie leaned into Joseph and he held her. She sobbed uncontrollably. He held her until she calmed down. Joseph got on one knee. "Willst du mich heiraten? *Will you marry me?*"

"*Jah*, Joseph. I decided today; there is no one I'd ever marry but you."

He kissed her cheeks, her forehead, her mouth. "I was so afraid you'd said yes to that Matthew guy."

"I-I told him no on the way over. I think he bid on the quilt, hoping I'd change my mind. He's a *goot* man, but I don't love him." She kissed Joseph and put both hands on his cheeks. "You're the only man I'll ever love."

Ginny came around the quilts. "Okay, what's the verdict? Do we have a wedding coming up or not?"

"Ginny, what are you doing here?" Katie asked.

"Someone had to drive Joseph, now that he's Amish."

Katie hugged Ginny. "I've missed you." She turned to Joseph. "It's time to go home to Smicksburg."

~*~

Granny Weaver stopped knitting and leaned forward. "So, Joseph bought Katie's quilt and then proposed at the money table?"

Ginny nodded. "Katie was so shocked she ran behind a quilt and he proposed there. I couldn't help but hear everything. It was so romantic."

Millie beamed. "I'm so happy to have him as my son-in-law. I hope in time, my Reuben will find love again."

Suzy wrapped more yarn into balls. "Love is definitely in the air. Judah and Maria, Noah and Kirsten…"

Sarah looked up. "We do love Kirsten, you know that, Ginny?"

Ginny looked over at Sarah. She was so at ease about her son's situation now. Or did she know something? Surely Kirsten would not be turning Amish.

"She learned a lot about the plain life in Italy," Sarah continued, beaming.

"That's because my cousins are rural, 'Old Order Italians', that's why. But Kirsten will be herself again, soon. Culture shock, is all." Ginny looked down to knit, glad it was a hard pattern. Her furrowed eyebrows would surely show her concern.

"Kirsten knows her own mind," Granny Weaver said. "I think Leah will be marrying Levi in the fall, too. God turned that poor girl's arthritis into blessing. If her joints didn't hurt so much in the snow, she'd never have come and lived with me…and meet Levi."

The little gold bell on the store door rang and Suzy got up. Soon Ginny heard Katie's voice. It had a lift in it, as if she was singing. When Katie appeared in the little side room, all the women got up and one by one embraced her. She went over to Ginny and put her arm around her. "You'll be my sister-in-law. I'll be a part of the Rowland family."

How she'd feared she was losing Joseph, and now possibly Kirsten. She never looked at it like she'd be gaining a sister. Ginny embraced Katie and then looked at the women in the circle. "A lot can happen in a year, that's for sure."

"*Goot* and bad," Sarah said. "Let's be praying for grace for Lottie and Eli."

Katie put her hand up. "Can we also pray that my friend, Matthew Yoder, finds a *goot* wife in NY? I'll see him when I go back up to finish out the school year..."

Ginny turned to Katie. "I met him and he's a dear. We'll do a 'casting off prayer' for Matthew.

The women joined hands and one by one cast their cares on the Lord, knowing he really cared about them, and continually knit hearts together in love.

The End

DISCUSSION GUIDE

Dr. Maryann Robert ~ Christian Counselor

❖ Joseph has an unraveled life before be comes to Smicksburg, First 9/11 and his mother's stroke woke him up to his self-destructive behavior. In light of Isaiah 1:18, do you think you can go too far from God to truly be forgiven?

❖ Ginny needs her family and friends to help her heal from grief. Ecclesiastes 4:12 says, *"A person standing alone can be attacked and defeated, but two can stand back-to-back and conquer. Three are even better, for a triple-braided cord is not easily broken."* Do you see, in your own life a chord of three? Or, what do you need to change to establish this for yourself? How does the busyness of your life make this difficult? How can you strengthen essential relationships?

❖ Ginny had a tendency to romanticize the Amish. Do you? Why is it reasonable to think that the Amish would have similar problems like the rest of us? (Rom. 3:23, 1 Cor. 10:13)

❖ Many Amish wish the *Englishers* would take to heart something an Amish man wrote in the *Budget* :

"If you admire our faith, strengthen yours. If you admire our sense of commitment, deepen yours. If you admire our community spirit, build your own. If you admire the simple life, cut back. If you admire deep character and enduring values, live them yourself."

This is quite a mouthful. What part hits you the most and what can you do to change? Do you need to become Amish to lead a simpler life? Can a person do this alone or does it take the power of community?

James and Ginny take the above statement to heart, what actions did they take? What was the impetus for the change? What were the benefits?

❖ Judah has quite a transformation in the book but it doesn't happen outside community. James Roland teaches him the Bible and Jerry and Janice Jackson take him in and counsel him. Do you need people to help you grow as a Christian? Who might those people be? Are you ready to be a part of the change in another person's life? In Matt. 18-20, what are we as Christians called to make? What would it require of you to do this time wise? Is your life ordered in such a way to obey this command?

❖ Solitude and silence seem to be a lost spiritual discipline. The story begins with Katie by the pond alone grieving the loss of her sister-in-law. Think about Matt. 14:13 and the following quote. Why is this an important part of grieving?

❖ William Penn said:

"True silence is the rest of the mind, and is to the spirit what sleep is to the body, nourishment and refreshment."

Finding time and a quiet spot can be a challenge. Discuss ideas on how you can incorporate more silence into your life.

❖ Joseph was seen to be impulsive in his early years, much to his destruction. Then he finds himself with a serious decision to make. How does solitude, community, patience and meditation on scripture (Jeremiah 6:16) benefit the decision making process.

❖ What did you find amazing about the true story of Eli Hershberger's buggy accident and the aftermath? Harry (Eli) wanted to show the love of God to everyone who stepped into his store. What does this tell you about how the Amish view the sovereignty of God?

❖ The Amish built Eli Hershberger a variety store so he could provide an income for his family. *Christian Aid Ministries*, an Amish and Mennonite ministry worldwide, hold to the saying; "You can give a man a fish and he will have food for the day, or you can teach a man to fish and he will have food for life." In light of the Amish hard working ethic and rejection of retirement in old age, do you think work and service add to your well-being?

❖ Kirsten and Noah don't see eye to eye on a church to attend. The issue comes down to worship style. Noah is uncomfortable with the change from the Amish slow acapella style of worship and his view of reverence. Discuss the concept of worship within various worship styles. Are there styles that are innately more reverent than others? How did Noah change his mind? What is the heart of worship?

❖ Jeremiah 6:16 is seen several times throughout the book between Joseph and Katie. They seem to use this verse as a lens to see situations that are happening in their lives as well as a truth to solving their problem. This can be seen as a type of meditation. In the Christian view (unlike the Eastern view of emptying the mind), the Christian fills it with a scripture. A physical example of this is to take a piece of quality chocolate and allow it to melt in your mouth, moving it across your tongue and feeling it as it goes down your throat.

Meditation is a truly lost discipline of the Church due to our choice to live a fast paced life. It allows time to reflect and savor God's truth, perspective and the power of God's word to act upon a person's life. Maybe this is a solution to a problem, a correction God wants to make in your action, thought, or attitude. Solitude is a key ingredient in allowing this experience to take place.

❖ What choices do I need to make to allow me to meditate on God's word? While I'm cleaning, driving, or gardening?

❖ Reflect on how the Amish and the Rolands celebrated Christmas. What was the main focus? How can our focus be distorted? What do you see as the remedy? Reflect upon Matthew 25:40 – *"What so every you've done for the least of these, you have done it unto me."*

❖ Mother Teresa didn't mince words:

You and I, we are the Church, no? We have to share with our people. Suffering today is because people are hoarding, not giving, not sharing. Jesus made it very clear: Whatever you do to the least of my brethren, you do it to me. Give a glass of water, you give it to me. Receive a little child, you receive me. Clear.

How can you reshape your Christmas priorities? My family started emphasizing that Christmas was Jesus' birthday and the gift's they receive are really just party favors. This allows for controlled spending and builds gratitude in our children. The focus became about what we would give Jesus for His birthday, because if we did it for the least of these, we were doing it for Him. What are some ways you can help those in need, giving Christ a birthday present?

❖ The *Serenity Prayer* and other poetry and saying from the English have been adopted into many Amish communities. The Amish collect wise saying, known as proverbs, and use them frequently. Why do you think they do this? Do you see the benefits?

❖ When Karen Anna Vogel lost her mom, after a long decline, and then two cousins to cancer, I helped her through the grieving process. The *Serenity Prayer* is a means to grieve and heal. Many don't know this whole prayer. Read it over a few times and see which part God may be using in your life.

> *God grant me the serenity*
> *to accept the things I cannot change;*
> *courage to change the things I can;*
> *and wisdom to know the difference.*
> *Living one day at a time;*
> *Enjoying one moment at a time;*
> *Accepting hardships as the pathway to peace;*
> *Taking, as He did, this sinful world*
> *as it is, not as I would have it;*
> *Trusting that He will make all things right*
> *if I surrender to His Will;*
> *That I may be reasonably happy in this life*
> *and supremely happy with Him*
> *Forever in the next.*
> *Amen.*

Chocolate Whoopie Pie Recipe

4 c. flour
2 c. sugar
2 t. soda
1 ½ salt
1 c. shortening (crisco)
1 c. cocoa
2 eggs
2 t vanilla
1 c. sour milk from the cow (and for the rest of us…1 tablespoon of lemon juice or vinegar plus enough milk to make 1 cup ;)
1 c. cold water
Cream: sugar, salt, shortening, vanilla and eggs. sift: flour, soda and cocoa. Mix ingredients together and slowly add sour milk and water until right consistency. Can add flour to mixture if too gooey. drop by teaspoonful. Bake at 350. put two cookies together with whoopie pie filling recipe.

Whoopie Pie Filling

2 egg whites
2 t vanilla
4 T flour
4 T milk
4 c. powdered sugar
1 c. Crisco

Beat egg whites until stiff. Add other ingredients. Spread between cookies and enjoy.

RECOMMENDED READING

Books mentioned in *Knit Together*

The following Amish books can be found at Scroll Publishing:
www.scrollpublishing.com

Pathway: Devoted Christian's Prayer Book

This small book is a collection of prayers from an Amish and
Mennonite prayer book that dates back to 1708 or earlier. It
can be used in daily devotions or on special occasions. The
book also includes the *Dortrecht Confession of Faith* and "*Rules of a
Godly Life.*" 124 pp. Hardback.

Family Life Magazine, a monthly magazine designed for adults
and families. It contains articles on Christian living, parenting,
and homemaking. It also contains editorials, letters from
readers, medical advice, poems, recipes, and children's stories.

Devoted Christian's Prayer Book. A collection of prayers from an
Amish and Mennonite prayer book.

1001 Questions and Answers on the Christian Life; This book covers
virtually every aspect of the Christian life: salvation, baptism,
the new birth, faith, prayer, discipleship, non-conformity to the
world, child training, courtship, dress, nonresistance, swearing
oaths, worship, and numerous other topics. The answers are
from an Old Order Amish viewpoint, and so this book serves
as a handy reference book on Amish beliefs.

The Martyr's Mirror Classic accounts of more than 4,000
Christians who endured suffering, torture, and a martyr's death
because of their simple faith in the gospel of Christ. Songs,
letters, prayers, and confessions appear with the stories of
many nonresistant Christians who were able to love their
enemies and return good for evil.

ACKNOWLEDGEMENTS

First Readers Betty Berkey, Karen Berkey, Bette Fisher & Karen Malena, Your encouragement gives me wings, and you corrections make me look better than I am.

Grace "Hawkeye" Yee, my gentle editor and friend. Someone who can say it like it is, but never leaving me discouraged. You're a gem.

Pittsburgh East Scribes writing group. I learn so much from you all.

My agent, Joyce Hart, who continues to believe I am a writer....

My readers...I keep writing by your encouragement.

CONTACT THE AUTHOR

Best-selling author Karen Anna Vogel is a trusted English friend among Amish in Western PA and NY. She strives to realistically portray these wonderful people she admires, most stories being based on true stories. Karen writes full-length novels, novellas and short story serials. She hopes readers will learn more about Amish culture and traditions, and realize you don't have to be Amish to live a simple life. Visit her popular blog, Amish Crossings at karenannavogel.blogspot.com

Karen is an empty nester, having four grown kids who flew the coop. Karen and her husband, Tim, enjoy homesteading in rural Pennsylvania. They run a family business, Thrifty Christian Shopper, an online business Karen created ten years ago

.   Karen would love to get to know you better on her author page on Facebook, where all things Amish, knitting, gardening, simple living, recipes…..all things downhome goodness are shared amongst Karen's readers. https://www.facebook.com/VogelReaders

HOW TO KNOW GOD

God so loved the world, that He gave His only Son, that whoever believes in Him should not perish but have eternal life. John 3:16

God so loved the world

God loves you!

"I have loved you with an everlasting love." — Jeremiah 31:3

"Indeed the very hairs of your head are numbered." — Luke 12:7

That He gave His only Son

Who is God's son?

"Jesus answered, 'I am the way and the truth and the life. No one comes to the Father except through me.'" — John 14:6

That whoever believes in Him

Whosoever? Even me?

No matter what you've done, God will receive you into His family. He will change you, so come as you are.

"I am the Lord, the God of all mankind. Is anything too hard for me?"

— Jeremiah 32:27

"The Spirit of the Lord will come upon you in power, … and you will be changed into a different person." — 1 Samuel 10:6

Should not perish but have eternal life

Can I have that "blessed hope" of spending eternity with God?

"I write these things to you who believe in the name of Son of God so that you may know that you have eternal life." - 1 John 5:13

To know Jesus, come as you are and humbly admit you're a sinner. A sinner is someone who has missed the target of God's perfect holiness. I think we all qualify to be sinners. Open the door of your heart and let Christ in. He'll cleanse you from all sins. He says he stands at the door of your heart and knocks. Let Him in. Talk to Jesus like a friend…because when you open the door of your heart, you have a friend eager to come inside.

Bless you!

Karen Anna Vogel

If you have any questions, visit me at www.karenannavogel.com and leave a message in the contact form. I'd be happy to help you.

Printed in the USA
CPSIA information can be obtained
at www.ICGtesting.com
CBHW072156090724
11385CB00025B/522

9 780615 941189